Praise for *He*

"Compulsively readable from the ... an expertly layered story of family ... an almost unbearable pace in this modern story of two sisters."

—Kelly Simmons, author of *One More Day* and *Where She Went*

"A beautifully written and intricate novel that delves into the complexities of sisterhood, relationships, love, and the ties that bind. Through her vivid characters, Taylor doesn't shy away from exploring challenging issues such as grief, shame, and infidelity with great honesty, insight, and sympathy. A very satisfying and emotional journey from an expert storyteller."

—Anita Kushwaha, IPPY award–winning author of *Side by Side* and *Secret Lives of Mothers and Daughters*

"A compelling debut novel of two sisters and how their ties to each other irrevocably change the lives of those they love. I couldn't put it down!"

—Shelley Noble, *New York Times* bestselling author of *Lucky's Beach* and *Tell Me No Lies*

Debut author Rebecca Taylor spins a superb story of two sisters who, despite growing up together, might as well have been strangers. Secrets, lies, and tragic truths unspoken swirl together through the pages, creating a sophisticated page-turner. It felt like sneaking a read of someone's fascinating private diary—and being completely powerless to put it down."

—A.G. Henley, *USA Today* bestselling author

"Sisters. Secrets. Suspense. Taylor's debut is a compelling dual-timeline story that centers around the secrets we keep from those we love, the secrets that are kept from us, and the secrets we keep from ourselves. A page-turner that keeps the reader wanting more until the very last page."

—Alison Hammer, author of *You and Me and Us*

Also by Rebecca Taylor

YOUNG ADULT FICTION

Ascendant

Midheaven

Descendant

The Exquisite and Immaculate Grace of Carmen Espinoza

Affective Needs

Published by Sourcebooks Landmark, an imprint of Sourcebooks
P.O. Box 4410, Naperville, Illinois 60567-4410
(630) 961-3900
sourcebooks.com

Library of Congress Cataloging-in-Publication Data

Names: Taylor, Rebecca, author.
Title: Her perfect life / Rebecca Taylor.
Description: Naperville, Illinois : Sourcebooks Landmark, [2020]
Identifiers: LCCN 2019045285 | (trade paperback)
Classification: LCC PS3620.A9653 H47 2020 | DDC 813/.6--dc23

LC record available at https://lccn.loc.gov/2019045285

Printed and bound in Canada.
MBP 10 9 8 7 6 5 4 3 2 1

~~A~~ Her

Perfect

Life

Rebecca Taylor

sourcebooks
landmark

For Rod, Beth, and Matthew.

CHAPTER 1

Eileen

SHE WAS HAVING ONE OF THOSE *EMOTIONALLY VULNERABLE* MOMENTS their therapist was often trying to get her to understand. All the signs were there: short temper, racing thoughts, catastrophic thinking—check, check, and check. All confirmed and completely undeniable in light of the huge fight she and Eric had last night.

The memory of it, with the morning hangover beginning to bloom, made her take a breath and hold it tight. Shit, what exactly had she been raving about? Because all of it was absolutely going to get rehashed at therapy next week. Eric certainly would not forget her every word; he never did. Eileen placed both her elbows on the desk and her head in her hands.

"A whole bottle of cab," she whispered to herself, shaking her head. "Come on, Eileen." The normally endearing expression broke her. The tears gathered and pooled behind her closed eyes.

Eric hadn't sung her that song in years.

No, not now. She sat up and checked the time on the computer screen. Shit and shit...what had she been doing? Twenty minutes before they were all supposed to be out the door, and not a single one of her kids was even out of bed. Lunches, the laundry she didn't move from the washer to the dryer last night, homework? Had she checked homework last night?

Time hated her—and it was so clearly personal.

Eighteen minutes. An impossibility. A series of miracles would not save them this morning. Everyone would be late, again. Well, everyone except Eric, of course. Eric was already out of the house, showered, dressed, pressed, and cologned. His lunch—the only one he ever packed—would be placed calmly and professionally onto the back seat of his immaculate and always client-ready car.

This, she remembered suddenly, is what had started the fight last night.

"I'm tired. I'm tired of doing everything," she had finally managed to say, standing at the sink and slamming a cast-iron frying pan into the stainless steel tub hard enough to dent it.

"Just tell me!" Eric said, throwing both his hands over his head. "What the hell do you want me to do?"

"Why do I have to tell you? Look around, Eric. The *To Do* is all around you. For fuck's sake, pick *anything*! Because I can't manage the kids, the house, the bills, the yard, the every-fucking-thing anymore. My car! My car has not had the oil changed in a year!"

"What?" Startled, he shook his head as if *this* was the most disturbing thing, the most pressing concern. "Eileen! A year?" His tone was accusing. "You're lucky it's still running. You can't let that go like that."

She stared at him. A swift and unexpected calm moved over her so fast it made the hair at the back of her neck stand up. She couldn't make him understand, but she absolutely knew what the next words out of her mouth needed to be.

"Will you please take my car and get the oil changed." It wasn't a question. It was a concession. She was telling him what to do. Never mind it solved nothing. Never mind her only thought was the impossibility of him ever understanding. Never mind the hopeless feeling creeping up her spine, squeezing her ribs, holding her breath and her words tight in her chest.

Eric looked relieved. "Yes. Yes, tomorrow I'll take it to my guy down by the office." For the briefest of moments, he had looked like he might have wanted to come to her at the sink, maybe kiss her forehead. *So happy we resolved all that. See, just tell me.*

She didn't want his kiss. She wanted him to know how hard it was to make all the pieces keep moving. She wanted him to help, not because she told him or gave him a list, but because he saw their life, their children...her. She wanted him to notice what needed attention because he cared—not because it was assigned.

That was the fight last night, and that was how it ended. Well, and with a bottle of cab as she finished the dishes and Eric retreated to his office for the work he'd brought home.

Fifteen minutes before everyone needed to be in the car.

She sat back in the kitchen chair she used when working on her laptop in the kitchen, felt the tears slide down her cheeks, and considered the implications of calling it a "mental health" day for everyone—not even waking the kids up. Let them sleep, the dogs sleep, the lunches go unmade, the laundry sit in the wash. Crawl back into bed herself even.

Twelve minutes.

An email alert slid onto the screen.

"News: Clare Collins"

Eileen stared at the rectangular notice box for the full five seconds it remained on her screen until it slid back off. She shouldn't. She didn't have time. Plus, there was the whole already "emotionally vulnerable" state of affairs. Reading internet alerts about her sister was almost guaranteed to make her more "emotionally vulnerable." She had promised herself, weeks ago, that she was going to turn these notifications off.

She stood up and walked to the bottom of the stairs. "Ryan! Paige! Cameron! Get up! Get ready!" she shouted before heading back to her computer.

Just a quick look, she told herself.

When she had learned you could do this, years ago, she thought it would be an easy way to keep up on any of the latest news about her sister and her books. Eileen never dreamed she would end up getting anywhere between five to ten alerts a day. She had always known her sister was a successful author. She could plainly see the evidence of it on the shelves of every store she walked into that sold books. It was only after she started reading about every book tour, new book contract, foreign rights deal, charity luncheon, celebrity book club endorsement, film adaptation option—only after seeing regular and daily evidence in the news of her sister's extreme success—that Eileen realized Clare was much more than a successful author whose books flew off the shelves and into shopping carts.

No. Her sister, Clare Collins, was, according to *Forbes*, one of the *Ten highest paid authors in the world*. Eileen remembered that morning, four or five years ago, staring at that ridiculously high number next to her sister's name sitting at the number-six spot on the *Forbes* list.

Fourteen million.

Dollars.

In a single year.

Her sister, the girl who had once shared a bedroom with her... who had loved eating Kraft Macaroni & Cheese after school...who used to sit next to her on their sagging couch and fight with her over the remote, now earned lottery win–levels of dollars—every year.

Eileen clicked open the email and steeled herself for whatever fresh self-esteem low she was about to plunge into.

It was a picture of Clare, poised and statuesque, long neck, face turned slightly away from the camera so her chiseled cheekbones and prominent chin were captured perfectly. A long, pale-blue dress looked poured over her toned body, revealing every tightly calculated proportion as it spilled into a short train over the red carpet beneath her silver-stilettoed feet. The second shot was from behind. Clare's long, auburn hair was styled in an updo so the dress's plunging back would not be hidden beneath her silky waves. The only flaw, if you could even call it that, was the hint of Clare's black inked tattoo, barely visible on her shoulder blade, creeping out from behind the dress. It hardly showed. Probably most people wouldn't even notice it—most people didn't even know Clare had that tattoo.

Eileen remembered the day she got it.

"Mom?"

Startled, Eileen jumped in her seat and turned to see her sleepy youngest child, Cameron, nowhere even in the ballpark of ready for school. "You're not dressed."

"I don't have any clean shorts."

She sighed and closed her eyes. Cameron's load of clean clothes was still sitting in a damp lump in the middle of her washing machine. "I know, I'm sorry." She racked her brains for some alternative. "We'll just put what you're going to wear today in the dryer. It'll be faster."

"School starts in five minutes."

Defeated, and obviously with no good solutions for anything this morning, Eileen nodded at her son.

"Is that Aunt Clare?" he asked, his eyes focused on the screen behind her.

"Yes."

"Why's she so dressed up?"

"One of her books was made into a movie, and she went to the premiere last night."

"Another movie?" Cameron beamed, his excitement erasing the last traces of sleepiness from his face. "Can we go see it?"

The pain—it was a real thing. Jealousy wormed through her gut like an infection. Eileen gave him a weak smile. "Of course."

Cameron, her most sensitive and emotionally attuned kid, narrowed his eyes at her. "What's wrong?"

"Nothing." She turned in her seat and closed the internet

browser on her screen so her glamorous sister was replaced by Eileen's tangled mess of desktop icons.

"Are you sick?" Both of his hands landed on her cheeks and drew her face back to his.

She looked into his bright blue eyes, took a deep breath, sat up straight in her chair, and conjured a real smile. "I'm only a little sick."

"Are you going to stay home today?" The hope in his voice gave away where this questioning would lead.

"No. And neither are you, or your brother, or your sister. We are all pulling it together and getting on with the day," she declared. She stood up and went to drag Ryan and Paige out of bed. "Go pick something to wear out of the washer and put it in the dryer."

Cameron, giving up any last hope that he might spend the day at home playing video games instead of at school, slumped his shoulders and moved like a snail toward the laundry room. "You know, class starts in two minutes," he called back to her.

"Just keep moving," Eileen yelled back. "Faster." Her own slippered feet raced up the stairs. "Paige! Ryan!"

An hour later, and after a frantic search for her car keys, which were eventually found in the sink of the downstairs bathroom, Eileen herded the last of her kids out the front door.

"I forgot my ID," Ryan said, rushing back inside the house.

Eileen closed her eyes and took a breath. Something was wrong with her… It simply wasn't this hard to get three kids to school and herself to work. She knew it. Every day, millions of families all over the world seemed to pull this off, on time.

Ryan finally came barreling back down the stairs, "Got it!" he said as he raced out the door. Eileen remembered to close the front door and lock it—something that hadn't happened yesterday.

She adjusted her tote and camera bags on her shoulder, leaning to counterbalance the weight, and pressed the unlock button on the key fob several times as she walked down the porch steps. When she rounded the edge of the house and could see the drive, she was surprised to see all three of her children, not inside her car waiting for her, but standing next to Eric's car.

Paige was pulling a large manila envelope from underneath one of the wiper blades on the windshield.

What is going on? Where is my car? Hasn't Eric already left for work? Then it hit her—their fight, her assignment for him. *"Will you please take my car and get the oil changed?"*

Ryan snatched the envelope from Paige and turned away from her, protecting the prize. "I'm opening it. It's probably for me!"

"I'm expecting something," Paige countered, trying to snatch the envelope back.

"I saw it first." Ryan clutched the envelope to his chest, his body turning and twisting against his sister's every attack attempt.

"Mom?" Cameron asked. "Can I open it? Please?"

They were about to get into a fight—a real one. She could practically smell kid fights rushing in, seconds before someone shoved just a bit too hard, initiating a return strike that actually hurt, leading to a defensive kick—running, arms flailing.

"Stop!" she commanded, rushing into the fray and grabbing the envelope from Ryan. "What is wrong with you two? Get in the car, now!"

"But—"

"Now!" Eileen finished. "For God's sake, we don't have time for this."

"Well, whose fault is that?" Paige added in a withering tone as she sauntered to the front passenger door.

"I'm sitting in front," Ryan called, rushing to get between his sister and the door. "I called it."

"You did not!"

"I did! Ask Cameron. I called it before we came outside."

"You can't call it when everyone's not there."

Movement across the street caught her attention. Her neighbor with her erect spine and size-two body was pretending to not hear this "poor parenting" episode unraveling. Eileen watched as she slipped into her shiny black Mercedes. Her children were already at school. The nanny got them there on time every morning.

"Stop it," Eileen hissed. "Get in the back, both of you. Cameron's sitting up front."

Paige turned on her. "Cameron's not even old enough—"

"I. Don't. Care. Get in the back. Now!"

Cameron beamed.

"It's not fair," Ryan whined.

Eileen ignored him and unlocked the doors. Finally, everyone got in the car—all unhappy except Cameron.

"What should we listen to?" he asked as he reached for the radio, defining the battleground for the fight that would happen on the drive.

Eileen put the key in the ignition and started the car, the

envelope from the windshield still in her left hand. Eric's full name was handwritten across the front in black Sharpie.

"No!" Paige declared from the back. "We are not listening to country music, Cameron!"

Eileen turned her body in her seat and stuffed the envelope down the side of her tote so she could give it to Eric later.

"No radio." She pushed the off button on the console. "We are having a moment of silence," she finished as she shifted the car into reverse and backed down the drive.

CHAPTER 2

Eileen

THE LIGHT WAS BAD. SHE HAD TRIED TO TELL THEM AT THIS TIME of day, on the east side of the lake, that they would be fighting the shadows. But when the client insisted on the location, you gave them what they wanted. Even though you knew ahead of time that it would lead to being unhappy with the results—you did it anyway.

"Okay, Mom and Dad," Eileen directed from behind her camera. "Let's try you two facing each other… Not quite that much… There you go." This whole shoot was turning into a complete disaster. "And we'll put the two tallest boys right in front of you. And the youngest in front of them, good, good," Eileen lied and pressed the button of her camera, capturing a series of rapid-fire shots.

"Okay, so," she started. Their middle child, one of the most sullen, uncooperative children she had ever worked with, refused to do anything but scowl. "I'm wondering if we can get a few with everyone smiling."

Middle boy narrowed his eyes and deepened the already dark, furrowed creases in his forehead. The father smiled while also looking completely annoyed, while the mother's eyes gave away her stress. The youngest child, a four-year-old girl in a florescent pink dress that would completely counterbalance every other person in her family wearing jeans and a white shirt, despite Eileen's explicit instructions to avoid white shirts, wandered away from the shot to inspect a black beetle on a flat, smooth stone nearby.

Only their oldest child, a boy of maybe eight, had enthusiastically smiled for every single shot they had taken so far.

Eileen sighed to herself, careful to do her best to hide her frustration from the clients. "Okay, so far so good. I'm thinking maybe now is a good time for a quick five-, ten-minute break."

"Sounds good to me," the father said as he pulled his cell phone from the back pocket of his jeans. The mother nodded and headed for her large purse, which she'd left on a nearby bench.

Eileen turned away from them. *It's money, Eileen.* Family portraits helped pay the mortgage—the same way weddings, graduations, promotional and publicity events, and the occasional bar mitzvah did. Landscapes, stills, and every artistic photo she'd ever taken did not.

"You're lucky to get to do it at all," Eric had snapped when she had once complained to him about a difficult family. "Would you rather be sitting in a cubicle? Would you rather be chained to a desk working on a spreadsheet, writing reports, watching the clock, and praying for five o'clock?" he had continued.

Because that was exactly what she used to do. And she had hated every minute of it.

Eileen closed her eyes, but she kind of hated this too. Not as much, that was true. At least she got to spend her days with her camera in her hands. And certainly it was miles away from the confinement of the cubicle. But spending her days directing and constructing sullen families into image-worthy poses—it didn't do much to alleviate that sense of abysmal failure that had begun a slow creep into her own life image lately.

Eileen grabbed a new lens and attached it to the front of her camera as she turned back to her client family. The dad was still on his phone, and the mom was waiting for the youngest to finish drinking from her spill-proof cup. That was when Eileen saw it, the top third barely peeking out from the mom's purse—Clare Collins, in a large gold font.

She had seen it in the grocery store just yesterday, her sister's latest hardcover release, *A Perfect Life*, filling the endcaps in the checkout line. She hadn't touched it. She had willfully ignored it, and she certainly hadn't bought it—but here it was, following her, haunting her, reminding her that complete strangers continued to finance and support Clare's art.

"Do you think we can wrap this up soon?" the dad asked, slipping his phone back into his pocket.

"Yes," Eileen agreed. "We've lost the light," she said, despite the fact that they had never had the light to begin with. "In fact...I probably already have something I can use."

Every single one of them looked relieved. Even the middle boy finally smiled, and Eileen, quick with the camera, snapped his picture several times before he could remember to be miserable again.

From the depths of her tote bag, her phone rang. The shrill, old-fashioned ringtone made her put her camera down and race to begin the frantic dig. Her tote was too big, filled with too much crap, and the phone was never, ever in the convenient phone-sized side pocket. By the time she managed to get her hands on it, the ringing had stopped—as usual—and she was left staring at a surprising notification.

Missed call, Simon Reamer

Why was Clare's husband calling her? When was the last time she had even spoken with him?

Christmas—three years ago? They had invited Eileen, Eric, and the kids to spend Christmas with them, in their huge cliffside mansion, and against Eileen's better judgment, they had gone. That was the last time Eileen had spoken with Simon Reamer, thanking him for having them and saying goodbye at the grand entrance to his and Clare's ridiculous house.

Eileen racked her brains. Clare's birthday was tomorrow, her fortieth. Given that Simon had rented out a ballroom at one of the most expensive hotels in San Francisco to celebrate Clare's thirty-fifth birthday with five hundred of her closest admirers, and fans, it wasn't hard to believe that he would be conspiring something completely over the top for her fortieth. Except, her birthday was tomorrow. If Simon were planning something, wouldn't she have received the ornate invitation by mail months ago? It wasn't like Simon to try to get away with a last-minute phone-call invite.

"So," the father interrupted her thinking. "We're good? What happens next?"

"Um…" Eileen tore her eyes away from the phone and stopped the thoughts that were forming about her mother and her deteriorating health in their tracks. "So I'll go through everything we were able to get today and send a selection of proofs for you to review. Once you've made some choices, I'll put the order together for you."

"Sounds good," the dad said.

"Thank you again," the mother added, unable to hide the strain in her voice. She shook Eileen's hand. "We hope there'll be some good ones."

Eileen smiled at her and the kids while the dad headed off to his car, presumably to get back to work. "I'm sure there are—you're such a photogenic family." There wasn't a single good photo of them on her camera; Eileen was almost sure of it.

As the mom shuffled her kids away from the lake and toward her own car, Eileen's phone beeped another notification.

Voicemail, Simon Reamer

Her mother. Was Simon calling because Clare couldn't? Had something happened to their mom? Clare had moved Ella into that retirement home right before Eileen and her family had gone out there for Christmas. The Regency in San Francisco, the best care facility to treat Alzheimer's patients Clare's money would buy, and close so Clare could visit her regularly.

Had her mother died? Is that why Simon, who never called her, was calling her now? She finished packing up her equipment, dreading every second that passed, knowing in only a few more moments she would need to stand here and listen to exactly what was going on. She tried to reassure herself that it was likely nothing—but she felt almost certain something was wrong.

She twisted the last of her collapsible light reflectors down into a smaller circle and pushed it into its black zipper case. The sound of her phone ringing again ripped the silence and sent an alarm out across her central nervous system. She lunged for her tote and grabbed her phone.

Simon Reamer

Eileen stared at it while it rang twice more, finally swiping to answer right before it could roll over to voicemail again. "Hello?"

Silence. Did they have a bad connection?

"Hello? Simon?"

"Eileen…Eileen," Simon said, his voice strained. Was he crying?

She tried to picture Simon crying… She couldn't. "Simon, is something wrong?" she asked. Her limbs suddenly weak, she sat down in the grass next to her bags.

A loud sob, unmistakable, erupted from Simon on the other end of the line. Eileen could hear his breathing, erratic and broken. Guttural sounds, like a wounded animal, kept him from speaking. "She… Oh my God. Oh, my God, Eileen. I'm sorry I can't say it."

Eileen's heart stopped. Dead in her chest. Frozen, her phone clutched in her hand, she waited for disaster.

"Clare!" he shouted, his sobbing wild with obvious grief. "She... she..."

"Simon," Eileen whispered into the phone, tears now streaming down her own face even though she had no idea what had happened. "Simon, please. Please tell me what's happened."

"She, oh...no, no, no. She's... I can't say it. I'm sorry. I'm sorry."

"Simon!" Eileen shouted. "What? What is it?"

A long silence stretched across the connection between them. Had she lost him? Had he hung up? A second later, she heard him gasp, then clear his throat. "She's dead," he blurted. His next inhale was deep. He held it for a long time. "I'm sorry, but she's dead. I needed to tell you myself...before you heard it...somewhere else."

"Clare?" Eileen whispered. "Clare?"

Another sob from Simon. "Clare," he said.

A feather, long and bright white, lay in a tangle of brown grass and small stones a few feet away. Eileen stared at it. Cameron would want that. She should collect it and bring it home for him.

"Eileen? Are you there?"

"Yes, I'm here."

"Can you...can you come? I need, um...I need help."

"Yes. I'll come," she said, pulling her eyes from the feather. "How? What happened?" And when? Hadn't she just this morning read about Clare attending the premiere of her movie last night? Was this even possible?

Simon sobbed uncontrollably into the phone.

"Simon." She kept her voice steady, her mom voice, the one she'd used when Ryan broke his arm. "I'm coming. I'll get a flight today. Tonight," she corrected. She'd need to make so many arrangements before walking out of her house with a suitcase. "But please, try to tell me what happened." Because Simon was right, the news would be reporting on Clare's death soon. They might already have more details than Eileen did. She didn't want to hear about it from the internet.

"Eileen…she shot herself." His voice was barely audible over the cell connection, but Eileen heard enough to understand perfectly.

She just couldn't believe it.

"No," Eileen said, her voice more matter-of-fact than she had intended. "Clare wouldn't…" Would she?

"People are here… I have to go. There's some other problem. Please let me know what flight you're on," Simon said, and hung up.

She sat, her phone pressed to her ear for a long time after the call had ended. Clare Collins was beautiful, talented, successful, internationally adored—but that wasn't what made it impossible for Eileen to believe her sister had committed suicide.

Long before Clare had become Clare Collins, she had been a force in the world. Audacious, fearless even. It didn't add up. It didn't make sense.

Why?

Why?

"Why would you do it, Clare?" she breathed.

She looked for the feather to take home for Cameron, but it was gone.

CHAPTER 3

Simon

Two years before Clare's death

"SIMON!" CLARE CALLED. HER BARE FEET RACED ONE AFTER THE other down the west side of the split marble staircase. "Simon! The internet is down!"

Simon Reamer, Clare Collins's husband and literary agent, sat at their kitchen table listening to his wife's voice echo through the hallways of their massive home. *Think, think, think,* he pleaded with his brain to come up with an acceptable excuse that she would believe. Because if she knew he had unplugged their modem to keep her from reading the *New York Times Book Review*—she would kill him.

"Simon!"

"In here!" he called back, his eyes closed, dreading the whole rest of this Sunday.

He couldn't keep it from her forever. He had slipped from their bed while it was still dark out, long before her alarm was set to go off, careful to take Charlie from his dog bed with him so the six-month-old Maltese wouldn't wake her. He had a bad feeling about this book. He needed to see for himself before Clare did.

With the puppy curled on his lap, Simon had pulled up the review section prepared to scan for the write-up of Clare's latest release, *If You Knew Her*. He didn't need to hunt for it; *If You Knew Her* was this week's lead title.

With one hand resting on Charlie's soft head, he scrolled down the page as his eyes raced over the recent National Book Award-winner, Donna Mehan's, scathing takedown of Clare's book. He finally reached its painful final conclusion, "Collins seems to have lost her footing, or perhaps worse, taken on characters and subjects beyond her ability to effectively convey." Simon sat back in his leather office chair and tilted his head back, eyes focused on the ceiling above him where his wife, and client, still slept, blissfully unaware of this public fallout.

She would hide it, even from him—but this was going to devastate her.

Without thinking, Simon stood up with Charlie cradled in his arms, opened the cabinet on the wall, and pulled the plug on the modem. "Come on, Charlie, let's get you outside."

"Simon," Clare said again, arriving at the entrance to the kitchen still in her midnight-blue satin pajama set with the matching robe cinched tight around her waist. Her hair, not yet brushed, hung over her shoulders just past her breasts.

Before they had gotten married, he had wondered if his amazement about this woman would eventually fade—if waking up to her every day for a lifetime might become commonplace. From his place at the kitchen table, his coffee still steaming, his toast now cold, he looked up into her frustrated expression. It had been fourteen years since he met her and six since their wedding day—she still devastated him. His chest tight with fear, he looked into her dark brown eyes.

"Yes? What's up?"

Her eyes flew wide with irritation. "Didn't you hear me? The internet! It's down!"

"Is it? That's weird. I'm sure it's the service provider. They'll have it up soon enough." He took a sip of his coffee. "Want some?"

Clare stood at the kitchen door, one hand on her hip, staring him down. She narrowed her eyes, then turned on a dime and headed across the marble entrance.

"Clare!" he called, sloshing his coffee down his T-shirt. "Shit. Clare, wait!" he shouted after her.

She was already past the mahogany circular table with this week's large floral display featuring five dozen white roses and light-blue hydrangeas, shoots of spiky green somethings that Simon couldn't identify reaching tall with the purple hollyhock. Her robe fluttered out behind her, her bare feet silent but determined and headed right for his office door.

"Please," he begged her.

She turned the handles on the double doors to his office and flung them both wide before her. In two steps, Clare had her hands on the cabinet hiding the modem and other various wires and receivers from view. By the time he reached her, she had the modem in her hands and was inspecting the backside.

"The provider is down?" she asked, her tone clearly accusing.

She grabbed the exact right cable and plugged it into the exact right port. Shit, he didn't even think she knew what a modem was. "How bad is it?" she asked, closing the cabinet and turning back to him. "I mean, for you to do this and imagine for even half a second you'd get away with it. It must be bad, right?"

Simon, his shoulders limp with defeat, stared at his wife. "It's bad, yes."

Clare's chin jutted forward, her nostrils flared slightly as she sucked in air and filled her chest. "Okay," she said, exhaling long and hard. She closed her eyes, shook her head once, and shrugged. "What can you do?" She was talking to herself. "A bad review from Donna Mehan...in the *Times*." She paced toward his desk, then back. "How bad? Be honest, because I'm going to go upstairs and read it anyway as soon as I calm down."

Simon hesitated for a moment. There was no way to even soft-sell it. The review was brutal. "Scathing," he said.

Clare sucked another lungful of air through her nose, chest full, shoulders wide, her hair a tangled halo around her face. "That bitch," she hissed. "That pompous, full-of-herself...overrated, bitch!" Clare spun away from him and headed for the office doors.

"Clare." He trailed after her. "Don't—"

"Don't what?" she snapped, already climbing back up the stairs.

"Don't do anything you'll regret." He raced after her and Charlie, the dog's long white hair bouncing as he chased his mom up the stairs. The puppy clearly thought this whole morning was fantastic fun.

"Like what? Shoving Donna Mehan's National Book Award right up her tight ass?"

"Yes, obviously don't do that. But moreover…" On the landing halfway up, where the single staircase split into two, he caught up to her and managed to grab hold of her wrist. Clare stopped and faced him. "I need you to make me a promise."

"What?" she snapped.

"No social media. Not today, not tomorrow…not for the whole week, in fact."

"That's barbaric."

"Can you honestly tell me you're capable of not biting right now?"

"Of course not."

"Exactly my point, and you haven't even read the review yourself yet. When that happens, your head is going to explode right off your shoulders. In that frame of mind, well, I don't like to even imagine the flame war you're likely to start." He tried smiling at her.

Clare pursed her lips and turned her head, softening…barely.

Simon took a step closer, then another, daring to pull his seething wife to him. He wrapped his arms around her. Charlie, feeling left out, pawed at their legs. Simon lowered his lips to her ear, "Besides, you're setting a bad example for Charlie."

They both looked down at the fluffy Maltese, wagging his tail, tongue hanging from his mouth. Clare's shoulders sank a few inches.

"Oh, you damn dog," she whispered, and bent down to pick up his squirming, happy body. "How's a woman supposed to stay enraged at her mortal enemy with you and that stupid cute face always ruining the moment?" She nuzzled the dog's ear and took a deep breath. "Fine," she said to Simon. "I promise, no social media for the day."

"For the week."

Clare scowled at him, but Charlie licked her face. "This dog, he's your dirtiest trick yet."

"A week?" He kissed her other cheek, then her lips.

"Fine, a week," she said, pulling away. "But if I'm even still a little mad by next Sunday," Clare declared and started back up the stairs with Charlie in her arms, "I'm going to find a way to publicly annihilate that puffed-up bitch. But don't worry, it'll be subtle."

So, that was settled. The plan was a *subtle, public annihilation*—they were maybe going to need two weeks.

CHAPTER 4

Eileen

THE LAST-MINUTE FLIGHT FROM DENVER TO SAN FRANCISCO HAD cost a fortune. Eileen put it on one of their almost maxed-out credit cards and hoped the charges would clear. For the last six months, the realization that she was almost assuredly going to have to go back to spending her days doing work she hated had sunk in deeper with the arrival of every ballooning credit card statement.

As usual, she pushed the thoughts aside. She didn't have the strength to mourn her sister and worry about money at the same time.

Her afternoon had been spent moving mountains. Buying a ticket, picking kids up early from school, cancelling afternoon music lessons, arranging rides for the rest of the week—trying to explain to everyone why she was leaving. A whirlwind of purpose driving her forward, keeping her busy, and her mind off the fact that her only sister was not in this world anymore.

It didn't seem possible.

"Aunt Clare?" Paige had asked, bursting into tears almost

immediately. Cameron and Ryan had followed her lead. Holding it together while her children had an opportunity to fall apart...that was the toughest mountain of all.

Next was walking out the door with a suitcase before their father was able to get home. "I'm so sorry," Eileen told her kids at the door.

Paige, who was only fourteen and had only that morning been fighting with her little brother, gave her a hug. "Don't worry, Mom. We'll be fine." She stepped back and placed her hands on both Ryan and Cameron's backs. "I'll make some mac-n-cheese. We'll do homework in the dining room."

Eileen stared for a moment at her daughter, suddenly taller than she remembered, then gave them all a kiss. "Thank you. And I won't be gone long," she said, although she had no idea if that was even true. "Sara's driving you for the rest of the week. You have her cell?"

"I've got it. You're going to miss your flight," Paige warned her.

"Okay, you're right." The tears she'd been fighting all afternoon welled up. "It's just..." Her voice cracked, and all three of her kids rushed in and held her.

"It's okay, Mom," Cameron said.

She took a breath and swallowed the lump in her throat. "Okay, yes, I'm okay."

"And we're okay," Ryan added.

Eileen nodded. "Okay." She picked up her tote and lifted the handle on her rolling suitcase. "Your father should be home"—she checked her phone for the time—"in three hours."

"We know... Go," Paige said and kissed her cheek.

She didn't want to leave them, but she gave them each a big hug, kissed their foreheads, then turned and walked out the door. "I'll call you when I get to the airport," she said over her shoulder as she dragged the case down the porch steps and out to Eric's car.

He would be stuck with hers for several more days.

Since she'd made it out of her house about two hours before rush hour, the expressway out to the airport had been practically empty. Denver International Airport, with its peaked white canvas roof, was a beautiful mini range of snowcapped mountains sprouting up in the middle of the Colorado plains, still mostly surrounded by nothing but grass. Only a few hotels and restaurants had staked claims. Suburban homes and neighborhoods were beginning to creep closer every year; and once the enormous convention center was completed, Eileen imagined this once-remote architectural wonder would eventually get dwarfed and hemmed in.

She parked Eric's car out in the economy lot, rode the shuttle bus with her suitcase and tote into the terminal, collected her boarding pass at the automated kiosks, and blew past security with no more trouble than an extra look at her camera and the one extra lens she'd packed safe into the center of her case. By the time she was on the concourse checking the departure board, she had an hour to wait before her flight boarded.

It occurred to her that she was both hungry and thirsty. She'd been in such a storm of activity all day that food had never even occurred to her. She turned away from the departure board, set on investigating the restaurants in the B concourse, and came face-to-face with her sister.

The Tattered Cover, one of Denver's independent bookstores,

had a small airport shop. She stood staring into it. Other passengers browsed the shelves. One man and his son were purchasing something at the counter, and two women stood at the center display table picking up copies of Clare's newest book, *A Perfect Life*.

Eileen watched the two women as they noted their common interest. She couldn't hear them, but the woman in yoga pants and a sweatshirt said something to the woman wearing the gray pantsuit. They both furrowed their brows, shook their heads, then took their copies of Clare's book to the register.

The news about Clare's death was out.

Eileen pulled her suitcase to the display table and stared down at the stacks and stacks of hardcovers with her sister's name. In true sibling rivalry fashion, it had been years since she had either purchased or read one of her sister's books. At the beginning of Clare's career, it had been easy to support her. A struggling writer, no different from the millions of other struggling artists, Clare had lived in a run-down one-bedroom apartment in Brooklyn with three other starving artists, subsisting on canned soup and apples. Back then, confident in her choice to put her camera down and pursue accounting as a major, Eileen had enthusiastically read every story draft her sister sent her. Most of them had been mediocre at best, and not a single one of them was ever accepted for publication.

Until one day, one was.

Eileen picked up her sister's latest book and got in line behind the two other women clearly eager to read Clare's last words.

After she paid, with another credit card that made her hold her breath, the cashier asked her, "Would you like a bag?"

Eileen forced a smiled. "No thanks." She picked up her book, along with the free bookmark, and opened her tote. "Shit," she said.

"Excuse me?" the cashier asked.

"Um, nothing. Sorry. I just realized—thank you," Eileen mumbled and headed with her suitcase out past the other passengers, who were now congregating around the table displaying Clare's book. Back out in the concourse, she opened her tote again and saw the large envelope addressed to Eric still in her bag. "Damn it," she whispered. She'd meant to leave it on his desk in his office before she left.

She pulled out her cell phone and checked the time; she still had forty-five minutes before they would start boarding her flight. She opened her recent calls list and tapped Eric's contact. With her phone pressed to her ear, she stuffed Clare's book in her tote next to the envelope and began walking toward the restaurants on the other side of the concourse.

"Hello?" Eric answered.

"Hey," she said, adjusting her bag on her shoulder and taking the phone back into her hand. "I'm at the airport."

"Everything okay? You made it on time?"

"Yes. I actually have a few minutes, so I was going to grab a bite."

"Is that Mom?" Ryan's voice echoed in the background.

"Yes," Eric said, his mouth aimed away from the mouthpiece. "She's at the airport."

"You're at home?" Eileen asked, surprised. All the kids were now talking at once in the background.

"Yes. Guys, be quiet so I can hear. Yes, after you called, I cancelled my last meeting and came home. How you holding up?"

Eileen found an empty table outside a Mexican food restaurant that looked cleanish and lowered her tote onto the empty seat. "I'm not sure. I think I'm just moving from one thing to the next."

"I'm so sorry. I wish I could be there with you."

Eileen closed her eyes. She wouldn't cry again. Not in the middle of the airport. "I wish you were too. But honestly, I'm glad you're home with the kids."

"Speaking of that…what have you told them, exactly?"

"I said she had an accident. Not that she shot herself."

"They're reporting her death on the news," he whispered into the phone. "It won't be long before the details come out."

Eileen took a deep breath. "I don't know what to do."

"I'll talk to them."

"I feel awful. I'm sorry. I never meant for you to have to handle that on your own."

"I think it will be awful no matter how they find out."

He was right, of course. "Anyway, I'm glad you're there. I love you."

"I love you, too. We'll get through this."

Eileen opened her tote, took out the envelope, and laid it on the table. "Actually, I was calling for another reason. Thank you, by the way, for taking my car in today."

"I'm happy to do it."

"But there was an envelope on your windshield this morning. I meant to leave it for you, but with everything, I forgot."

"An envelope? That's weird… Oh, I bet it's from Carl next door. We were talking last week. He's started selling insurance on the side, trying to make some extra money. He hit me up. I didn't know what to say. We don't need to be messing around with insurance right now. He was going to put together some quotes."

"Do you want me to open it?"

"Sure."

Eileen bent back the brass tabs holding the flap in place.

"I'd say just throw it away, but I'm probably going to have to talk with him and find a way to tell him we're not interested right now. God, I hate when friends try to sell you shit. No," Eric said to the kids, his mouth away from phone. "I did not say the S word... Well, how about you mind your own business?"

Eileen reached into the envelope and pulled out several thick pages.

As she stared down at the pages in her hand, she vaguely heard Eric ask the kids, "What do you want for dinner?" She didn't breathe. A sickness rushed through her bloodstream, stunned her senses, paralyzed her limbs.

They were large, eight-by-eleven-inch black-and-white pictures. There were six. Her fingers gently pushed them apart, spreading them out across the table to reveal different scenes, different settings, but always the same main characters. Each picture a punch in her gut more powerful and painful than the last.

She stared at them.

There was a handwritten note in black ink torn from a spiral notebook paper-clipped to the photo that most clearly showed Eric and Lauren's faces. The note was signed—*Dave, Lauren's husband.*

A man in a dark gray suit walked toward her table. Pulling a black carry-on suitcase, he held his phone in his free hand as he spoke into the headset attached to his ear. His eyes swept over the table as he passed by, then met hers for the briefest of moments, understanding igniting between them before he looked away. Eileen heard him keep speaking into his headset. "What was that? Yeah, sorry… Brian's quotas weren't met for that quarter."

She looked around, suddenly remembering she was in an airport surrounded by people. A woman with two small children sat at a table only three feet away, their paper-wrapped tacos half eaten.

"Eileen?" Eric asked. "Are you there? Can you hear me?"

She listened to the sound of her husband's voice. She loved him. Too much—that's what Clare had once told her: "You love him too much."

"Yes," she managed to say. "I'm here." She raked the photos and the note together, aligned their edges, and hid them back in the envelope.

"What was it?" he asked her.

"What?" Eileen pressed the flap of the envelope down over the sharp brass tabs and spread them flat.

"The envelope? Quotes from Carl?" he reminded her. "Are you okay?" She could tell from his tone that he was referring to Clare's death. He was asking if she was okay. He was implying that maybe she wasn't, because she had learned a few hours ago that her sister had shot herself. He had no idea what she'd just seen.

"Eileen? Can you hear me?"

"Yes. It was just insurance sales stuff…from Carl."

They had been married almost fifteen years. They had three

children. She loved him more than she should—too much. "Sorry," she choked. "Um, they're actually boarding. I made a mistake about the times."

"Are you sure you should be traveling alone right now?"

"I'm fine."

"You don't sound fine."

"Eric… I have to go. They're boarding my flight," she said.

She hung up and placed her phone facedown on the table next to the envelope. Near her spine, a black hole cracked open and spread across her back, through her stomach, wrapped around her heart, pressed her lungs. An empty space of loss so large, her whole life fell inside out.

Eileen closed her eyes, willed herself to breathe, and swallowed back the agony clawing its way up her throat. The images of her husband fucking Lauren Andrews were burned into her field of vision, as if she had been staring at the sun. Their entwined limbs, his naked ass, her spread legs. Eric on top of her, behind her. His exposed throat, her full tits. Expressions contorted at the height of orgasm.

And worse. Their bodies spooned, outlined by only the drape of a sheet, faces slack with sleep. Eric's arm hung over Lauren's thin waist, her cropped brown hair spread across the pillow they shared, his lips resting at the base of her neck.

Eileen put her hands over her face, pressed her eyes, willed the scenes to disappear. Images she knew she would never unsee.

"You love him too much," Clare had once said.

CHAPTER 5

Clare

Two years before her death

IT WAS ALL A SHOW, BIG TALK, PLAYING THE PART. ONCE CLARE HAD convinced Simon she wouldn't go online and start a public grudge match with Donna Mehan, she was free to retreat to the solitude and safety of her study. With only her little Charlie to bear witness, she locked her door, took a deep breath, and turned off her Clare Collins act.

She could be fun, for short periods of time. She could also be useful—in television interviews, for example—but largely, being Clare Collins was exhausting.

With the internet now functioning again, Clare sat at her desk and pulled up the *New York Times* to read for herself Donna's "scathing" review of *If You Knew Her*. She didn't have to look; it was the first one on the page.

For years, international bestselling author Clare Collins has churned out book after book that has appealed to that wide audience that is either devoted, or addicted, to Collins's signature, if often-times repetitive, plot structure: love gained, love lost, love gained again with a twist. So it was with great anticipation that readers, including this reader, who generally prefers a meatier book with more depth and substance than a typical Collins book, awaited the release of *If You Knew Her*. It's Collins's first self-confessed attempt at elevating her prose and leaping the chasm between an all-you-can-eat buffet and a fine dining literary experience.

One can imagine Collins scratching at the surface of the story she wanted to tell, but when it came time to dig deep, she pulled back before truly daring to break ground with her characters. The result is a setup that makes a heady promise—a promise that Collins's unexcavated characters are unable to deliver.

Collins has indeed leapt; however, *If You Knew Her* has botched the landing and unfortunately ended at the bottom of the canyon.

Clare stood up from behind her desk and crossed her expansive study to face the floor-to-ceiling glass wall that looked out over the Pacific crashing below her. The overcast sky met the gray ocean out on the horizon and promised a storm to match her mood. She would give Donna her pound of flesh and read the rest of the review, but

Clare already knew two things: Donna's review had little to do with *If You Knew Her*, and it wasn't going to get any better. This was personal, and ten years in the coming. Apparently, Donna's National Book Award and subsequent improved sales had done little to help her move on.

They had been friends, once upon a time in Brooklyn. Two struggling writers, going hungry together, sleeping on couches in an over-occupancy one-bedroom apartment. Hunting for silence, space, and the time to get words on pages. Wading through drifts of rejection, rejection, rejection, together with their other two roommates. It had been the four of them. Flynn had also been a writer back then but now worked as an editor for a midsized publisher uptown. Sergio was an actor who had eventually given up chasing off-Broadway and now lived in LA. Back then, their professional struggles were best weathered together, the pain of every "Thank you, no thank you" washed down with the biggest bottle of Boone's Farm Strawberry Hill they could scrape enough change together to afford from Roy's Liquor around the corner.

Their miseries loved each other's company, but the company started to shift the day she came home, bottle in hand, wanting to celebrate some success. Clare's struggle ended first and the most dramatically, despite the fact that it was Donna who was, without question, the most singularly talented of them all.

She had her reasons to hate Clare, and in truth, Clare understood those reasons perfectly. It was easy to imagine being Donna, that very specific pain of watching your friend achieve professionally everything you ever wanted. Honestly, everything Donna deserved.

Clare looked down at Donna's book, *Messages from the Shadowlands*, on the glass coffee table. It was an advance copy that Simon had requested from Donna's publisher before the hardbacks hit the shelves, and long before the National Book Award medallions were placed on the covers. It had sat on her table ever since Clare had stayed up until three a.m. to finish it. When she had closed the book, she sat with it, silent, her pristine white-walled study dark beyond the reach of her crystal table lamp's glow.

Stunned. Moved. Affected by Donna's story, yes, she had been all of those things. And also, for the first time since Simon had plucked her from that wood-worn book bar in Brooklyn, the Blue Spruce, Clare felt shame creep over the grand facade of her own oversized success.

Had any of her many books, even one of them, ever made a single reader feel what Donna's symphony had accomplished?

Clare picked the book up off the table. It was the reason Clare had reached and, as Donna so accurately pointed out, *lost her footing, or perhaps worse, taken on characters and subjects beyond her ability to effectively convey*. Because she had wanted to do more—she had wanted to do what Donna did, but instead she had *landed at the bottom of the canyon*.

Clare threw Donna's book against the thick glass wall. The thud of its spine, first on the wall and then on the floor, broke the silence of her study. Several pages broke loose and littered the floor next to the large white shag rug and roused Charlie from his spot nearest the heating vent to sniff and investigate.

"You can go ahead and pee on those," she told him.

He gave the pages a single snort, then trotted across the rug, under the glass table, and jumped up onto the white couch behind her. "You're not supposed to be up there," she said, and shook her head as she bent down to nuzzle his stupid, cute face and let him lick her cheek. She pulled the pale-blue throw from the back of the couch, laid it out, and positioned Charlie in the middle—pushing the extra fabric up and around him into a puppy nest. She kissed his face once more then headed to her desk to do the one thing Simon had expressly begged her not to.

Poised in her office chair, one hand on her mouse, she opened Facebook.

Her official author page popped up, the stream filled with her publicist's recent posts—dates and locations for the thirty-city book tour she would still have to attend, despite her bloody, mangled corpse of a book being dead on arrival at the *bottom of the canyon*.

But Clare Collins wasn't who she wanted to be right now, so she logged out of this account and typed in the user ID and password of the person who she needed to be in this moment: Sara Smith.

Sara Smith was no one. A low-profile, lurking plain Jane with a stock photo profile pic so innocuous, so truly forgettable, friend requests made by her were almost never rejected. It was easy to believe Sara Smith was someone who went to your high school, was someone you forgot. Maybe she was that wallflower in your junior year chemistry class who sat in the far corner? No, was it econ? Whatever, she's already friends with everyone else you went to high school with—*Accept Friend Request*.

With Sara Smith's help, Clare had, one by one, become social media friends with eighty-four people from her high school class. If any of them ever suspected Sara was really Clare Kaczanowski, the girl from their yearbook who had defied all their expectations and actually become "The Most Likely to Succeed" by changing her name to Clare Collins and writing loads of books, they never called Sara out on it. Which would be mortifying, especially since she had, from time to time, contributed to some of the comments when former classmates occasionally posted news stories about her.

"Hey, I went to high school with this woman!" Daniele Stephens posted several months back, along with the *Forbes* article detailing their guesstimates about Clare's current net worth. The picture the article had used was of Clare at one of her book signings, a long line of readers stretched away from the table where she sat, pen poised over an open copy of *Would I Lie to You?*, smiling up at the elderly man waiting for his autographed copy.

Not that she really cared about impressing her old high school friends. Well, that wasn't completely true. At first she had, in those early years when fame and success were still new, still fun. Now she really just liked looking at people's family pictures, seeing how they had changed, and sometimes, like now, pulling up Kaylee Collins-Hensel's profile and seeing if she'd made it public yet. Clare had always been too afraid, even hiding behind her Sara Smith mask, to send a *Friend Request* to Kaylee.

She always worried that Kaylee would see right through her Sara disguise.

Even if Kaylee didn't suspect Sara was really Clare, what would she maybe have posted about Clare over the years? Clare had obviously taken Adam's last name, and Kaylee would know that, but what did she *think* about it?

She stared at the photo she kept always on her desk, the four-by-six snapshot now almost twenty years old, in a thin silver frame to the right of her monitor—Adam and Clare. It was her eighteenth birthday, right before Adam had given her a tiny chip diamond ring. The ring had been a secret from everyone, everyone except his twin sister, Kaylee, who had helped him pick it out.

Next to the frame, in a small two-drawer lavender velvet box, Clare kept a few of her most precious items. She pulled the dark purple tassel hanging from the handle and opened the top drawer. Inside, all the way at the back, she found the small white ring box she kept hidden, took it out, and placed it on the desk in front of her. She slid off the four-carat emerald-cut diamond engagement ring and matching wedding band Simon had bought her six years ago, with money he'd earned off her books, and placed them in the shallow dish next to her keyboard.

With careful fingers, just like she'd done that day, Clare pried open the box to reveal the tiny chip of a diamond, held in place by four thin silver prongs, on a delicate gold band. She pulled it from the black fabric-covered sponge holding it in place and slipped it on her finger. Adam had shoveled driveways all winter through their senior year to afford it before their graduation in May.

Twenty years ago. How was it even possible that so much time had passed? She'd lived an entire lifetime since losing Adam, but every time she thought of him, it was a new knife in an old wound that refused to heal.

Clare leaned over her desk and pulled the photo closer, ran her finger across those two faces. They were so young, so happy. So desperately in love with each other—and for practically their whole lives. They had grown up on the same street in the same small town. He had always been part of her life.

Until that night.

Clare sat back in her chair, the photo resting against her chest. She let her head fall over the back of her chair and welcomed the tears that always came whenever she thought about Adam. She still, even now, loved him. Spent too much time imagining so many versions of lives she could have had with him.

Clare wiped her eyes and sat up, stared at the computer screen in front of her that was still illuminating Kaylee's profile picture. Like Clare, she was now thirty-eight. Unlike Clare, she had what looked like a normal life, if you could assume such a thing from a nuclear family photo complete with husband, wife, and two children—a boy and a girl. But that was all Clare had ever been able to see. Sara Smith and Kaylee Collins-Hensel were not Facebook friends.

Clare reached for her mouse and moved the cursor to hover over the *Add Friend* button.

Maybe she should leave Kaylee alone. Was this weird? Or even worse than weird, totally *wrong* to be social-media-stalking your old boyfriend's twin sister? She twirled Adam's ring around her finger with her thumb.

Donna's most accurate critique from that morning came back to her. *One can imagine Collins scratching at the surface of the story she wanted to tell.* It was an old accusation now freshly thrown down, publicly, whereas eighteen years ago it had only been witnessed by their other roommates.

"What are you afraid of, Clare?" Donna had asked and tossed Clare's pages on the table between them. "You have to dig deep, get into your characters' guts. I mean, what is the fucking point of writing anything if you're not willing to tell your reader a painful truth?"

Donna's criticisms had always been so hard because of their laser-like accuracy. Clare wanted to tell that story, the one burning inside her, the one she'd been scratching at the surface of for over sixty books.

Donna was right. Clare was afraid of that story, but twenty years was long enough.

Kaylee was an important part of getting it right. Clare couldn't envision telling it, diving into the guts of it, if she didn't know what happened. Clare stared at the photo of Kaylee and her family, evidence of how she had moved on with her life. Had Kaylee really moved on? Before Clare could change her mind, she clicked her mouse—*Friend Request Sent*—and sat back in her chair staring at her screen.

For the first time in years, she didn't know what would happen next.

CHAPTER 6

Eileen

EILEEN WAITED WITH THE HORDES OF OTHER PEOPLE IN THE LAST boarding group outside the gate. Stunned, numb, unable to believe she was about to get on a flight to San Francisco while still clutching explicit photographs detailing her husband's affair with Lauren Andrews.

Lauren and Eric had worked together at the same consulting company for years. Dave, Lauren's husband, had left the photos and the note.

Eileen had been to their home twice—once for a Halloween party, where Lauren had dressed up as a belly dancer, and once for a Memorial Day office barbecue. Surrounded by other people, she obviously couldn't take the photos out of the envelope right now to check, but she was pretty sure every picture was from inside Lauren and Dave's house. There was no way Dave had taken them himself without Eric and Lauren knowing; the photos looked like they were probably stills from an in-home security system. Did Lauren know her husband had installed a camera security system throughout their home?

Obviously not.

Actually, Eileen suddenly thought, wouldn't it be more likely that it would be a *video* surveillance system? She felt ill all over again. Of course, because who had a single-shot photography home surveillance system? Which meant Dave had watched entire videos of Eric and his wife fucking, repeatedly, throughout his home. The envelope she held were just a few of the choicest shots Dave had prepared to... What? Why had he made them? Why had he left them on Eric's car? Was Dave trying to blackmail Eric? Leaving it on Eric's car, obviously Dave had not intended Eileen to see it first, or—*oh God*, their kids.

Because that had almost happened. How close had her kids come to ripping Dave's message open themselves? What if she'd been five seconds later getting out of the door this morning? She tried to imagine Ryan and Paige's reactions—no, she couldn't. Cameron begging to see too, clawing at the photos, Eileen trying to process what the photos meant in front of her kids—with them. All while the smug neighbor bitch across the street bearing witness before sliding into her Mercedes.

Eileen handed her boarding pass to the gate agent.

"Have a wonderful flight, Ms. Greyden." The woman smiled at her.

Eileen, still processing the family earthquake that had barely been avoided on her driveway this morning, nodded and kept walking through the door, down the jet bridge, and toward her plane.

The flight attendant near the door was busy with a first-class passenger, threading a coat hanger through the arms of his sport coat. Eileen didn't want any more greetings or smiles. Just her seat, a drink—and eventually, when she was ready, Dave's note.

Once she got to San Francisco, Clare would know what to do about all—

Eileen stopped dead in the middle of first class. Clare wouldn't know anything. Like a bucket of ice water, the reason why she was even on this flight shocked her from her train of thought. The weight of loss crushed against her chest.

"Excuse me?" the woman behind her asked. "Are you here? My seat's farther back."

Eileen shook her head and kept walking past the divider separating first from economy class. Her rolling suitcase caught on the arms of the seats every few rows, and she yanked it hard to keep it moving. She looked up at the row numbers and letters running the length of the overhead bins. She had no idea what her seat number was.

Where was her boarding pass? She'd just had it in her now-empty hand. Eileen tried to keep moving down the crowded aisle while reaching into the side pocket of her yoga pants. Her suitcase caught on another armrest while her tote slid off her shoulder, down her arm, and against the head of the man sitting in 27D.

"What the hell!" the man said, shoving her bag away and back at Eileen. "Watch it!"

"Oh my God… I'm so sorry," she said to him, clutching her offensive bag to her body. "It slipped. I'm so sorry. Are you okay?" She leaned in to touch his head.

The man jerked back and raised his hand to block her instincts to mother. "I'm fine. Fine," he spat, and turned away from her and toward the woman sitting next to him, who was also glaring at Eileen.

Eileen stood up straight and took a deep breath before continuing toward the back of the airplane, trying her best to ignore the smattering of other passengers who were stealing furtive looks at the frazzled woman causing a scene.

She glanced up at the row numbers again, still with no idea where she needed to be but probably long past her seat, too afraid now to again stop the train of passengers intent on riding her ass.

At the very back, standing in the last row, a young male flight attendant with a kind face stood with both arms over his head in a V, his palms resting flat against the overhead bins. He was poised, professional and would know how to help her find her way to her seat. All she needed was to get to him.

Don't cry, Eileen. Don't you dare. She bit the meaty back of her tongue between two molars and forced her mind to not think, no, not one single thought, about every shitastic thing that had happened in the last six hours to completely upend her whole life.

"Hello," the man greeted her with a large, white-toothed smile. He sized her up for a split second and then asked, "Can I help you?" His face suddenly morphing into an expression of extreme concern.

Eileen nodded. "I…um." She swallowed hard. "I can't find my seat." Her voice came out a whisper.

His brow furrowed as he cocked his head. "I'm sorry, what was that?"

She licked her lips. *Don't cry.* "I…I can't." Helpless, she looked up into his now very concerned face. Eileen shook her head. She could feel herself losing control right before the tears filled her eyes and blurred her vision. She swiped them away with her one free hand, sending her tote again sliding off her shoulder and down her arm to her elbow.

The flight attendant's hands pulled away from the bins and reached to take her bag from her. "It's okay," he said as he motioned with his hand, *follow me.*

She stumbled after him, farther back into the galley, so the passengers right behind her could make it to their seats in the last row. He placed her tote on the floor next to the jump seat. "How can I help?"

A weird sound, like a horn, echoed out of Eileen's strained throat. Embarrassed, she hoped he hadn't heard it. "My seat," she managed to say, "I can't find it."

"Okay," he said, his voice reassuring. He smiled at her. "I think we can get that figured out for sure. My name is Chris."

Eileen's lips pressed hard into a straight line as she looked at him, so grateful. She nodded. "I'm Eileen. Thank you, Chris. I'm not normally... It's just been a really hard day."

Chris sighed. "I'm sorry about your day. It looks like it was maybe a whopper."

Eileen nodded and resisted the urge to pull the envelope and book from her bag and launch into an explanation—see this, this is my sister, she's dead. And these, these pictures are of my husband, and fucking Lauren Andrews, the bitch. Instead, she said, "My worst day, yes."

Chris nodded. "Well, let's at least help you find your seat. Do you have your boarding pass?"

Now with Chris's authoritative presence, and some space, Eileen was able to check her every pocket and her catastrophe of a bag. She finally located the rectangular piece of paper in a side pocket where she had absentmindedly shoved it. Her seat assignment was 22B. Once there was a break in the aisle traffic, Chris carried her tote and rolled her suitcase back up the aisle, past the man she'd almost concussed in 27D and his angry wife.

Eileen didn't dare even glance at them.

"Here we go." Chris pointed to what seemed to be the last empty seat on the whole plane, a middle seat in the middle of the plane.

Eileen died a little more when she saw the cramped little space she would be spending the next two hours inside. The passenger between her and her seat stood up while Chris opened the overhead bins all around her seat to try to find a spot for her suitcase. "I'm sorry, they're all full. We'll need to gate-check it," Chris informed her.

Of course.

Resigned, Eileen nodded and held onto the seat back in front of her and shuffled with her tote into her seat.

"I'll bring you back a gate-check receipt in just a minute," Chris said. "You'll pick your bag up in baggage claim once we're in San Francisco."

Eileen collapsed backward into 22B. "Thank you," was all she said as she shoved her tote beneath the seat in front of her and searched for the seat belt.

Chris disappeared toward the front of the plane while her

seatmate to the right of her squeezed back into their row and began the process of readjusting himself, his seat belt, bottle of water, phone, and headphones, in preparation for the next two uncomfortable hours ahead of them.

Eileen sat back and stared at the blank screen embedded into the back of the headrest in front of her. Maybe this was all she would do for the whole flight—stare in a stupor of disbelief for two hours. Completely surrounded as she was, she couldn't risk pulling Dave's note out of the envelope and reading it. She couldn't trust or predict what her reaction might be. Already an exposed wire of raw emotions, the last thing she needed was to start sobbing uncontrollably while trapped dead center of an airplane hurtling through the skies at forty thousand feet.

"Eileen?" Chris called her name gently from the aisle.

She looked at him, expecting to get her bag claim ticket from him.

"Eileen Greyden?" he clarified.

She nodded her head stupidly.

Chris smiled. "I need you to gather your things and come with me," he explained.

Her shoulders sagged—what now? "Is something wrong?" she asked.

"No, not at all." He glanced at her seatmate, who was clearly trying to hide his extreme annoyance at having to, yet again, reshuffle himself and his things so Eileen could, yet again, get past him. "There's just been a last-minute alteration to your flight itinerary."

Eileen blinked, still not understanding exactly what that meant, but she felt fairly positive she was getting bumped off the flight.

Never one to question authority, she pulled her tote from under the seat and unfastened her seat belt.

Does it even matter? she wondered as she slid back across the seat. She kept her eyes down to avoid the angry expressions of her now ex-seatmate, waiting in the aisle with his open laptop in hand.

"Should I just stand here?" the man asked Chris, not bothering to hide his annoyance. "Is someone else coming?"

"No," Chris said, politely ignoring the man's rude tone. "Sorry for the inconvenience. Please go ahead and take your seat."

"Again," the man said, relishing the savor of the last word.

Chris smiled and nodded, then ushered Eileen back toward the front of the plane.

"Is something wrong?" she asked him as they navigated the aisle.

"No, not at all. You've just had a seat change," he explained as they passed the curtain dividing the economy section from first class.

"A seat change?" she asked.

"The gate agent just came down. Your seat has been upgraded," he said.

"Upgraded?" Eileen asked, still confused. "Not bumped and reassigned…like on a later flight?"

Chris smiled and shook his head, then pointed to the large cocoon-looking seat contraption next to the window behind her. "No, not bumped…upgraded to first," he whispered. "Your new seat is 3D, Ms. Greyden."

Eileen turned and stared for a second, looked back at Chris like maybe this was a joke, and then finally slid, dumbfounded, into the large seat.

"I've taken the liberty of placing your suitcase above your seat," he explained with his hand on the bin over her head.

Eileen scanned the rest of first class and its passengers, then waved Chris closer. "I can't afford this," she admitted in a whisper.

Chris crouched down beside her individual first-class pod. "You don't have to. Someone else called in the reservation change." He pulled a folded note from his blazer pocket and read aloud. "A Mr. Simon Reamer?" Chris raised his eyebrows. "That's who called the airline and upgraded your seat. Ring any bells?"

Understanding washed over her. Eileen sat back in the spacious seat and nodded.

Satisfied that she was settled, Chris nodded once and stood back up. "Now, we still have a few minutes before we close the doors and prepare for takeoff. Can I bring you a preflight cocktail?"

Eileen shifted her gaze from her chipped toenails peeking out from her comfy sandals—if she'd known she'd end up in first class, she would have worn different shoes—up to Chris's friendly face. "The drinks are complementary?"

"One of the perks."

"I'll have a Scotch, please. Straight."

"Coming right up."

Eileen managed to lift the corners of her mouth enough to approximate a smile.

Once he left to pour her drink, she pulled her bag onto her lap and reopened the envelope. Careful to not look at any of the pictures, the images already seared permanently into her memory, she found Dave's ragged edged note and took it out.

"Your drink, Ms. Greyden," Chris said, placing the tumbler on the small table next to her seat.

"Thank you," she whispered leaning toward him.

After he walked away, Eileen took a sip from her glass, felt her throat burn, and sat back. Her single pod angled toward the window, which gave her a bit of privacy. She unfolded Dave's note on her lap.

Eric,

As you can see, I know what has been going on between you and Lauren. I have no idea for how long, but as I think back, I realize there have been plenty of clues and red flags I've obviously ignored. I suspect it's been years.

I love my wife. I can't imagine living my life without her. I am giving you this envelope, with only a fraction of the evidence I have, as a warning—stay away from her. Stay away from her or the next envelope I deliver will be to Eileen. So unless you're ready to end your marriage, break up your home, have your kids find out what you've done, stay the fuck out of my house and my bed.

I don't think your wife would be as willing to try to forget as I am.

Dave

As soon as she finished reading Dave's threat, the neural wash of memories rushed up against the floodgates of her consciousness.

Fourth of July. She had stood at her kitchen sink—rinsing vegetables. Their house had buzzed with neighbors and friends. Kids tore through the house, upstairs, out the backdoor. The doorbell continued to ring as more and more people arrived, eventually getting directed to the kitchen or out the backdoor to the cooler filled with beer. The grill, manned by Eric's brother, pumped out the smoky promise of perfectly grilled gourmet burgers, sizzling bratwursts, and hot dogs for the kids.

Eileen had yet to escape the kitchen and join the chaos. Refilling chip bowls, laying out the vegetable tray, monitoring the last pie in the oven so it didn't cook too long and burn. Their wide kitchen windows overlooked the backyard and were pushed open to help with airflow. Outside, many of the guests were standing and drinking; others were seated around the patio table, talking, laughing. Cameron had managed to wrangle the music flowing through the outdoor speakers onto a country music channel; only Paige seemed to notice and complain.

Eric and Lauren sat in chairs next to each other around the outdoor table, crammed closer than usual to fit more people. When she first noticed them, Eileen had only wondered if Lauren might prefer a glass of wine. She was about to open a bottle for herself and anyone else that didn't want beer. But then what happened? Eileen got busy again, she supposed. She did manage to open the wine but never made it over to the table to offer Lauren any.

Someone handed her a paper plate with a burger. "You're working too hard, Eileen," Cara from down the street said with a smile. "Go sit down and enjoy your party."

Eileen shrugged. "I enjoy it," she said, but managed to slow down playing hostess long enough to doctor her burger with ketchup and add a handful of rippled, greasy potato chips to the side of her plate. She stood at the kitchen counter with Cara and took a bite.

The sun had moved, casting her east-facing backyard into the relief of the shade.

Eric and Lauren hadn't moved.

That was all she had thought at the time. The natural flow of the party had shifted. People had finished eating, some had picked new cold cans of beer from the cooler, some stood in the far reaches of her yard smoking cigarettes, others had abandoned their crowded collection of chairs around the table to go play cornhole on the side of the house.

Eric and Lauren had been sitting together under the shade of the patio umbrella hours ago. And they were still there.

...but as I think back, I realize there have been plenty of clues and red flags I've obviously ignored. I suspect it's been years.

That was it, and Dave was right. Eric and Lauren sitting together, pushed close by necessity but remaining there by choice, taking advantage of the obvious excuse to be so near to each other. They enjoyed the physical proximity to one another, neither one wanting to jeopardize their spot.

Once they were at cruise altitude and the captain's pleasant and competent voice let them know it was "now safe to move about the cabin," and she heard the auditory cue, *ding*, of the seat belt sign going dark, Eileen folded Dave's note and put it away.

Red flags. Even though Eileen had never allowed what she noticed that day to take full shape, had never entertained a real suspicion, it all now seemed so painfully obvious. The other flags: the office Christmas party, late nights, Eric texting on their driveway, so many times she thought something was... What? A little off? Memories that now rushed in to crush her with her own, now obvious, stupidity.

How could she be so oblivious? So blind?

"You love him too much," Clare once said.

Eileen's throat and face tightened again with the threat of tears. She forced herself to take a breath, big and deep, just like she'd coached the kids when they had been little and wrecked their bikes or cut their fingers. *Take deep breaths. Try to think about something else.*

But there were no safe thoughts, so Eileen shut them all down. *Emotional vulnerability. Yes, that is happening right now.*

She only wished she could call their fucking brain-dead therapist, *Rachel*, and self-report this moment of control. *See, see how I am not reacting with my emotions first. See how I am capable of calming myself first—big, deep breaths, counting slowly down. Look how I am reaching for this flight attendant call button.* Ding.

Within seconds, a smiling middle-aged flight attendant with a bright blond bob cut arrived next to her seat. She reached down, deactivated the call light, and asked, "Yes, Ms. Greyden?"

Eileen smiled back at the woman, then glanced around the cabin before settling her gaze on the space between the woman's light brown eyes. "Could I please have a glass of cabernet?" she whispered.

"Of course." The flight attendant nodded. "I'll be right back."

I'm calmly ordering a glass of wine, Rachel, instead of standing up in my seat, mouth wide, screaming at the top of my lungs as I run wild up and down and up and down the aisles, arms waving over my head. Yes, Rachel, you late-twenties know-it-all who's never been married or had children but still feels qualified to counsel those of us that end up blindsided—BLINDSIDED—by photos of our husband fucking Lauren Andrews.

Speaking of that, would you like to see those pictures? It's only a fraction of the evidence *Dave has, but you get the idea. So, and this is just a suggestion, and I realize I don't have a master's degree from our local state college, but maybe next session we could discuss these photos with Eric, spend a bit more time digging below his excellent example of* emotional stability, *because I can't help feeling like these photos suggest, I'm only suggesting, perhaps some culpability?*

But just think about that, Rachel, because maybe I'm wrong. I have been feeling quite emotionally vulnerable.

The bob-cut flight attendant returned with the bottle. "Your wine, Ms. Greyden," she said as she placed a short-stemmed glass on the table and then expertly held the bottle between both her hands. Eileen watched as the woman filled the empty glass with the deep burgundy-colored wine, careful to wipe the mouth of the bottle with a white linen as she exited the pour.

"Thank you," Eileen said, as the flight attendant finished and stood straight.

Eileen picked up her glass and took a drink. She was unaccustomed to having people wait on her, *do things* for her. It was unfortunate that this normally wonderful surprise of a circumstance was completely overshadowed by so many horrific realities battling for space and attention in her mind.

She considered sending a series of text messages to Rachel with cell phone snaps of the photos. *We need to cancel our appointment next week. Also, you're fired.* She imagined the stunned surprise on Rachel's face; it brought her the smallest sense of smug relief.

It wouldn't last.

Her sister was dead.

Her husband was sleeping with Lauren.

She wanted to rage. To scream, howl, to hit something hard and repeatedly—like Eric's face. She finished her glass of wine in one long swallow from behind the half privacy screen of her pod and stared out the oval window at the bright expanse of clear blue sky beyond.

Maybe their plane would crash.

The image of her three children immediately floated up, sobbing, standing at her funeral. Eric holding Lauren's hand next to her grave. "I swear," Lauren pledged. "I will be a good mother to—"

Don't be stupid, Eileen. Of course you don't want the plane to crash.

She leaned forward and pulled Clare's book from her bag. She couldn't even fathom having the ability to focus her attention long enough to read right now; she just wanted to sit with something her sister had created in her lap. Hold on to it. Stare at the blur of words filling page after page, words that had come from Clare's mind.

They had grown apart, but Eileen loved her sister. She couldn't imagine Clare really gone from the world.

It didn't seem real, or possible.

Eileen ran her hand over the cover, feeling the raised gold letters, *Clare Collins, A Perfect Life*, beneath her palm. She opened the cover, felt the new spine release some stiffness, and flipped past the title page to the dedication.

For the love of my life.
Finally, our painful truth.

Eileen stared at those words. She read them several times, tried to shape them into an understanding that fit with Clare as Eileen knew her. She placed her hand over the dedication and stared out the window; two thoughts struck her.

Clare had always dedicated her books to her readers.

Clare would never call Simon the *love* of her life.

It was true, it had been several years since Eileen had purchased one of Clare's books; she supposed something may have changed for her sister in that time. Maybe she had grown to love Simon.

"More wine, Ms. Greyden?"

"Yes, please."

CHAPTER 7

Clare

Two years before her death

LIKE SOME WEIRD, OBSESSIVE STALKER, CLARE KEPT REFRESHING HER *Sara Smith* Facebook page every ten to twenty minutes, checking to see if Kaylee had accepted her. After an hour with no response, Clare got up from her chair and paced her study, from her desk at one end to the floor-to-ceiling bookshelves on the other. She twisted Adam's engagement ring round and round her finger. On her third lap, her eyes fell on the bottom three shelves of her bookcase. Her journals, every one of them she had ever filled since she was eleven years old. The one constant thing that had followed her from her childhood in Casper to New York and then back across to the other side of the country. Her documentation of life as she had lived it—she'd kept every one.

Her eyes found the first one, crammed tight between the whitewashed wood of the shelf and the hundred other journals she had filled with ink over the years. She knelt in front of the shelf, her finger working to dislodge the thin spine from the tight space until the slim volume came loose in her hand. With her legs crossed beneath her, Clare held the now limp and faded book closed in her lap. A kaleidoscopic swirl of rainbow colors overlaid with a translucent, shiny foil that had lifted and peeled away from the edges of the cover over the past three decades—*My Diary* was centered in a large silver script.

It had been a birthday gift from Adam. Clare held the book between her palms and closed her eyes.

"Tell me a story, Clare."

Her eyes flew open, the sound of Adam's voice still clear in her mind, but also, it was as if she had heard it in the room. His sound, his exact pitch and tone, the lifetime she'd lived with that voice—the eternity it had been since she'd heard it.

"Adam?" she whispered into the room. Only the sound of her own heart rushing in her ears answered her. Twenty years. In a few months, it would be twenty years since that night. The thumb of her left hand pressed against his ring on her finger.

She opened the journal and stared down into her eleven-year-old handwriting. Looking at the loopy and irregular, slightly wild cursive that had improved only a little in the last twenty-seven years, Clare read the first line she'd ever put down into the world.

Mama said Daddy isn't coming home.

Clare took a breath and held it. She remembered that day, standing next to Eileen, their mother still in her cop uniform just home from her shift. "Your father is back in the hospital... They don't think he'll be coming home this time."

She remembered her mother unfastening her duty belt, placing it on the table, removing the gun from the holster, checking the safety, and walking it back to the bedroom, where she kept her gun safe behind the folding closet door. It wasn't her mother's words that had made Clare's heart stop in her chest that day; it was the resignation of her tone. As if their father were already dead.

Clare had left her little sister standing there, sobbing and hiccupping alone over the back of their polyester couch, and wandered two doors down to Adam and Kaylee's house. Adam was in the front yard, digging a hole with a stick in one of the many dirt patches where their lawn stubbornly refused to fill in. He looked up, his eyes on hers, the second he heard her tread-worn sneakers on the cracked concrete walk.

"What's wrong?" he asked when he noticed her tears. Standing up, he dropped his stick.

Later, in the tree house Adam and Kaylee's father had built for Christmas four years ago, Adam had given her his birthday present two days early, hoping it would help cheer her up and take her mind off her father dying in the hospital two miles away.

"What should I write in it?" she asked him.

Adam, his head in her lap, looked up at her with his bright blue eyes and smiled. "Tell me a story, Clare. You always make up the best stories. You should write them down."

Later, standing beneath the tree, long past when it had gone dark and Clare was expected to be home, Adam kissed her lips for the first time. She could still remember that first soft press of his mouth against hers, the moment they became more than best friends, the moment everything between them changed forever.

Later that night, after Eileen had finished crying herself to sleep on the other side of their shared bedroom, Clare wrote her first words in her first journal. *Mama said Daddy isn't coming home.* The next three pages had poured out of her as she had sat upright, her diary resting on her knees under the covers of her bed, straining to keep her words on the lines with only the soft glow of their night-light to help her.

Their father had died the very next morning. He was thirty-one.

Clare closed her first journal and placed it next to her on the white shag rug; she was now seven years older than her father had been when he died, alone, in that hospital room.

She stared at the hundreds of other journals before her, remembering clearly what was in some, frightened by what revelations were held in others. These books, collectively, held the essence of what Donna Mehan had been dogging her about for years. In these books was the meat of a story Clare was afraid to tell.

She leaned forward and touched the tops of several spines all at once. She pulled them out, three, four, five. She used both her hands and pulled journal after journal into a heap on the rug in front of her until she had cleaned three shelves worth bare. By the time Roberto arrived for his scheduled weekly private piano performance, Clare was busy stacking the books in piles of ten on her glass coffee table.

Clare had met Roberto at a private party in Pacific Palisades, hosted by the director of the movie based on Clare's thirtieth book, *She Knew You When*. Roberto had told her he and his wife were retiring to San Francisco after a long and successful career as a studio musician who had played backup piano for major artists for more than forty years. "It's my fingers that are needing to quit, damn arthritis. My heart and my head would keep at it right up until they shoveled the dirt into my grave."

It had been months later that she'd called him. She'd been working on *What We Lost*, annoyed with her inability to find exactly what she was wanting for mood music. When she'd realized what she wanted, needed, was live piano music, she'd called Roberto and asked if his arthritic fingers would be able to manage one session a week. She'd had a very specific playlist. Music from her past, once played in this exact order by someone she loved very much.

"Shall I play the usual, Ms. Collins?" Roberto asked, his eyebrows raised at the sight of her hauling books from a perfectly useful bookshelf to a cluttered construction of paper in the middle of the room.

"Of course, please don't mind me," she said as she leveled one stack and returned to the pile for two more handfuls.

"Do you...would you like a hand?" he asked, making his way toward the pile and moving to pick some books up himself.

"No!" she shouted and held up her hand. "Don't touch them!"

Roberto stopped midstoop, then stood up slowly, like a man suddenly realizing he was not in a petting zoo but a bear's den.

"I'm sorry," Clare recovered. "They're...special. I'm sorry I shouted."

Roberto shook his head twice. "No need to explain to me." He pointed to Clare's white Steinway and Sons grand piano, Her Majesty, as he often called it, and tilted his head. "I'll just play?"

"Please." Clare sighed, relieved to get back to what she was working on before his interruption. It wasn't just someone else touching her books, although admittedly that was part of it, the physical act for her, the intimacy with this past, the memories that were opening up to her—her mind was going to *that place*.

That place was where her books had all started. A smorgasbord of thoughts, emotions, images, snippets of dialogue, characters were forming in her head—Roberto was, unintentionally, interrupting that flow. She wanted him to play her songs but didn't want to get sidetracked from the thoughts that were starting to coalesce in her mind. As soon as she had all the books stacked, she grabbed several new notebooks and her pens from the desk.

Roberto played, and Clare wrote.

With notes and pens and various journals spread out around her on the shag rug, with Donna Mehan's sharp critique still stinging, and Adam's ring on her finger, Clare began working out her next book. With a new, acrid black Sharpie, she wrote out her title across the first of the many notebooks she would use for her notes and character sketches: *A Perfect Life*.

When Roberto finished the set of songs, she lifted her head from the pages. "Do you have time today to play the list one more time?"

He smiled down at her from Her Majesty's shiny bench and shrugged. "I think I could squeeze you in before my next appointment with my rocker recliner."

"Thank you, Roberto." The music he played for her was always transportive, dredging up memories and moments she never wanted to forget, but today it was helping her resurrect more than memories. It was helping her summon the ghosts she needed to craft this book. When he had run through all but the last two songs again, Clare noticed that she had filled most of her first notebook and her hand was cramping.

She flipped through her notes with only a vague sense of what she'd put down. As if she'd barely been conscious while writing and was only now waking up. Charlie shifted on the couch and drew her attention, then she glanced at the computer and remembered—her friend request to Kaylee.

She sat upright and stretched out the kinks that had roped across her back and up her neck from sitting hunched over on the floor for too long, then stood up and moved to her desk. She glanced back at Roberto, all his concentration and efforts focused on his fingers and the keys in front of him as he began the final song. Clare sat down and shook her mouse to life, placing each of her noise-cancelling earbuds in her ears to now drown out the piano—she felt heavy, and she recognized the feeling. It was the grief come back. She found a track of music she had recently purchased, nothing from her past— she needed to wake back up to the here and now.

With two clicks of her mouse, she learned that Kaylee and Sara Smith were now Facebook friends. What's more, Kaylee had sent Sara a direct message. She hesitated. Did Kaylee suspect it was really Clare? She envisioned some sort of horrible message: *I know it's you, Clare. Oh and by the way, so does everyone else. You're not fooling anyone, "Sara," so how about you cut the crap? Or are you just too famous now?*

Clare sighed. Kaylee had always been a very sweet girl; it was hard to imagine this now mother of two suddenly morphing into a mean-girl bitch. She was always friends with everyone. Clare clicked open the message.

Hi Sara,

Thanks for reaching out! I see you are friends with lots of people from Cleaver High. Are you an alum? I'm sorry I don't remember you off the top of my head, which is weird, but twenty years is a long time! But if you are an alum, and didn't already know, I'm coordinating the class of '98 twenty-year reunion. It will be in Casper, of course, in May. Click the link I'm adding at the bottom of this message to go to our official page—hope to see you there! Best, Kaylee Collins-Hensel

Clare clicked the link for the reunion page and sat back in her chair. Kaylee maybe didn't know it was her, but she had to suspect. *I don't remember you off the top of my head, which is weird.* Of course it was weird. They had gone to a high school with less than three hundred people in their graduating class—everyone knew everyone. If Clare Kaczanowski (a.k.a., Collins) was the only one missing, and no one really remembered *Sara Smith*, it didn't take Sherlock Holmes—

Something touched her shoulder—she screamed.

CHAPTER 8

Simon

Two years before Clare's death

IF HE WAS HONEST WITH HIMSELF, AND HE SUSPECTED THAT MAYBE he hadn't been in a very long time, he hated living in this place.

He stared down into the green, swampy-smelling pool that no one ever used and considered a list of things that could possibly be wrong. The pump was running; he could hear it humming softly through the open doors of the low-slung equipment shed. The chemicals had just been checked last week. There was no way a week of nonuse left the water looking like this unless it was something more serious, like a cracked pipe.

With his hands on his hips, Simon sighed, suddenly aware of the tension that had been building all day, ever since sneaking out of bed before Clare to read Donna's review.

He stared at the sky above him, gray and overcast. The wind blowing in from the ocean picked up speed and smelled like a storm. He walked away from the pool. It wasn't like he possessed even the most basic of mechanical skills; what was he going to do about it? Once he was back inside, he'd call their pool guy, see how quickly they could get out here.

Their house had been built on a vacant five-acre lot, naturally secluded on a jut of cliff. Three sides of the property were surrounded by steep, rocky drops that overlooked both the crash of the Pacific Ocean and Muir Beach. Should any of their closest neighbors—not that they knew any of them—happen to decide to drop in, they would either have to scale the three hundred wooden steps leading from the beach below or announce themselves at the fifteen-foot-high security gate protecting the fourth side of the property.

With bare feet and his pants rolled at the ankle so they wouldn't get wet messing around with the pool, Simon crossed the stamped concrete pool deck to the grass yard that led out to the three-foot black wrought-iron fence, the one barrier between him, the cliff, and the Pacific. When the house was first built, they hadn't even bothered with the fence. When the contractor mentioned putting it in, Clare had scoffed.

"What for?"

"Well, it's pretty dangerous," he advised them with a nervous glance over his shoulder. "A child, or adult, for that matter, in the dark, let's say, could easily wander too far. Those cliffs are sheer. There's nothing to stop them going right over."

"We don't have small children," Clare announced like a declaration. "And we are likely the only adults who will ever be here—adults who are smart enough to not fall off a cliff," she chided. "Right, Simon?"

"Um...of course," he agreed, which was pretty much all you could do with Clare once she had made up her mind about anything. What had she meant about being the only adults? Like ever? This huge house and pool, the outside deck, surely there would be people over—parties?

"Besides," she added, striding right over to the cliff's edge and throwing her arms wide. "I like to stand here... It's one of the reasons I specifically chose this property." She whirled around to face them, her heels right at the rocky lip, making Simon's stomach queasy with fear. If she lost her balance, fell back even half a step—she'd be gone. "I don't like the idea of *anything* between me and this ocean. I like the feeling, the *power* of it."

The contractor had raised his eyebrows and shrugged as if to say, *It's your homeowners insurance, not my problem which of you, or your drunken friends, goes careening over the edge to their certain death.* It wasn't until Simon brought Charlie home four months ago that Clare had called the contractor back and explained their new circumstance.

Because she couldn't bear the thought of *Charlie* getting hurt.

Simon stood at the fence now, his hands gripping the cold wrought-iron bars. The crash of the sea nearly drowned out the tinkling notes of piano spilling from Clare's open window high behind him.

This was not his home.

It was his first honest thought in a long time, and it scared him. Simon took a deep breath of the cold sea air. It made his lungs constrict, and he coughed the salty, wet air back out. She had never, not once, even asked his opinion on anything with regard to *their home.*

This place, a secluded and sleepy seaside enclave forty minutes north of San Francisco, this plot of land, chosen by Clare without consulting him, even the design of the house, also all Clare's idea. Everything about this place originated from what she wanted, where she wanted to be, how she wanted to live. One day, four years ago, she had made the executive decision to completely change their lives.

He had come home from his office and ridden the elevator up to their fourth-floor apartment in SoHo, and Clare had simply announced what she had done.

"I've purchased some land. I'm going to build a house."

She was standing in the kitchen, glass of white wine in hand, slouchy wool socks, and her pajama shorts. Her long auburn hair was piled on top of her head in a sloppy bun, and he knew right away she had been writing all day. Clare never bothered getting dressed when she was writing.

He let his computer bag slide from his shoulder to the wood floor. "What?" he asked, still half thinking about the two foreign deals, German and French rights that had come in that morning. He'd been planning on surprising her, but she had surprised him first. "Land?" He shook his head. "I'm not following."

"My book signing last month, in San Francisco?"

He nodded, yes, he remembered. San Francisco had been the last stop of the book tour.

"Well, and you know how I spent a few days there after…as a break?"

More nodding, yes, he had flown back to New York for a meeting he had on the Monday or something. He had to get home, and she had stayed. "Yes."

"Well, I don't know if you remember, but at the end of the tour, I was coming out of my own skin and needed some headspace. Some *physical* space."

Simon was now shaking his head. "You never told me that."

Clare waved this statement away. "Anyway, I got to talking to this guy in the hotel bar. We had this…connection, I guess. And it turned out he was a real estate agent. After we'd been talking for about an hour, I asked him, please take me anywhere, away from cities, people. Take me somewhere I can just be, just think."

"Wait." Simon put up both his hands and took a deep breath. "You asked, what, just any guy to take you…anywhere? And didn't tell me or anyone where you were going? You didn't even know yourself where this guy might take you."

Her shoulders sank, and she gave him her annoyed look. "Are you listening to what I'm trying to tell you, or are you trying to micromanage my past? I'm telling you now where I went."

"But what good would that be had this guy been some crazed lunatic that hauled you off to some basement for the rest of your life?"

"What the hell are you talking about? He was a *Realtor*. He drove me to Muir Beach. He parked the car near a cliff and showed me how to find the beach access."

"Lucky for you…for us both!"

"He was a perfectly nice man!"

"How can you take risks like that? You're Clare Collins! He could have been anyone!"

She stared at him, raised her wineglass to her mouth, and took several large swallows of the Silver Oak special reserve he could see she had opened to celebrate her news. When she lowered the glass, she also lowered her tone. "Simon, my husband, I have bought some land overlooking the Pacific Ocean, with beach access to a lovely strip of sand. I have fallen in love with a place and have decided to make it mine. I am looking at architectural designs for a home. I am celebrating these facts this evening with a very nice bottle of wine. Please join me." She walked back to the counter and poured wine into the second glass she had waiting and ready for him for when he got home.

"Additionally, while finding this bit of heaven on earth, I managed to not get abducted, raped, ransomed, or sold into a human trafficking ring, despite being *Clare Collins*." She raised her glass to him. "So, we also can celebrate that good news." She brought the glass to him.

"Please, I don't want to fight—not tonight. I've been *so* happy all day thinking about this." She smiled and kissed his lips. "Let's have a good night."

He took the glass and a drink from it, trying his best to return her smile. He hated making her unhappy. When Clare was unhappy, the stormy silence could stretch for days, weeks even. He took a deep breath and sighed it out. "You just caught me by surprise."

She gave him a wicked grin. He could tell she was already half drunk. It was very likely the Silver Oak was not the first bottle opened in celebration. "Of course I did." She shifted into her coy expression. "Surprises are what I do best. I have to keep you on your toes. Wouldn't want you getting bored, trading me in for one of your new, young, *up-and-coming* girl-authors." She pinched his belly gently.

When Clare had first brought him out to this very spot that was to become the edge of his new home, Simon had experienced a creeping panic that grew with every mile that separated him from the life he had known and this isolated existence. Back then he had held out a small hope that she would grow tired of the idea. A phase. A project to distract her from the pressures of being Clare Collins, but with every step she took, finalizing a design, hiring the contractor, breaking ground, Simon's hope that she would eventually give up the idea diminished. Brick after brick, one gallon of cement at a time, Clare built the daily existence she wanted. An existence three thousand miles due west from where Simon wanted his life.

He was a New York man, born and bred. He missed the noise, the pulse, the people. Nights out, the subway, the smells—constant activity, the hustle. This life he had now, it was like being trapped on a deserted, albeit luxurious, island.

Simon turned away from the roiling ocean and felt the wind blow hard against his back as he headed up to the house. Clare's personal pianist, Roberto, was halfway through the last song of his set, the same exact set of songs he always played, per Clare's request. When Roberto left, that would be a good time to try to intercept Clare. He was hoping to pry her out of the house and into the city for the evening.

By the time he was back inside, through the darkened living room, and up the marble staircase, Roberto had finished playing.

Outside her door, Simon couldn't hear anything; the pianist would be making his exit as soon as he'd gathered his music and packed it away in his satchel. The handle of the door turned, and a beam of light shot through the crack of the open door into the dark hallway, where Simon waited to see his wife.

Roberto slipped out the door. Almost seventy, his back bent and fingers crooked from his lifetime devotion to classical piano, he pulled the door shut behind him.

"Roberto," Simon said.

The old man startled and dropped his slim leather bag with a thud onto the hardwood floor.

"Sorry," Simon said and placed his hands on the man's shoulders for reassurance. "I didn't mean to frighten you."

Roberto turned around, relief washing over his face as he pressed one hand to his heart. "You got me good, son."

Simon bent down to pick up the man's bag. "I'm so sorry. I was just wanting to quietly slip in as you were leaving." He motioned toward the still-open door and handed Roberto his satchel back. "How's she doing?"

Roberto adjusted his glasses and took a moment to think. "Quiet, I suppose. But she's always quiet when I play. Today, though, I guess something felt a bit different, maybe a bit off," he finished in a whisper. "Everything okay?"

Simon bit the inside of his bottom lip then scratched his chin. He'd need to shave before they left, assuming he could get Clare to come with him. "She had some not great news this morning, a bad review from another author."

Roberto nodded. "Usually, she sits on the couch, looks out at the ocean when I play. Lost in her thoughts." He shrugged. "Barely said hello when I came in today and was poring over some books most of the time, then on her computer for a bit. I imagine she's pretty distracted by the news."

Simon furrowed his brow and nodded, suddenly worried Clare had gone back on her earlier promise to stay off of social media until the news about Donna's review could blow over. He reached out to shake Roberto's hand. "Thank you," he said as the old man placed his gnarled, knuckled hand in his own. "Until next week?"

Roberto smiled and nodded before he turned to leave. "Oh, one more thing. It's probably getting about time to have Her Majesty tuned. She's not too far gone just yet, but I can hear her starting to go wrong."

"I'll call the piano tuner tomorrow, see if she can get out here in the next week or so." The piano tuner and the pool guy. All Simon needed now was to find a leak in the damn roof. He thought again of how much he missed the simplicity of their two-bedroom New York apartment.

"No rush, when she can get to it." Roberto raised his hand once in goodbye and started his slow and careful descent down the wide staircase.

Simon turned his attention back to the light streaming from the crack in Clare's door. She wouldn't want to be disturbed. She never did. He pushed the door in anyway, revealing her lavish white enclave, her sanctuary, as she called it. The designer had cautioned Clare, "Maybe, just one or two spots of color?" But Clare had been insistent. White walls, white couch, white shag rug.

He hadn't done it on purpose, but even the dog he picked out for her was snow white. Charlie, lying curled in a blanket on the couch, lifted his head when Simon came in. His tail wagged violently and thumped against the taut buttoned leather. Simon couldn't help but smile at the always-happy dog, before turning his eyes to his wife. As Roberto had described, her back was to him, her entire focus and attention aimed at the wide, flat computer monitor in front of her. But on the coffee table, and strewn all over the rug and couch, hundreds of the journals from her shelves were stacked, open, resting on the arm of the couch. He could also see a pile of pens on the floor and new notebooks with Clare's handwriting.

She was writing a new book.

This both excited him, as Clare was his client and he always loved her work, and depressed him, as she was also his wife who always worked. When Clare was in the throes of a book, she rarely left the house, rarely left this room. The thought of her entrenching for the next several months made his own feelings of entrapment swell. Resisting the urge to go peek at what she was working on—it would make her angry—Simon instead headed over to Clare, who was still oblivious to his presence.

The sound of his shoes on her marble floor could be heard, but she didn't move a muscle to suggest she noticed. When he was only a few feet away, he could see she had her earbuds in. She always listened to music when she wrote.

Except, she wasn't writing.

On the huge screen, he could clearly see that Clare was on Facebook; she had promised him. A nervous dread wormed its way around his spine. What damage had she already done? A public social media throw down was the last thing he felt like trying to clean up.

"Clare?" he said, placing his hand on her shoulder.

She screamed and jumped sideways in her chair. She whirled around, startled and angry. It took her a moment to register it was him. "Jesus, Simon!" Her voice echoed through her study. She yanked one of the earbuds from her ear. "You scared me to death."

"Sorry," he said flatly, then pointed to the screen in front of her. "You promised."

She wrinkled her face, deciphering what he meant, and it dawned on her when she glanced back at her screen. "What, this?" She reached for her mouse, aimed her cursor, and with a single click, she shut the whole show down. "I didn't break my promise. It has nothing to do with Donna Mehan."

He cocked his head. "Well, what does it have to do with?"

"As if it's any of your business," she shot back. "I am still entitled to some privacy, yes? No? You tell me, Simon. Do I need to consult you before I look into the specifics of my high school reunion?"

This. He wasn't expecting this. "What? Reunion?" He shook his head. "What are you talking about?"

"It's nothing. This year is my high school's twenty-year reunion."

Dumbfounded, he stared at her. "And? You're thinking about going?" It was impossible to hide his sarcasm.

Clare shifted in her seat, her chin raised a fraction of an inch. "Maybe, I don't know. I was just looking into it."

He closed his eyes and took a very long and deep breath. It occurred to him, and not for the first time, that he quite possibly didn't know his wife, and most successful client, at all. He had no idea what to say to any of this, couldn't find the words to explain to her something that seemed obvious to him and yet she, repeatedly, seemed to fail to understand. She was Clare fucking Collins. What exactly did she think was going to happen if she RSVP'd to her high school reunion?

This wasn't why he'd come in here.

He opened his eyes and found her staring back at him. "I came to see if you'd come with me into the city. One of my other clients has a signing at City Lights Books."

"Which client?" she asked, something like jealousy coloring her tone.

"William Cleary."

Clare rolled her eyes. "That wordy windbag?" She rotated her chair so she could get up from behind her desk. "Have fun." She walked over to the couch, and Charlie, who was now standing on his hind legs, his head peeking over the back of the couch, was eagerly awaiting her attentions.

"Yes, well, your personal opinions aside, I was hoping you'd come with me."

She picked Charlie up under his front legs, his back legs squirming until she cradled him on his back. Bending her head low, she loudly kissed the side of his face. "Who's the best dog ever?" she cooed. Charlie licked her cheek several times. "Charlie is. Charlie's the best dog ever."

The dog, clearly in heaven, looked adoringly up into his mother's face.

"Clare," Simon interrupted them. "Will you come with me? I thought we could make a night of it." He moved in to pet Charlie's belly and tried smiling at her. "I'm sure we could still get a last-minute table for *Ms. Collins* at a good restaurant." He wanted to turn this around, be fun, convince her to come out with him, leave the house, enter into the world. "We can stay the night at the condo. We'll take Charlie with us. And tomorrow, we can get up and have breakfast at that cafe on the corner you said you loved. They have that outdoor patio. We can walk Charlie to the dog park on Blake—he'd love that." He was begging her. He wasn't even trying to play it cool at this point.

He needed to get off this desolate rock. *They* needed it.

He was so goddamned lonely out here.

CHAPTER 9

Clare

Two years before her death

WHEN SHE TURNED, SHE HAD SEEN SIMON HOLDING UP HIS HANDS, both sorry and surprised. Roberto had finished and left already, not wanting to disturb her. Now Simon was trying to coax her out of the house and into the city for the night. He was even using Charlie as bait.

His desperation, it hung all over him—she found it nauseating.

Clare looked at the stacks and stacks of journals littering the coffee table and floor, her notes—the beginning of her new book. "Why don't you go ahead?" She placed her hand on his cheek for a moment before returning it to Charlie, cradled in her arms. "I've started something new. I don't want to get distracted right now. I don't want to lose this thread." She turned away from him and stared out the glass wall, the sky darkening so that the lights of San Francisco to the south reflected off the Pacific in the distance.

When she turned back around, he was staring at the piles of papers and books. "You've already started," he said.

Clare sighed. "Yes. It just hit me. You know how it is—creative feast or famine."

He turned to face her. She knew he wouldn't press her to come with him. "You've never had a famine," he said, trying his best to smile. "Don't get me wrong, I love your books as much, probably more, than anyone. I just miss you when you're working on them. I guess I thought we might have a bit more time, you know, before." He gestured to the mess.

"I'm sorry, Simon. Really."

He shook his head. "How ridiculous that my most lucrative client apologizes for making money."

Clare shrugged. "I guess that's one of the problems that comes with shitting where you eat... Isn't that what your mother warned you about?"

Simon didn't move a muscle; only his eyes shifted up to her face. He held her gaze for several long, uncomfortable seconds before turning to the glass wall himself. It was a low blow, dragging his mother in, but the impact was effective.

When he had first started dating Clare, his mother, an editor who had married a writer, Simon's father, had tried to warn him about falling for the client. "It's hard, Simon. They're temperamental, fragile...and, I'm sorry to say, downright infantile at times. You know the old adage about shitting where you eat—it isn't pleasant." Fifteen years ago, he'd made the mistake of joking about his mother's warning with Clare—and she never let him forget it.

"I'm going to get going, then. William's signing is at eight; if I leave now, I'll still have time to get some dinner in the city."

"You'll be staying at the condo then?"

He nodded and turned back to her and Charlie. "And I'm going to catch a flight to New York tomorrow."

Clare raised her eyebrows at this unexpected news. She tried to not look pleased. "New York? Okay."

"I have some meetings I've been putting off," he explained as he closed the distance between them. "I've been out west too long." He tried to smile, but Clare could see he was hoping she would ask him to stay, or take her with him. She would do neither.

"It can't be helped," she said, knowing it wasn't true but not caring. There wasn't any reason Simon *needed* to be in New York for work. He handled everything over phone and email.

"That face-to-face…editors," he added lamely, not even believing it himself.

"Well…" She kissed his cheek. "We'll miss you. Be safe."

Simon stood there a moment longer, staring at her and her dog.

"Do you want help packing some things?" she asked, hoping to hurry him along but also praying he'd say no.

He shook his head, his mouth flattening into a line. He looked into her eyes. "I'll miss you. I love you."

She smiled, but felt flat and emotionless. Her eyes rested on the top button of his white oxford shirt. "I love you, too," she replied before letting him kiss her goodbye.

CHAPTER 10

Eileen

IN THE SAN FRANCISCO AIRPORT, EILEEN STOOD WITH HER BAGS AND her sister's book in her hand staring up at one of the overhead signs, unable to bring the words into focus.

Dammit, she was really drunk.

As other passengers pulling bags rushed past, she took a deep breath and held it as she squinted and forced her eyesight to untangle the blur of swimming words above her head. After several seconds she was finally able to make out *Passenger Pickup* and *Lower-Level* along with the direction of the arrow she needed to follow, right. Eileen hefted her tote back onto her shoulder and grasped the handle of her suitcase before heading off toward the escalator.

"Excuse me," a woman said as she touched Eileen's elbow. When Eileen turned to face the heavyset, middle-aged woman with a mass of unruly curls that didn't look to have done battle with a comb in quite some time, she was surprised to see a copy of *A Perfect Life* raised from the woman's purse like it was a coded communication between them. The woman smiled and pointed to Eileen's copy of the same book cradled in the crook of her arm. "I couldn't help but notice a fellow fan."

"Oh." Eileen managed to find her voice. It sounded slow and too drunk in her head. "Yes." She nodded.

"Isn't it just the most horrific news?" The woman's expression suddenly turned sad, like a poor actor in a community play. She shook her head and furrowed her brow. "You have heard, haven't you? About Clare Collins? I'm just devastated. I've read every single one of her books, some more than once. I just can't believe this will be her last."

Eileen's mouth went dry. It was impossible to think of what words to say. Should she admit Clare was her sister? Would that make this more or less horrible? She couldn't decide, mostly because her brain was drowning in gallons of wine. She stared blankly at the woman and waited for whatever came next in this surreal moment.

"Oh God!" the woman exclaimed as she reached out and grasped Eileen's arm. "You *do* know, don't you? That Clare Collins died last night?" She had the decency to whisper her last sentence. The woman removed her hand from Eileen's arm and placed it over her heart. "I hope I'm not the first one to break the news."

Eileen shook her head. No, she had heard.

"I was this close." The woman pinched the ends of her pink manicured fingertips together. "This close to going to see the movie last night. I couldn't believe they were releasing the movie and book at the same time! But no." She held up her hand like a stop sign. "I always, always read the books first, just in case, you know, they get it all wrong and the movie's terrible."

Eileen swallowed. "Clare…wen to the premi lasss nigh…*t*," she slurred.

The woman recoiled a fraction of an inch, her smile turned uncomfortable. "I'm sorry. What was that?" She tilted her head.

Eileen bit both her lips between her teeth. She hadn't meant to say anything at all, and now had zero confidence in her ability to execute a whole new sentence, especially since her last one had just tumbled from her loose and drunken mouth. She shook her head, her hand haphazardly waving in front of her, as if this could somehow wipe away what was now clear to this woman with her *Oh, oh I see* expression.

"She'sss my siiiisster," Eileen explained.

The woman took half a step back. "Well, I hope you *enjoy it.*" She pointed her index finger to Eileen's copy, took another step away, then turned and left.

Eileen watched the woman retreat. "Bissch," she breathed. It was not like Eileen was the one bothering strangers in airports.

She had sipped glass after glass of cabernet from Denver all the way to San Francisco, never waving off the generosity of the first-class flight attendants, who were always ready with the bottle when she needed a refill. As she cut a weavy, uneven path for the escalators, it became embarrassingly obvious that drinking large quantities of wine while trying to process soul-crushing life events was a huge mistake. Especially since once the flow stopped, it wasn't like she could simply climb the familiar staircase in her own home and pass out on top of her bed. No, she actually needed her brain to be working here. It needed to function and navigate her through this airport, find a taxi willing to transport an obviously inebriated passenger, and somehow communicate her sister's address without slurring and drooling all down the front of her shirt.

Why on earth had those flight attendants allowed her to drink so much?

How could she have been so stupid?

As she stepped onto the descending escalator, she nearly lost her rolling case behind her when it got hung up on something and refused to follow her. Thankfully, she was saved by the irritable man boarding the stairs behind her with reflexes quick enough to shove her bag into alignment with his foot.

"Thank…you," she said to him, raising her hand in apology before turning back to face the ride down. Everything about her, words, gestures, facial expressions, moved in a painful and obvious slow motion. This is how people went missing, their bodies discovered weeks later dead in a back alley or beheaded and floating in with the tide. Drunk beyond belief, one stupid choice after another, accepting the kindness of a serial killer who knew an easy target when it came along.

From deep inside her tote, she could feel her cell phone vibrating. She sighed. "Shit," she whispered while reaching into the bag's cluttered abyss and eyeing the ever-approaching end of the escalator that required her to dismount while remaining upright and in total possession of both her bags. Somehow, her hand closed around her phone, her left foot led her smoothly off the moving staircase, and the wheels of her bag barely hiccupped as they passed over the threatening metal teeth swallowing the stairs. A thought suddenly occurred to her as she stopped to answer her phone—maybe she could get through this day.

"Hey!" the man behind her shouted, right before careening into her back. "Jesus Christ, lady!"

Eileen threw both her hands wide, her cell phone flying, as she pitched violently over her own bag and tumbled onto the linoleum floor. The heavy weight of another human falling on top of her—it was chaos.

"Who the hell stops?" a man was shouting.

More people were yelling, shuffling, trying to get around the pileup of people at the bottom of the escalator. "Hit the emergency stop button!" a woman yelled.

After a bit more shouting, untangling of strangers' limbs, righting of upended bags, someone reached out a hand to Eileen. She looked up from the floor, confused. "What happened?" she asked and took the man's outstretched hand.

As he helped hoist her up from the floor, he looked into her eyes. "There seems to have been…uh, a bit of an accident," he said.

"Damn right there was a bit of an accident!" another man standing nearby began yelling at Eileen. In two steps, the man's red and enraged face was right in front of hers. "Who the hell stops at the bottom of a busy escalator to answer their phone? What the hell is wrong with you?" The man raised his hand and shook it at the now-paralyzed stairs behind them. "You could've killed me! Me and at least five other people!"

Eileen shrank back from the man's rage. "I…I don't know—"

"What the hell you're doing? You got that right, lady!"

"Hey now," the man who had helped Eileen up from the floor suddenly interjected, taking a step between Eileen and her angry victim. "It was an accident."

"A completely preventable one!" the furious man yelled. "Here's an idea—how about you *stay off* your goddamn phone while you're on an escalator and shit-faced drunk!" he crescendoed while snatching both his suitcase and computer bag off the floor.

Eileen stood, mortified, squeezing her two hands together until the knuckles turned white. "I'm sorry," she whispered as the man shook his head and stormed off through baggage claim and toward the sliding glass doors.

As the rest of the crowd began to disperse, some continuing to give her sidelong looks and whispering, the man who had been kind enough to help her up off the floor began trying to collect the multitude of crap that had spilled from her tote far and wide all over the floor. Ready to die now, Eileen bent to her knees and swiped up several pens and, oh God, two tampons, and shoved them back into her bag.

When the man returned to her, he had a handful of loose papers, her sister's book, the envelope of photographic evidence, and her cell phone. "Um, I think there's someone on the line."

Eileen took her phone from the man's outstretched hands and saw her husband's name and number on the screen. "Eileen? Eileen, what's happening?" She remembered her phone ringing right before disaster struck. Obviously it had been Eric.

She couldn't be drunk, have her shit spread all over the San Francisco airport, and deal with her lying, cheating, son of a bitch husband right now. Eileen made the only reasonable choice open to her and hung up the phone before switching the whole thing off. "Thank you," she managed to say as she looked up into the man's face and took the rest of her belongings from him.

She froze. She recognized him. From before her flight, at her table near the food court, the pictures of Eric and Lauren spread all over, and this man walking past bearing witness to the whole ugly scene. He had been on his Bluetooth headset, noticed her and the failure of her marriage on display, and had been kind enough to avert his eyes.

Not thinking it was physically possible, Eileen slipped a whole degradation level lower. She pursed her lips and repacked her tote.

The man stood up and looked around, as if to make sure she wouldn't be verbally assaulted by any more of the passengers she had nearly killed trying to exit the escalator. "Are you going to be okay?" he asked her.

Incapable of speech, Eileen closed her eyes and nodded before standing upright and taking hold of her suitcase again.

The man nodded once, seeming uncertain of how to exit their uncomfortable social situation. "Okay," he finally said and started to walk away.

Eileen breathed a sigh of relief, but the man only got five steps before he turned back around.

"I'm sorry," he continued. "Are you *sure* you're okay? It's just, I'm pretty sure you're having a really horrible day. I was on your flight out of Denver...across the aisle three rows up in first class." He shook his head. "I'm sorry, I know this is weird and completely none of my business, but we *have* met before. Your daughter is Paige, right? She plays soccer with my daughter, Kimmy."

Of course she did.

"I don't know if you remember me." He stuck his hand out to Eileen again, this time to shake it. "I'm Samuel Cramer."

Eileen took his hand in hers, shook it twice, and thought about how convenient it would be to drop dead, right then and there in the middle of the San Francisco airport baggage claim. "Eileen," she mumbled, still too afraid that any speech that required more than one or two syllables would completely expose her for the disorderly public drunk she was.

"Yes, I remember." He smiled at her. "I used to stand on the sidelines with your husband, Eric, and—" He stopped cold. "Well." He glanced at her tote bag and then up to the ceiling. "I shouldn't keep you, but are you... Do you need me to get you a cab or a car?"

She realized two things all at once. One, he had clearly seen the photos of Eric and Lauren. And two, he absolutely knew Eileen was completely wasted. She sighed, not wanting to accept help from Samuel, who just might end up telling other people, who would then tell more people.

"Did you hear about Eileen and Eric. Oh God...and what her sister did? And, this guy I know, he was on Eileen's flight, he said she was completely three sheets to the wind—hammered. Almost killed people when she fell off the escalator."

"Thank you," Eileen said, still deciding if it was better to risk the suburban public shaming or try to navigate a major city she didn't know while possibly needing her stomach pumped. She should probably accept his help, and was about to, when she looked up and noticed her name written across a folded white piece of paper being held by a wide-stanced driver.

Simon, of course he would send someone for her.

"But I have a ride." She pointed to the evidence waiting patiently for her.

Samuel's gaze followed her finger and then turned back to her with a smile. "Good," he said, seemingly genuinely relieved. "Sometimes the cab line can go on forever here."

Eileen nodded. "Thank you, again. It was…nice…seeing you." It wasn't, not at all, but this was the way to try to exit a horrifically embarrassing situation when there was a very high likelihood of seeing the witness of your bad behavior again. She raised her hand in a lame goodbye gesture and started toward her name on the paper.

"Eileen," Samuel said.

Jesus, please, please, please, she thought. When she turned, she could see that he was holding a business card out to her. He walked toward her, and she took the card from him. *What the hell?*

"I'm in town for the month. I don't know…" He shrugged, as if he also could plainly see how awkward this all was. "If you need anything…when you're away from home, it's always good to know some people, you know?"

She didn't know—but seriously, what-the-fuck-ever right now. All she wanted was to escape this never-ending nightmare. "Sure." She nodded. "Thanks." She dropped the card into her black-hole bag, most likely to never be seen again, and headed for her driver.

"Ms. Eileen Greyden?" the driver asked her when she approached him.

"Yes," she answered.

The man nodded, and an unmistakable sadness pulled at his features. "Hello, I'm your sister's driver, Henry. I'm so sorry for your…" His voice broke. He cleared his throat. "For your family's loss," he managed to finish as he stepped in and hugged her.

Surprised, overwhelmed, still a drunken mess, Eileen let this Henry person wrap her in his arms before leading her out the tinted double doors.

CHAPTER 11

Eileen

HENRY LED EILEEN TO THE BACK SEAT OF A CHAMPAGNE-COLORED four-door Bentley he had parked nearby in the short-term lot. As he loaded her bags into the trunk, Eileen crawled onto the two-tone beige-and-white leather back seat. When Henry finished with the bags, he returned, shut her door softly, then climbed into the driver's seat.

The car smelled like money. Rich, full-bodied luxury. Eileen hated that she thought it, but her sister was so ridiculously rich.

Was. Eileen thought. Clare *was* so ridiculously rich… She started to cry again, quieter, tears that originated in her belly, seized at her heart. Tears that rose up from some deep, dark well at the core of her—tears that would weep out of her forever.

Her sister was dead.

Her sister had killed herself.

Why, Clare?

Eileen lay down across the dewy, soft leather and closed her eyes.

"Ms. Greyden?" Henry asked. "I'm sorry to disturb you. But if you could please buckle your belt?"

Eileen pushed herself up, grabbed the middle seat belt, and wrapped it around her waist while leaving the shoulder strap up against the seat, then lay back down and closed her eyes. She was exhausted, sick, drunk, and sadder than she could ever remember being in her whole life. Clare and Simon's house was at least a forty-minute drive from the airport. She wanted to spend it passed out.

"Thank you, Ms. Greyden," Henry said, then left her alone until they pulled into Clare's garage in Muir Beach.

When Henry opened the back door, it woke her up, and Eileen's brain felt like it was going to explode all over the inside of her skull. He handed her a large glass of ice water and two brown pills. "I thought you might want these," he said. "I'll get your things and take them up to your room, third door on the right after the stairs. Mr. Reamer is in his study on the first floor…whenever you're ready. He told me to tell you there's no rush, so take your time."

Eileen threw both pills—they looked like ibuprofen—into her mouth without question and chased them down with four large swallows of the water. Oh God, had water ever tasted this good? She continued to chug the entire glass down, then wiped her mouth with the back of her hand. She took a deep breath that filled her lungs till they felt like they might burst, then let it out in a loud rush through her mouth.

Henry had pulled the Bentley right into the garage. The large door was closed behind her, and she could see he'd left the door to the house cracked a few inches. There were three other cars also parked inside the garage, with plenty of room for more should Clare and Simon decide they needed more than four cars between them.

Should Simon decide, she reminded herself. For half a second, she had forgotten again. It just didn't really seem possible that her beautiful, talented, simply awe-inspiring older sister wasn't inside that house waiting for her to come in.

It wasn't possible.

Eileen heaved herself from the back seat of the car and went inside to find her brother-in-law.

The door from the garage led into a slate-tiled mudroom with an upholstered bench seat and custom shelving and cabinets. A woman's black trench coat hung from a nickel-plated hook, and a large gray leather handbag sat slouched open on the bench beneath it. From the mudroom, Clare and Simon's large, airy family room opened up before her. The soft white walls and ceiling reflected the light from the setting sun that radiated through the glass walls on the far side of the room, turning the whole space into a warm, luminous cocoon of soft couches and silky upholstered chairs.

She had only been here once before, for Christmas with Eric and the kids three years ago, but she thought she remembered where Simon's office was. She turned right, passed several closed doors, and saw the large mahogany entrance table with an enormous arrangement of birds-of-paradise, wide palm fronds, and artfully added red and peach roses. One pointy orange beak with its arched stem of a neck seemed to leer down at her as she passed.

The kitchen, lights out and desolated, was on her right; Simon's double office doors were to the left. A numbness spread out from her belly through her limbs, and she placed one hand on the table for support. The heat from her hand created a moisture vapor on the shiny wood surface. Worried about the fingerprints, she snatched her offensive hand away and cradled it between her breasts.

Simon's door was half open. He knew she'd be coming. She took a deep breath of the rose-heavy air and pushed his door with one hand, more than a little terrified of how she might find him. "Simon?" she whispered, glancing around the darkened room. "It's me, Eileen," she continued, thankful for the improved clarity of her speech. She wasn't sober by any stretch, but at least the outward signs of her drunken stupor were shoring up.

Movement in the far corner of the room caught her attention. It was Simon looking disheveled in a wrinkled shirt, his hair standing out from his head in a riot of angles. He sat in a brown leather wingback placed in the corner where the wall met a bookshelf that stretched from the floor to the ceiling. He had a book spread open in his lap, but his eyes stared blankly out into the room.

She moved closer on quiet steps, bending her head to try to intercept his frozen stare. "Simon?" she whispered. "It's me…Eileen."

His eyes shifted and met hers. "Hi, Eileen," he whispered back, his voice hardly more than a breath. His eyes, still glassy and unfocused, welled up fast before tears spilled down his cheeks and disappeared into the gruff of his unshaven face. He shook his head once and spread his hands out over the pages of the open book in his lap before his fingers curled around the edges and gripped it so hard she heard pages tear.

"This isn't happening," he whispered. It reminded Eileen of something Ryan or Cameron might say in response to tragedy. Simon looked up at her, pleading, as if she somehow had the power

to set everything right, turn back time, bring his wife back. "I can't...
I can't do this," he said like it was a matter of fact. "It's too hard."

She stood watching him, frozen herself in disbelief. She couldn't
do this either. After several ragged breaths, Eileen managed to make
her body move. She walked toward him, took the book from Simon's
lap, closed it, and placed it on the bare, clean surface of his wide
desk. The familiar dust jacket with its bold gold font and her sister's
name caught her eye, *A Perfect Life, Clare Collins*.

She rested her hand on the cover, blotting out the center. Simon
would have read this book many, many times already—long before
it was ever published. Was he, like Eileen had done earlier, simply
trying to hang on to one of the last tangible pieces of herself that
Clare had left behind?

"Why would she do it?" Simon's voice suddenly broke the
silence. "I can't understand it."

Eileen turned to face him with no answers to help.

"I didn't even know she owned a gun," he whispered to her like
a confession. "How could I not know that?"

Eileen's heart beat hard against her chest, and a sickening realization took shape in her head.

"A gun," Simon mumbled to himself, trying to configure the
Clare as he knew her with this secret weapon that he hadn't even
known was in their house.

"Our mother gave it to her," she said. "She gave us each one,
when we moved out. To protect ourselves."

Simon stared at the floor in front of him for a long time; it was
impossible to guess what he was thinking. "I'm so sorry, Simon."

He nodded in a series of quick up-and-down movements that looked more like a mild seizure than agreement. He placed his hand over his mouth, rubbed his lips and chin, then started shaking his head with the same spastic force, as if trying to counter his earlier thinking. "For her protection?" he asked, his voice breaking on the last word.

"It was over twenty years ago," Eileen tried to explain, as if somehow the age of the gun, or their mother's good intentions, could help Simon understand the destruction of his life today. She regretted the words. "Our mother…" What? What pearl of wisdom about their mom could possibly make any of this better? "She was a Wyoming cop, Simon."

His lips flattened into an angry line. He needed someone to blame, and he couldn't possibly blame Clare right now. Eileen braced herself for some displaced fury, prepared herself to not defend the twenty-year-old actions and intentions of a mother who had loved both her and her sister fiercely—but she didn't have to.

Simon took a breath and stood up. "I'm not in a good place," he said as he grabbed *A Perfect Life* from the desk where Eileen had placed it and walked to the door. With his hand on the handle, he stopped before leaving. "Can you find your room?"

"Yes, I think so."

He nodded once and started to leave again before stopping himself. "I'm sorry. I just… I'm sorry," he finished and left.

Eileen stood staring out the door after him for several seconds. Her mind, exhausted, wrung-out, and still addled with wine, refused to try to work anything out beyond what she needed for basic life support. Her heart was beating, her lungs still breathing, and she would need to get herself to the kitchen and find a glass of water soon.

She tipped her head back and looked up at the heavy-beamed wood ceiling. This room, with its dark wood and heavy upholstery, was so unlike the whole rest of the house. It was Simon's space, she realized. This was the one room that looked like a historic library. Everywhere else was entirely her sister's style: white walls, high ceilings, bright spaces. Clare had built her home as she'd wanted and given this space to her husband. Eileen stared at the large bookcase before her, her eyes focusing on titles that lined shelf after shelf, multiple copies of each book Clare had ever written, she realized.

Clare had allowed him this space to make as his own, and he had filled it with his wife's work.

A memory came to her, Eileen and Clare standing at a white linen–covered high-top table in a swanky Manhattan bar, glasses of champagne in hand. Simon was surrounded by his friends and coworkers. His face beamed with obvious joy as he accepted slaps on the back and congratulations on his recent engagement.

"You love him?" Eileen had suddenly asked her sister.

Clare took a sip from her long-stemmed flute before placing it on the table in front of them. She tilted her head, her eyes watching her future husband for a moment before turning to meet Eileen's. "No."

Eileen had been stunned by Clare's brutal admission, but not surprised. She had always suspected. "So why?" Eileen asked, glancing down at the new four-carat rock pinning Clare's left hand to the table.

"Because…if I could love someone again, I think it would be him."

"Clare," Eileen had said, attempting to find some way to express that something was wrong without fully understanding it herself. "He *adores* you."

Her sister had nodded. "That's why I'm marrying him," she'd explained, then raised her slim glass for another sip of champagne.

Eileen left Simon's office and headed for the kitchen. After rooting through several cupboards with no success, Eileen finally located the glasses near the sink. Too exhausted and already over-whelmed to try to figure out the NASA-looking water system built into the refrigerator, Eileen filled her glass at the sink and went to find her room.

At the landing where the grand single marble staircase split into two heading off in opposite directions, Eileen veered right. *What were Henry's directions again?* She continued up until at the top she faced a long hallway with several closed doors. She couldn't remember which room Henry had said was hers, but she hoped she wouldn't accidentally stumble into Simon again so soon.

Without a clue, she cracked the first door off the second floor landing slowly, just in case Simon was in there sleeping, changing clothes—crying. She absolutely did not want to disturb him right now. When she didn't hear anything, she dared to push the door further.

She remembered this room. It was Clare's study. Three years ago she had sat on that white couch, drinking a glass of wine with her sister, watching the sun set over the Pacific. The room looked exactly the same as she recalled. No furniture had moved; no new artwork filled the walls. Even the early evening light flooding in through the massive glass walls was the same. Eileen's eyes were drawn to the sun on the horizon, the radiant half disc throwing a shattering of orange and yellow light out across the ocean.

She came fully into Clare's room and closed the door behind her. Standing with her back pressed to the door, Eileen stared into her sister's space. The silence—it was so profound, so pervasive, it struck Eileen with a chill.

Eileen's life, filled with her children, her dogs, her phone, her... husband—it was a constant chaos. Silence never had any chance of taking hold anywhere at any time. When she had been here before, in this very room, Eileen had dragged all that life chaos with her. She hadn't realized before, not really, what Clare's daily world was like—the stillness, the eerie quiet of a day not filled to overflowing with other needful bodies. Eileen had been unable to see how her own family had come in and filled up this empty house. It seemed very different to her now.

Was this really how Clare had wanted to live?

Eileen headed for the couch and the view of the sun setting on one of the worst days of her entire life. She lowered herself onto the taut, buttoned leather and gazed out at the sparkling lights dancing across the ocean. Only last night, Clare had been alive. Dressed in a beautiful gown, attending the premiere for her new movie—how was it even possible for a person to die so suddenly? To move so quickly from being a part of your life, to gone forever? Eileen spread her hands out onto the cushions on either side of her. When was the last time her sister had been here, in this very spot? Less than twenty-four hours? Eileen sat upright and looked more closely at her sister's room. Where had Clare been when she'd killed herself?

Simon hadn't yet told her where he'd found Clare.

This room? It seemed impossible that a violent suicide could have been cleared from this pristine space in only a day. It *was* impossible, Eileen decided. She didn't know where Clare had taken her life, but it wasn't here.

She swallowed back a fresh wave of tears. She didn't want to cry anymore today.

On the glass coffee table in front of her, a slim notebook caught her attention. A rainbow of shiny colors, peeling edges, and *My Diary* stamped across the center in silver—a child's book, something Paige would have had five years ago. It didn't belong in this very adult space. Eileen leaned forward and picked it up off the table before settling back in the cushions. It was old and very familiar. Eileen sucked her breath when the connection came to her. This was Clare's. Back in their small house in Casper, Wyoming, they had shared a bedroom, and Clare had kept this diary under the corner of her mattress. How many nights had Eileen fallen asleep to the sight of Clare sitting up in bed under the dim glow of their shared night-light, scribbling in this book? This book and so many others, Eileen suddenly remembered.

She ran a finger over the book's peeling edges; Clare had kept it all these years.

Eileen opened the limp and tattered cover to the first page. There it was, Clare's looping and sloppy penciled script. The words had faded over the years, but she could still clearly read Clare's first words.

Mama said Daddy isn't coming home. And her next—*I hope to God it's true.*

The words surprised her. She placed the tips of her fingers on them. Eileen had been nine when their father died, so Clare would have been eleven when she wrote this—almost the same age as Ryan was now. Her memory of their dad had always been hazy, more a vague remembrance of the emotions she felt whenever he was around—which wasn't that much, she thought—but that fear, the sharp tension even the sound of his voice in the house always created, that's what she remembered the most about their dad.

There were also the moments, highly detailed moments of horror. Her parents shouting late at night, the sound of bodies slamming into walls and the crash of furniture as it overturned. The day their mother came home and installed two locks on the inside of Clare and Eileen's bedroom, one on the doorknob and another sliding bolt. Still in her cop uniform, she had sat on Clare's bed and given them explicit instructions to lock the door every night from then on. No matter what they heard, they were never to unlock the door or come out if they heard their dad was home.

There was also the time at Christmas when their dad bought both Eileen and Clare matching porcelain piggy banks and then filled them with fifty dollars in quarters.

Eileen closed her sister's childhood journal. Their father was a drug addict, heroin to be specific, but in the end he would take almost any kind of pill, powder, or injection he could get his hands on. There were pictures in their house from before, when he and her mother were younger and he was healthy—but Eileen had no real life memories of him without a gaunt and haggard complexion made terrifying by his erratic, unpredictable, and often-violent behavior when he needed money for drugs.

Clare had *hoped to God it was true* that their father wouldn't come home that night from the hospital—that childhood, dredging up those sepia-colored memories, Eileen couldn't remember if she had felt the same. She had always felt like her father was someone she had barely known; had she wished him dead as well? When he was around, he frightened her and hurt their mom. It wouldn't surprise her if she had felt the same as Clare; she just couldn't remember.

With the notebook in hand, Eileen stood up and scanned Clare's study again. This was the first of Clare's journals, but there had been many, many more, and those were just the ones Eileen knew about from their childhood together. Had Clare kept journaling all this time?

The room was falling into shadow as the sun on the horizon dipped deeper into the Pacific. She got up, flipped the switch next to the bookcase, and cast the entire north side of the room out of the creeping darkness. She scanned the shelves for several seconds before noticing the bottom; row after row of slim volumes pressed tight against one another. She crouched down and pried several out from the middle—they were journals, a hundred at least. Clare's words about Clare's life?

Eileen stood up with the books in hand, and considered all the other journals still on the shelves. It was like holding on to a piece of her sister, an intimate part of Clare's world, her experiences, her feelings, her perceptions. As kids, Clare had caught Eileen reading her journals many times—her wrath and retribution had been swift and usually painful. But even back then, Clare's life was so much more interesting than her own. She looked up to her sister, envied her. Reading her journals was Eileen's way of both finding out about Clare's life and measuring her own uneventful days. Was it wrong to read these now? She imagined Clare chasing her around this room, as adults, screaming at the top of her lungs for Eileen to "give me that back, you little bitch!" right before she caught the back of Eileen's shirt and wrestled her to the posh white shag rug. The ridiculous thought made her smile—until reality rushed back in.

Eileen held Clare's journals to her chest. How could she have let her own sister drift so far away? She took a ragged breath and let it go. "I'm sorry, Clare," she stated. "But I don't give a shit about your privacy," she whispered. She knelt back down in front of the shelf and grabbed another handful of books. "I need to know, okay? I need to know why you would do this to yourself, and I'm going to find out," she said.

When she stood up, her arms now loaded with Clare's journals, she carried them to the door, checked to make sure Simon was nowhere nearby, and shuttled them into the hall. She had to open and check two more rooms before discovering where Henry had put her bags.

With her elbow, Eileen pressed the wall switch to turn on the chandelier hanging over the center of the room. It was exactly as she remembered it. She and Eric had slept here three years ago at

Christmas, while the three kids had shared the room down the hall. This room had the same west-facing view of the Pacific out of the glass wall that, just like the larger version in Clare's study, slid open to a private balcony.

Eileen placed the journals on the dresser, found her tote, and dug her phone out from the bottom. Three missed calls, two from Eric and one from Paige. Eileen lowered herself onto the bed and tried to imagine speaking with Eric right now.

Should she lay it all out, confront him about Lauren, the affair; tell him about the photos Dave sent? She couldn't. She had no idea what she'd say or how he would react. And the kids? It was too soon. She needed to think, but she also couldn't imagine pretending like nothing was wrong either. She pulled up a group text with her whole family instead.

Arrived safe. There is a lot to manage, and I'm exhausted. I'll call tomorrow. Good night.

She hesitated a moment, then finished, *Love you, Mom,* before hitting send. It was for her kids. Eric could go fuck himself, even if she couldn't say as much right now. Eileen put her phone facedown on the bed beside her and stared at the stack of journals in front of her. She was exhausted—that was no lie—but she pushed herself up off the bed anyway and grabbed one of the books off the top stack. She pressed the button that controlled the sliding glass door to the balcony. As the wall opened, a rush of cold sea air blew in off the ocean. It made her eyes water and swept her hair back off her shoulders. The briny scent filled her senses and the room behind her, blowing open several of the journal covers and rustling the pages.

It was early evening; the light was fading and the temperature dropping, so she turned on the balcony light and started up the outside gas heater. She remembered that Clare and Simon kept a small wine rack and a mini fridge with other drinks and snacks in the closet for their guests. She placed the journal on one of the outdoor loungers and went back inside, pulled opened the cabinet, and grabbed a bottle of sparkling water, a bottle of red wine, and a small bag of mixed nuts before settling in on the balcony with the blanket from the bottom of the bed.

Until she started reading, there was no way of knowing when in Clare's lifetime this was created. Was this one from her childhood? Her life after she moved to New York? Or here in California? If Clare had kept them on the shelf in chronological order, this was likely one of the earlier journals, but there was no way of knowing until she dove in.

She pressed open the spine with her palm and read her sister's words.

CHAPTER 12

Clare

Twenty-two years before her death

IN THE THEATER SEAT NEXT TO HER, KAYLEE NUDGED HER ARM WITH her elbow. "Adam's next," she whispered and pointed to his name on the single sheet program Bobby Wright had handed them at the entrance to the Cleaver High auditorium.

Clare gave her a tight-mouthed smile and nodded. She knew perfectly well that Adam was next. She had suffered through the first eleven acts, along with everyone else in the packed auditorium, simply to get to this moment. With her eyes glued to the stage, she could feel her heartbeat in her throat. Everyone knew Adam Collins would be the best act in this year's annual Cleaver High talent show. He had been the best act since seventh grade in the Ralston Middle School annual talent show. That was why they always scheduled him last, so people didn't simply get up and leave as soon as they'd heard Adam play.

Adam walked out from behind the red curtains, pushed open at both sides of the stage. The entire auditorium erupted into spontaneous applause the moment they saw him, long before he was anywhere near the old grand piano in the center of the spotlight. As soon as he heard the roar, the whoops and whistles, the loud and booming "Aaaaduuuuum" being chanted by the standing-room-only crowd, a smile spread over Adam's face. He lowered his head and gave the people of Casper a one-handed salute wave and continued toward the piano bench waiting for him.

Clare, neither clapping nor shouting, squirmed in her seat. Clare knew there was more than one person in the audience watching her, judging her. Wondering, still, why the hell Adam Collins, with his good looks, good family, and good chance of one day playing professional basketball, wasted his time with Clare Kaczanowski. Clare could practically hear them thinking, feel their eyes on her back.

Next to her, Kaylee sat upright in her seat and clapped furiously for her twin brother until someone a few rows in front of them caught her attention. Craning her neck, Kaylee stopped clapping and leaned toward Clare. "Take a look at Ms. Homecoming," she whispered, nodding her head in the direction she wanted Clare to look.

Three rows in front of them, Heather Roberts was surrounded by her friends and beaming up at Adam, who was taking his seat in front of the piano. Clare watched her turn to her left and whisper something to her best friend, Winnie, who nodded approval. Clare bristled, and a white-hot flame of irritation ignited in her gut. It was no secret Heather Roberts wanted Adam.

"Such a bitch," Kaylee whispered. "As if Adam would ever… Why doesn't she give up already?"

Her mouth suddenly dry, Clare swallowed hard and gave Kaylee a grateful smile, despite the fact that her words did nothing to relieve Clare of her dread. Heather Roberts was exactly the kind of girl this whole fucking town thought Adam *should* be with. Good looking, good family, and a good chance of making something of herself since she would be heading off to the University of Chicago with her full-ride academic scholarship next fall.

Heather Roberts would be less than two hundred miles from where Adam would be playing basketball for the Hoosiers and majoring in music at Indiana University.

One thousand three hundred miles from where Clare would be, right here in Casper, working as a receptionist for Carter's Moving and Storage out on Old Round Road. Her mother had set up the job for her, bragging to the owner, Roland Carter, about Clare's "exceptional typing skills." That's what Mrs. Cartwright had written on her last report card along with the A+ she'd received in her typing class. "Clare has exceptional typing skills!"

Exactly what Roland Carter needed in a new receptionist. A pleasant phone voice and fast, accurate fingers on the new computer he'd just invested in. He'd hired her right away. Part-time after school for now, full time starting in less than a month once she graduated from school.

Less than a month.

Up onstage, Adam placed his hands on the keys and waited while the noise from the audience died down by degrees until the whole room sat in silence and waited. In a town like Casper, where almost nothing truly special ever happened, Adam Collins was extraordinary. He was this town's high school basketball star, good enough to lure scouts from a dozen big universities to the middle of Wyoming to watch him practice and play, and turn down offers of full-ride scholarships to other schools before accepting Indiana University. And if that weren't enough, having the best local teacher for a mother, he also played the piano like he'd been born in front of it. In a town without many cultural highlights, Adam Collins working his way through Chopin's "Polonaise No. 6" was almost, almost, as great an evening as watching the kid orchestrate the basketball with the fluidity and grace of a ballet dancer.

Why Adam Collins wasted his time with a girl like Clare Kaczanowski was a big mystery to most everyone in Casper. A girl whose mother, the only woman on the police force, was the butt of every female pig joke that could be thought up over a few beers. A girl whose father ended up just another dead junkie. A girl so clearly headed nowhere, so undeserving of the most special someone this town had ever produced.

Adam had always been Clare's best friend, but the older they got, and the more amazing Adam became, the more she had begun to wonder *why* herself. She watched him, in that spotlight, lean into the keys and away again, the music flowing from him, through his hands, and touching every person in the room.

He was beautiful, mesmerizing. She already missed him and felt the impending loss of him rising up like a claw in her throat. She was going to lose him. The best thing she'd ever known, the person she loved most in the whole world—he was leaving. She was staying. Everyone here knew it—but no one but her felt the excruciating pain of it. The reality of it was a weight on her heart, the pressure building, squeezing harder every day that brought them closer to their graduation day.

What would she be without him? Who? A handful of their friends were staying in town, working for family businesses or picking up shifts at the Exxon. Some would be heading to Laramie to go to the University of Wyoming. A couple were going to Colorado for school. It felt to Clare like being left behind, left alone.

She would be forgotten, her and her amazing typing skills, sitting at a secondhand metal desk out on Old Round Road taking calls at Carter's Moving and Storage. She could have done better in school, easily—she just didn't do the work. Or care to, except now it mattered. Now, four years too late, every stupid assignment, quiz, test she'd half-assed her way through—it all mattered. She half-assed her way right into a dead-end job she already didn't want.

Onstage Adam began playing a crowd favorite, Beethoven's "Moonlight Sonata." When they heard the familiar start, a few people clapped before they were shushed back into silence. Most of the people in this room hadn't heard Adam play since they saw him on this exact same stage last year. Clare and Adam had grown up less than a block away from each other; she'd heard him play almost every day of their entire lives together. Sitting on the sagging couch in his parents' front room, she'd read, or sometimes write in her journals, and Adam would practice the piano before his parents got home from work. None of that would be happening anymore. It was all coming to an end.

Three rows in front of her, Heather Roberts made an act of

sighing and placing her hand over her heart as she tilted her head to the side. Winnie smiled and nudged her friend before whispering something in Heather's ear that made her turn, bite her bottom lip, and grin.

To Clare, it felt as if something monumental had already happened. Or was about to. Something huge and painful and terrifying. A rift opened up inside her, an enormous vacuum of space, a giant nothing that had for years been filled with a knowing, a connection, with another person who felt like a piece of her own self. She lifted her eyes again to Adam on his stage, his back tall and straight, his perfectly muscled arms, long fingers, and mop of blond hair that fell like a disaster over the brightest blue eyes. She loved him. Desperately, completely. She had no plans, no life, no real future she wanted to live without him.

He was leaving her. And maybe it wouldn't be Heather Roberts… but it would be someone, because Adam was that guy, handsome, talented, kind, and so good that it was simply impossible to not fall in love with him. How long until he figured out that there was a whole world outside of Casper, Wyoming, filled with exactly the kind of girls everyone already thought he should be with? Girls who were beautiful, talented, kind, and good—girls who had more going on than excellent typing skills.

"You should kick Heather's ass," Kaylee whispered in her ear. "You could easily take her."

Clare nodded and forced a smile to hide what she was really feeling. If Kaylee took one look at her and sensed enough to ask, "What's wrong?" Clare would break into tears right here, right now.

"Maybe I should jump her in the parking lot after the concert," Clare joked.

"I'll hold her down."

"Like I would need you to hold her." She reached across the armrest separating them and took Kaylee's hand in hers.

Kaylee looked at their clasped hands for a moment and then leaned in again. "I'm going to miss you so much, Clare."

Clare shook her head, forcing down the sob that threatened to break loose. "Don't," she warned. "Not here…not now." Her voice broke on her last word, and Kaylee squeezed her hand.

Clare closed both her eyes tight and willed herself to not cry as Adam finished playing for the last time in the Cleaver High School auditorium and the crowd broke their silence and stood up to applaud him.

"I'm going to go find Carl and Denise. They're here somewhere," Kaylee shouted over the noise as she hugged Clare goodbye. "We're supposed to meet up after."

Clare nodded. "See you later," she said before turning toward the aisle. She excused herself past the people in her row, still standing and clapping for Adam, who was standing and smiling on the stage. She rushed up the threadbare red carpet toward the exit, catching Mrs. Collins's glance as she passed.

She refocused her eyes on the double exit doors in front of her, pretending to have not noticed Adam's mother. It was easier than suffering through her fake smiles and ministrations. When they were younger, and obviously just friends, Mrs. Collins had been more welcoming to Clare, more genuinely interested in her stubbed toes and need for snacks. She would bring Clare and Adam cups filled with ice and homemade lemonade as they raced down the lawn and threw themselves down the bright yellow Slip 'N Slide.

Homemade lemonade had stopped sometime during the summer after ninth grade—soon after Mrs. Collins ascended the ladder to Adam and Kaylee's tree house and found Clare and her son shirtless, limbs tangled, and lying on an old sleeping bag. She still smiled at Clare, outwardly welcomed her into their home, but her facade of social graces was a poor cover for a protective wariness—as if Clare had grown from the girl next door into a dangerous predator stalking their home. Mrs. Collins smiled at Clare, but her eyes gave away her true feelings.

My son is too good for you.

Outside, Clare found Adam's beater blue pickup in the lot and waited for him outside the passenger door. It was the first Friday in May and warmer than it should have been. The air on her skin barely registered a temperature, like a tepid bath. She didn't bother putting on the sweater she held in her hands. Across the street, just above the squat two-story Motel 6, the half-moon inched into the cloudless, star-filled night. Normally, she loved nights like this—a calm, warm night, the air heavy with the scent of growth and fresh-cut grass. Tonight, it only made her more uneasy, visceral reminders of the change that was coming, unstoppable, unending.

Groups of people, twos, threes, families of five, trickled from the double doors and into the parking lot. Heather and Winnie, now with four of their other friends, strolled past Adam's truck in their pack. They knew Clare was there, waiting for Adam to come out and open the doors, but all six girls, especially Heather, were very careful to not turn their heads and notice her. Their silence, carefully structured smiles, and unblinking straight-ahead focus communicated their intentions perfectly. Clare was an unimportant, and temporary, obstacle unworthy of acknowledgment, an unfit contender for the attentions of Adam Collins. Clare imagined that Heather, with the help of her gaggle of gal pals, would figure out a solution to this pesky problem. Even if it meant having to wait until she and Adam had thirteen hundred miles of help.

"Fuck you," Clare whispered into the night and turned her back on them.

She heard a rhythmic slap of leather-soled shoes, a slow jog, on the pavement behind her.

"Hey Adam!" a girl's voice called out. "Nice job on the keys," the voice sang through the night, the tone unmistakably flirty, teasing and inviting Adam to take the bait.

Clare turned back around and watched Adam raise a hand and smile at Heather and her friends. "Thanks," was all he called back, then turned his gaze back on Clare and broke into a huge smile. "Well, what did you think? Was it great? Did you love it? Wasn't I fantastic?" He laughed and, in two long strides, swept Clare up into his arms, pressed her carefully up against the side of his truck, and kissed her neck. "Say it." His lips moved beneath her ear. "You thought I was amazing."

Clare smiled. "Okay, I thought you were amazing."

He nodded and smiled. "Oh, yes you did." He kissed her mouth, and she felt him press his hips against hers. God, she hoped to hell that fucking Heather Roberts and all her bitchy friends were watching this right now.

"But you should stop trying to take advantage of me in the school parking lot, Clare," he said as he pulled away from her and pretended to straighten his shirt. "It's tacky and, quite frankly, a little slutty."

She laughed and slapped his chest. "You're a pig."

"And yet you sexually attack me? In public, no less." He leaned forward and kissed her cheek, then reached around her to unlock and open the door that squealed loudly on its rusty hinges. "My lady." He swept his free hand out and bowed, ushering her onto the passenger seat. "Your chariot."

She shook her head and climbed onto the springy seat. She watched him through the dingy window as he shut the door, gave her a wicked grin, then turned and jogged around to the driver's side. Adam was always goofing around, but he seemed especially weird tonight. When he climbed onto the seat next to her, he leaned into the steering wheel and placed his keys in the ignition.

"What's up with you? Where are we going?" she asked him.

Barely able to contain himself or his conspiratorial grin, Adam only shook his head. "It's a surprise," he said in his best showman voice before cranking the ignition and pumping the gas. Once the truck's engine finally roared to life, he turned to her and wrangled the gearshift into reverse. "You're just going to have to wait and see."

"I don't like surprises."

"Well, you're going to love this one."

As Adam backed out of the parking space, Clare turned in her seat to watch out the rear window. Several packed bags in the bed of the truck caught her attention. "What's all that in the back?"

Adam shifted the truck into first and cranked the wheel hard to the left. "Part of the surprise. Now no more questions," he said as they accelerated out of the parking lot, passing Heather, Winnie, and company on the way. Clare resisted the urge to roll down her window and flip them all off.

Adam's *surprise* amounted to his two-man tent, a bundle of fire-wood, a pile of sleeping bags and blankets, a six-pack of Coors Light, a bottle of Cook's sparkling wine, and his secret fishing spot on the North Platte River. Clare offered to help him set up the tent, but he settled her onto a nearby log overlooking the river and told her to give him ten minutes.

She sat, listening to him unpack the back of his truck and pull the tent material and poles from their bag. Five feet in front of her, the North Platte rushed over submerged boulders and uneven ter-rain, the moonlight reflected off white-water cascades, wet dirt, and the tall grass near the bank. Since it was so warm, Clare slid off the dress shoes she'd worn for Adam's performance and dug her toes into the grass and dirt. The rapid current mesmerized her, made her wonder about where the water had come from, where it would eventually end up.

After several more minutes, she called out, "Are you sure I shouldn't help?"

"Already finished," Adam said, suddenly beside her and making her jump. "I told you I only needed ten minutes. I could set up that tent blindfolded."

He reached out a hand to her, and when Clare took it, he pulled her gently from her log and into his arms. She rested her head against his chest, listening to the sound of his heart beating hard beneath his dress shirt. "What exactly are we doing out here?" she asked.

Adam took her hand again and guided her to the campsite he'd constructed. As promised, the tent was up, filled with the sleeping bags and blankets, and two low-slung camping chairs she hadn't noticed before were arranged near a circle of large river stones that would act as a firepit. He'd arranged the wood into a teepee and surrounded it with dry grass and kindling. Adam led her by the hand to one of the chairs. "Your seat, my lady."

Filled with questions she didn't think she'd get answers to right away, Clare sat down and looked up at Adam. He reached into the small Igloo cooler between the chairs, took out a bottle of beer, and twisted off the top before handing it to her. "A cold beverage?"

She took the beer from him and sighed.

Adam held up both his hands. "All your questions will be answered shortly. But first, we need some fire."

Deciding to be patient, Clare sat back in her chair and sipped her icy beer while she watched him take a lighter from his pants pocket and get the campfire up and roaring before her in record time. "I'm not exactly dressed for camping, you know," she said. "With a little warning, I could have ditched this dress and grabbed some jeans and a sweatshirt. I would have been happy to get you something other than your best suit and dress shoes as well."

Adam grabbed a beer for himself and took the seat next to her. "I don't know." He looked down at his own dress clothes and then pretended to appraise Clare's, as if seeing her for the first time tonight. "I think we're dressed perfectly for the occasion." He met her eyes, still playful and acting weird, but a strange seriousness, an unspoken tension ran underneath every word he said, everything he was doing.

"What is going on?" she asked, holding his gaze so he couldn't slip into another silly answer. "It's been kind of a hard night for me, and I can't say that all of this is exactly putting me at ease."

In his chair, Adam looked up at the night sky and took a deep breath that filled his chest. The light from the fire danced over his features and threw half his face into shadow. It was impossible to tell what he was thinking. "Okay," he said, letting his breath out with the word. "I was going to wait until a little later in the evening, but…" He slipped out of his chair and onto one knee in front of her. His hand shook as it reached again into his pants pocket and took out a small white box.

Stunned, scared, uncertain if what she thought was maybe happening was actually happening, Clare sat speechless, watching him and waiting for whatever came next.

Adam opened the box. In its center sat a thin gold ring with a tiny chip of a diamond. "Clare Kaczanowski." He looked up into her eyes. "I love you. I have always, my whole life, loved you. And…I know I'm leaving…soon. I can't bear the thought of being without you…of you, maybe…" He shook his head, as if to clear it. "Clare, will you marry me?"

She stared at him. Her heart was beating so hard it made her feel like she was out of breath even though she hadn't moved a muscle.

Was he crazy? Was she? She didn't want to lose him, but did she want this? Yes, she did, but now?

Fear, that was what she felt. Sharp and distinct, something about this was making her want to run, making her wish she was anywhere else but right here, right now. He was waiting for her to say yes, but her mouth felt like paste. Her head was a confusing swirl of pressure. He was looking at her, waiting—and she was taking too long to answer. She could see the slight shift in his expression, the way he held the box before her was flagging. This wasn't the reaction he had been expecting. This wasn't exactly how he imagined she'd respond.

She wasn't ready for this.

But she was going to lose him.

"Yes," she blurted. "Yes, I'll marry you."

CHAPTER 13

Eileen

THE COLD WOKE HER UP. FRIGID AIR CHILLED HER BARE SKIN, RAISED goose bumps across her arms and back. The cold, and the sound of a fan? No, was it water? Not steady like from their faucet, a rhythmic rush that came and went. She felt for the blankets with her feet, expecting them to be at the bottom of their bed, but all her toes found was more cold mattress.

"Eric?" she asked, rolling over and dragging open scratchy lids against her dry eyes. She reached for him with her hand. More cold, empty mattress.

This wasn't their bedroom.

Eileen propped herself up sideways on her elbow and tried to focus her eyes on the bright white– and soft gray–colored room. One by one, the horrible realizations returned to her. This was Clare's spare bedroom she was sleeping in—alone. The dread and hurt she had managed to escape while asleep came sweeping back like a tidal wave. She let herself fall back onto the mattress and stared at the ceiling over her head.

It hurt to breathe.

She rolled onto her side and scanned the wood floor; all the blankets and top sheet were in a heap next to the bed. She must have kicked them off in the middle of the night. She leaned over the edge and grabbed hold, pulling the cold, downy pile back up and around her shoulders as she swung her legs over the side of the bed and sat up. She'd left the sliding doors to the deck open last night. That was why the room was so cold this morning. The rushing water was the crash of the ocean against the cliffs below her room.

The light drew her eye, the soft, pale blue of the clear early morning sky stretching out over the Pacific. Eileen forced a deep lungful of the salt air in and stood up. With the down comforter as her robe, she grabbed a pair of socks from the tumble of clothes spilling out of her open suitcase on the floor and her camera.

Outside, the deck sent a cold chill up through the bottom of her feet. She placed her camera on the side table next to her empty wineglass from last night and Clare's journal, then sat down to pull the socks over her feet. She had sat outside reading and drinking until her brain became too fuzzy from exhaustion, alcohol, and grief that she couldn't keep her eyes open any longer. Clare's journal had surprised her. She had no idea Clare and Adam had been engaged.

She grabbed her camera off the table and stood up. The balcony was enclosed in a glass half-wall. Eileen remembered Clare showing her and Eric the room three years ago. "It'll keep you from stumbling to your death while not impeding your view when you sit and have your morning coffee," Clare had joked. In that moment, standing here, with Eric gazing around and adding it all up, and her children off in other rooms marveling at their aunt Clare's unbelievable wealth, a jealousy unlike anything she had ever experienced had settled like a stone in her mind. Eileen had looked at her sister, her long auburn hair blowing away from her beautiful face in the ocean breeze, her slim, lithe body, long bones, tasteful clothes, perfect skin, her beautiful full smile—every aspect of her perfect older sister made Eileen feel small, painfully common by comparison. It always had.

She had always been a little envious of Clare, but that moment, with the material evidence of Clare's success, wealth, and fame surrounding her and sinking in for the first time, her simple jealousy had mushroomed into something larger, darker, a feeling much closer to hate. Eric and her children were so clearly impressed by Clare. No, not just impressed—awed. Because Clare hadn't simply fallen ass-backward into money or married it; Clare had built this. All of it. Clare had harnessed her talents and constructed a life, a world for herself. All this was hers. And no one else, not Simon, not their mother, not even Eileen, could say they had any real part in what Clare had accomplished.

"Do you like it?" Clare had asked her.

Eileen had nodded. "It's nice. A little sterile, and certainly not kid-friendly, but that's not an issue for you and Simon." She had smiled at Clare and pretended to not notice the hurt in her sister's eyes. "Speaking of that—I better go find my three monsters before they drag their grubby hands all over your perfect walls."

Haunted by her own words that day, sickened by her capacity for cruelty, Eileen raised her camera's viewfinder to her eye and snapped several photos of a lone gull picking over a tangle of seaweed on the rocks below. She had known full well Clare couldn't have children.

She lowered her camera and watched the pewter, shifting swells of ocean water rise and fall, the sound of it crashing against the rocks directly below her. Its rhythm connected with her own pulse, the beat of her heart. The wind picked up, cold and unforgiving, and blasted her flesh like ice. Clare had wanted her approval that day, had wanted Eileen to say how proud she was of her.

She wished, now, that she'd been able to hug her sister. Marvel at her beautiful home, congratulate her on her success, tell her how amazing it all was, truly. Clare had dragged herself up and out of their broken, dysfunctional home in the middle of nowhere Wyoming and built her own American fucking dream, book by book, with her own two hands. The truth was, Eileen was proud of Clare and all she'd done. How could she not be? But Clare's every success had cast Eileen's every choice deeper into the shadow of *so what*. Everything Clare accomplished made Eileen wonder, *what if*, with regard to her own life, her own abandoned dreams. Armed with the only accomplishment she knew Clare could never have, Eileen had lobbed Clare's most painful truth into her face.

Her body, broken in the accident that had almost killed her, wasn't capable of creating a child.

CHAPTER 14

Clare

Twenty-two years before her death

BRIGHT LIGHT, LIKE TWO SHARDS OF GLASS, SLICED THE DARKNESS. Garbled voices filled her ears. Clare swallowed, and her throat burned. She opened her mouth, took a breath. Pain registered, a nauseating wave of signals firing throughout her system but with no specific source. It was simply everywhere. Her lids fought to open, erratic and hard to control. Her eyes were uncooperative. It would be easier to just close them again, pull back closed whatever heavy curtain was lifting and taking its protection away, letting in light and sound and pain.

What was happening?

The voices grew louder, and a dark image moved into her sight line, an eclipse breaking up the intensity of the white glare. A head, a person was in front of her and they were speaking, their voice impossible to make out. It was like when she and Adam were kids and on hot summer days, bored with cannonballs and searching the bottom of the city pool for pennies, they would try to speak to each other underwater. This person sounded exactly like that, but she knew it wasn't Adam because...why? Why did she know that?

Adam.

Something was wrong. Something had happened. It was why she couldn't see or hear right. It was also why she hurt so much.

Adam.

She was angry and hurt so much so that it felt like an enormous hole had opened up inside her. A large, empty vacant lot. She noticed this space, felt it now because of what it no longer contained. Like being untethered, drifting, terrifyingly free, as if nothing were holding her to the earth anymore.

She had lost something. It was huge, it was everything, and it was gone. Forever it was gone. She knew that, and pain that had nothing to do with her physical body broke open in her heart and spread through her like liquid ice.

Sorrow, a deep well of abandon, her own destruction—she felt it, trapped inside a body that wasn't working. "What happened?" she tried to scream, but not even her voice functioned.

Someone was holding her arms. She felt more hands on her shins. Then two hands, large and soft and familiar, cupped her face and tried to keep her from thrashing her head. Clare turned her lips against the woman's palm. She knew these hands, the weight of them, the scent.

"Mom?" she whispered against the fingers.

Her mother's face was next to hers, cheek to cheek. Her mother stroked her forehead, then her hair, trying in the ways she always had to comfort, hush, soothe.

Where was she? What was happening?

What had happened?

All she could remember was the sound of her shoes in the gravel as she ran for Adam's truck, the music from the party in the distance, the wind rushing through the tall cottonwoods lining the road leading to the Robertses' ranch, and Adam calling after her.

Three months after Heather Roberts's graduation party, Clare opened her eyes in the Cheyenne Regional Medical Center to a life she now barely recognized. She had pressed and prodded and pushed her brain again and again through that night, the days and weeks that led up to it, and even the painful details of seeing...

But no matter how many times she went over it, her memory ended with her running down that dirt road.

It was a movie that faded to black before her eyes. Frustrating her over and over because the next images were there. She could feel them, skimming just beyond the grasp of her neural reach, devastating because they were the last moments of her old life, the minutes that changed everything forever.

She ran down that dirt road, and Adam called after her to stop. Faster, stronger than she was—he was going to catch up to her.

Then she opened her eyes.

Eventually, her eyesight began to focus, her hearing cleared up, and her throat, sore from being on a ventilator for over twelve weeks, was able to scratch out the most rudimentary of sounds. Her mother and Eileen took turns at her bedside, shaking their heads to her notepad full of the same scrawled questions. *What happened? Where is Adam?* Until finally, three days later, she was able to vocalize the questions she needed answered, and they could no longer avoid the facts. Her mother sat at the side of her bed, took hold of her hands, and whispered the horrible truth.

"Clare, there was an accident." Her mother stared into her eyes, waiting, watching Clare absorb this information before pressing on. "Do you remember anything?" Her gaze broke from Clare's as Ella shifted her eyes to their hands clasped on the bed between them. "Do you remember anything about the accident?"

Clare stared at her mother, scrutinizing her expression, her every facial muscle, looking for something she couldn't put her finger on. "No," she croaked. Clare cleared her throat and tried again. "No. We were at Heather's party and… " Clare stopped talking. She had seen them and had run. "I left," she finished. "I don't remember an accident."

Her mother, still not meeting her eyes, nodded her head. "Try for a second, please. Think. You were in Adam's truck. What do you remember before the wreck?"

Clare shook her head. "Running away from the party. I wanted to leave. That's it. That's all I remember." Frustrated, Clare shook her head hard, and a desperate sob rose up and filled her chest. There was all this empty space inside her now. So much loss where she once felt complete and whole. She was afraid of what her mother would say next while also already knowing, somehow, exactly what this hole inside her meant.

"Honey, I need you to really—"

"Tell me now! I told you, I don't remember. Please," she sobbed. "Just tell me!"

That was when her mother raised her eyes and squeezed her hand. She nodded. "That night, after you left Heather's party, Adam wrecked his truck off Old Round Road. About a mile from Heather's house, the truck was found at the bottom of the embankment just past where the road crosses the North Platte. It drops down…" Her mother paused, swallowing down her own emotion. "The truck rolled five or six times. They think he was driving pretty fast. His blood alcohol was over two… Yours was…higher." Her mother stopped talking.

Clare turned her head and looked at her sister sitting in the chair pushed into the far corner of the room, her head hung, hands folded in her lap.

Clare turned back to her mother. "Where is he?"

"Clare…"

"No, where is Adam? Is he here?" She moved to get out of the bed, forgetting she was still hooked up to two IVs and strapped to a monitoring system that tracked her vitals.

Her mother stood up and grasped her shoulders with firm but gentle hands. "No, he's not here. He…died, Clare. I was the one to find you. He died in the wreck. But you were still alive," she cried. "Like a miracle, I found you thirty feet from where the truck was, still breathing, barely, but you were. You were alive."

Clare stared at the white blanket covering her legs and tried to make sense of what her mother was saying.

"Do you have any idea how lucky you are to be alive?"

She felt numb, disconnected, surreal. None of this could really be happening. Adam wasn't dead. He was going to Indiana to major in music and play basketball on TV. "There's been some mistake," she whispered.

Her mother sat back down. "I'm so sorry," she said. "But he's gone."

It was a hot day in mid-September when they released her from Cheyenne Regional. The trees clung to their wilted leaves, and the earth seemed to beg for the relief of fall rains and winter snow. The temperature gauge on the cruiser's dash said it was ninety-eight degrees out; the backs of Clare's legs burned when she slid onto the old, cracked leather of her mother's patrol car. Beads of sweat rolled down Ella's temples as she loaded the small duffel bag with the few belongings Clare was taking home with her from the hospital: her toothbrush and paste, a few changes of underwear, the plastic, kidney-shaped barf tray that Clare had come to depend on, magazines from the gift shop, stuffed animals from a few get-well-wishers, a tattered copy of *Catcher in the Rye*, and five slim journals that Clare had nearly filled from cover to cover in the last four weeks since she had woken up. She stared out the window and waited as her mother closed the trunk with a bang and got behind the wheel. Clare didn't care about anything in that bag except the journals and the barf tray; she still sometimes had a hard time keeping food down.

"Ready?" Her mother looked over at her and gave her a weak smile as she turned the ignition key.

Clare nodded once, fastened her seat belt, and tried not to think about everything that would be different from now on. Her mother had been reluctant to offer up details, but when Clare had found herself alone with her sister, she had been able to pry the essentials out of Eileen.

"What are people saying about all this?"

"Everyone was pretty shocked, what, with it being Adam and all."

"What do you mean?"

Eileen whispered like she was telling a dirty secret. "He was like the town hero. And he gets drunk at a party, crashes his truck, kills himself and almost kills his girlfriend. Some people have been weird about it. Almost like it affected them, somehow, personally. Saying things like, Adam was no good, and that they always thought something wasn't right with him. Other mean things, like he wasn't really all everyone thought he was. Mom says that some of them are taking it personally because it's like they lost something special, even if it was just being close to someone else's greatness. I think they should just get their own lives."

"What about Kaylee?"

"After the funeral, she and her parents left town."

There had been a funeral for Adam, and Clare had not been at it—that in and of itself was hard to comprehend. Adam's body was in a box in the ground. "Left town for where? Did they take Kaylee to school?"

Eileen shook her head. "I don't know. Maybe, but I think they were also getting some phone calls, people saying things about Adam and hanging up. Someone..." Eileen started but snapped her mouth shut.

"What?"

Eileen sighed, obviously wishing she hadn't said so much. "Someone, in the middle of the night, threw a brick through their living room window and then a basketball. At least that's what I heard."

The cruelty of people was astounding. The Collinses were good people, people who had lost their only son.

"Who would do that?"

"Assholes."

"It was an accident," Clare said. "It's not like Adam meant to hurt anyone."

"Yes," Eileen said. "But he was really drunk, Clare...you could have died."

Clare could have died, and on the ride home from the hospital, she wished she had. As soon as she was more stable on her own two feet, Clare would walk the mile from her house to Saint Joseph's Cemetery to see Adam's grave for herself. She didn't think she would be able to believe he was gone until she had seen his headstone with her own two eyes.

"When we get home, I want you to head straight to your own bed and get some rest," her mother instructed.

"I've done nothing but rest for the last four months."

"Your body was busy healing, not resting. Plus, a hospital bed is not like your own. I imagine your first night back at home you'll sleep like the de—"

They both let the poor word choice slide away without comment or apology. "When is Roland expecting me back at work?"

Her mother shook her head. "He's not. He needed to get

someone in there answering the phones and running the office. Since we didn't have any idea how long you might be in the hospital…" Her mother shrugged. "I told him it was probably best for him to get someone else hired as soon as possible, so he did."

The news didn't upset Clare, only unsettled her even more. It was yet another tether come undone, disconnecting her from her places in this world. "So I don't have a job."

"Not right now. You should give it at least another month of healing anyway. Something else will come along. Maybe something down at the library. You always liked it there." Clare watched out the windshield and wondered if she would ever like anywhere, anyone, or anything again in her life while pretending to not notice her mother driving two blocks out of their way to avoid passing the Collinses' house on the way to their own.

CHAPTER 15

Eileen

Eileen found Simon in the kitchen, standing in front of the sink, staring out the window at the palm tree–lined driveway in front of the house. Barefoot, he wore a limp flannel robe; his dark hair was disheveled and slept on.

"Simon?" Afraid of startling him, she kept her voice soft.

When he turned to face her, his bloodshot eyes and sallow complexion told of a sleepless, tear-filled night. He looked down at the cup he held in both his hands and then back up at Eileen with some confusion, as if he had forgotten she was even in the house. Seconds passed. He nodded once, confirming some unspoken logic to himself, then turned back to the sink and dumped his coffee into it. "Would you like some coffee? Mine's cold."

"Yes…please."

Simon walked around the large center island to a complicated contraption of levers and dials on the opposite side of the kitchen. He flipped a switch, and a loud whir of electric blades followed by the crush and grind of whole coffee beans filled the kitchen. The aroma, rich and robust, floated into the air and pulled Eileen's senses beyond the semistupor she'd been hiding in. With the sound and the smell, the desolate white kitchen seemed more alive, and she could remember a time when this pristine space with its polished surfaces had been filled with family, food, sounds, voices, stacks of dishes, and a concoction of delicious aromas—the chaos of a Christmas shared.

Simon shut off the machine, and the silence swept in again.

"Here you go." He carried a cup for her around to her side of the island and placed it with a clink onto the white marble in front of her. "Do you take anything in it?"

"Just cream. I'll get it." She waved off the idea of him doing anything further for her and moved to search the industrial-sized refrigerator for a carton of anything dairy-like. Simon's grief was so palpable, the weight of it filled the whole house. She considered sending him back to bed and wondered if Simon and her sister had been the sort of people that might have a leftover prescription bottle of something that might help him sleep. When she returned to her cup with the closest thing she could find to cream, a thin container of nonfat milk, she noticed Clare's new book on the kitchen table.

"I can't help but think," he said when he saw her staring at the book, "that I missed something. Some clue. Some answer to Clare, some reason for why she'd…do this."

Eileen poured the watery milk into her coffee, glanced at Simon to make sure he wouldn't object, then picked the book up off the table and brought it over to the island. She held it between her hands and stared down at the cover.

Simon sighed. "I've read everything she ever wrote at least ten times. Partly because it's my job, mostly because I'm her husband, but always because I loved her stories. That book." He pointed to *A Perfect Life* in Eileen's hands. "Something was different. I knew it right from the start. She wouldn't let me read any of the early drafts, wouldn't tell me what it was about. She would even stop writing and close her computer if I happened to walk in on her while she was working on it." Simon stared at the bare marble countertop in front of him, as if some answer to Clare could maybe be deciphered in the randomness of black and gray swirls. "All her other books, except for that first one…she'd never acted like that before. We always consulted, brainstormed. She'd let me read her works in progress so we could discuss direction, theme, the current market, what her fan base expected. But not that book… So I keep thinking, because of what she's done, that maybe there's some message, some clue. Something I might have caught in time, if only I'd *made her* let me read it."

Eileen looked up at Simon, his pained expression, his false belief that he might have somehow saved Clare from herself. Her sister, Clare, the same girl who had always, always, fearlessly marched ahead into God-knows-whatever unknown and hardly blinked an eye. That he even entertained the idea he could have deciphered Clare made Eileen seriously wonder if he had ever really known his wife at all. Because to know Clare, truly, was to accept the fact that you couldn't ever know what was swirling beneath her beautiful surface. She was a mystery, and aside from the money and fame that Clare manifested, the mystery was her single greatest draw, and certainly the most enduring. Had Simon never realized it? Really? Because Eileen had managed to work that all out by the time she was twelve.

"Why not her first book?"

"Hmm? Sorry, what was that?"

"You said, aside from her first book, she'd included you in creating every other one. Why not the first?"

"Oh." He shrugged and raised one eyebrow. "Well, she wrote that first when we were only getting to know each other. Before we fell in love, I suppose."

Eileen racked her brains, trying to remember. "Which book was that? I can't remember the title of her first book."

"Yes, well that's because it was never published. She wrote it during her short story days back in—"

"Brooklyn," Eileen finished. "And actually, I think I did read it. I must have. Back then I used to read all Clare's stuff."

Simon, despite his haggard and grief-stricken self, cracked a small smile. "Of course. You were her only fan." He nodded.

"What?" Eileen tilted her head to the side.

Simon took a sip of his now-fresh cup of black coffee. "When I first met Clare, in that run-down bar on its way out of business trying desperately to stay afloat by holding readings for local writers, she told me her sister was her only fan." Simon raised his coffee cup to Eileen across the island. "So, brava, sister Eileen. If not for you, one of the most prolific and popular fiction writers of our time may have thrown in the towel before the world had a chance to show up and kneel at her door." He took a long drink from his coffee and lowered the cup to the counter with a clank that rang out.

"Some fan. I can't even remember now what that book was about. Why didn't it ever publish?"

Simon stared at his cup and took a breath. "If I recall, editors far and wide said something along the lines of, while the writing was fantastic, they had a hard time connecting to the main character. They couldn't determine a market audience. They *liked* it but didn't *love* it, and some of them simply didn't respond at all. Clare was a nobody, and I was a nobody agent. Collectively, we were easy to reject out of hand at that point in our careers." Simon shrugged. "All of that, it's fairly typical actually. It's what she and I did after that first book—that's the stuff of literary dreams." His voice broke on the last word.

"Simon…" she said, her voice soft and trying to comfort.

He raised his hand to stop her, sucking air fast and hard through his nose. He shook his head once, as if trying to push away the sudden tsunami of grief that had washed over him again. "My every thought leads to her, and it's like breaking in half over and over, and over. I don't want to move. I don't want to breathe… Why would she do this? Why would she leave me like this?"

Eileen shook her head. She had no idea what Clare could have been thinking, feeling—what might have driven her to something so desperate, so irrevocable. By all accounts, Clare's life was perfect. At least that was what Eileen had always thought. Clare was beautiful, talented, successful, rich beyond belief, and adored by both her husband and her fans. She looked down at the book she still held in her hands, *A Perfect Life*. She now wondered if Simon's suspicions could be correct. Was there something about this book that was different? Some message from Clare that someone who knew her could possibly decipher? But if Simon couldn't see it…

He had been the closest person to Clare for the last sixteen years. Simon and…

Eileen looked up at him. "Has our mother been told?"

He closed his eyes and sighed, as if just now remembering the elderly woman in the assisted living home who had lost her eldest daughter but had no idea any of it had happened. "No… I don't know. Maybe someone from the Regency… God, I completely forgot about—"

"I'll figure it out. I'm sure the home wouldn't have told her without consulting one of us first. It will be best if I tell her."

Simon nodded. "She didn't even know who I was the last time I went with Clare to visit. It was like the last twenty years had disappeared for her."

Eileen nodded. "I'll go today." She stared down at her milky coffee, dreading the moment she would have to try to explain to her mother that Clare was gone. It would be awful under any circumstances, but how would it play out with a woman whose mind slipped further and further every day into a tangled gray fog of confusion and loss? Would she even understand what Eileen was telling her? "What about…what other arrangements still need to be made?"

"I don't know. Everything, I guess. Clare's publicist is coming. She's hired someone to help us, some sort of professional planner."

"A funeral planner?" Eileen asked, never even considering once in her life before this moment that such a profession existed. "Like a wedding planner?" she clarified and immediately regretted mentioning two disparate life events that threw their current situation into such a stark contrast. "I'm sorry… I just—why a planner? Won't someone at the funeral home just sit down with us and help us pick out... I mean, go through the details, let us know what we need?"

"If it was me that had died, yes," Simon said. "But it's not me; it's Clare Collins. I don't think you're realizing this could turn into a circus, a total media shit storm. And the sheer number of people who will try to be there—her most devout following? We need more help than a funeral director can offer. I'm sure you saw what happened when the publicist released the initial announcement, just the basics?"

Eileen thought of the two women in the airport bookstore, commiserating and buying Clare's new book. Obviously, people knew her sister had died, but Simon was alluding to something more. "I guess I didn't. I've been pretty out of touch since your call yesterday."

He nodded and pulled his phone from his robe pocket and swiped the screen awake. "I told the publicist, just a basic announcement that she'd passed away, here at home. That we wanted some privacy. She had advised being more forthcoming. She wanted us to verify the death was a suicide." Simon handed Eileen his phone so she could see what was happening for herself. "I just couldn't do it—I still can't. But people are speculating wildly now. Some are even wondering if her death was drug-related, or even murder. There's all sorts of theories all over the internet and social media, people making wild leaps of logic, some based on characters or plots from Clare's books—especially because of *that* book." Simon pointed to his copy of *A Perfect Life*. "That's part of the reason the publicist and planner are coming today."

"Damage control," Eileen offered.

"Exactly."

"How much information will you release?" she asked.

"You mean, how much will *we* release?" Simon shook his head. "I don't know. I can't even imagine getting dressed, never mind trying to think this all out. It wasn't just a courtesy asking you to come. I really need you here, Eileen. It's too much, and I can't manage it alone."

"Of course," she said. She took a deep breath and held on to it for several moments before letting it go.

"They'll be here at three. They want us to hash out a plan and come out with a revised statement by the end of today. They hope it will help squelch the rumors starting to fly."

Eileen nodded. "We're going to tell everyone, aren't we? We're going to let the world know what Clare did?"

Simon swallowed, the corners of his mouth pulling down. "I think we might have to."

"I need to tell our mother first. It needs to come from me—not some news report or nursing assistant."

Simon looked at the time on his phone. "Yes, absolutely. You're right," he said, the tone in his voice giving away the fact that he hadn't even considered this. "That would be the right thing to do. And you should have time to get there and back before everyone arrives if I call Henry right now and arrange for him to drive you." Simon pulled up the contacts on his phone. "Can you be ready in twenty minutes?"

"Yes," she said, largely because *no* was apparently not an alternative. She picked up her coffee and turned to head back up the stairs and into a very quick shower. She stopped at the door and looked back at Simon, who was just finding Henry's number. "You said especially *that* book. Why? Have you figured out what's so different about it? Aside from her not letting you read it right away?"

"You haven't read it?" Simon asked as he lowered his phone.

Feeling slightly ashamed of the fact, Eileen shook her head. "Not yet. I just picked it up."

Simon sighed. "Well, apart from it just being a very different book from what she usually wrote, the main character, in the end... she kills herself."

Eileen stared at him.

Simon looked up and met her gaze. "So you can understand why I feel like I should have known my wife needed help." He looked down at the space of counter between them and shook his head. "I should have known. I should have been here." He placed his hand on his forehead and held it there for a moment before slamming his fist onto the marble. "I should have fucking been here," he whispered. "I could have stopped her...saved her...fucking done something other than...find her."

On instinct, Eileen went to him and wrapped her arms around his shoulders.

"I don't... It doesn't make sense to me," he whispered while his shoulders shook. He pulled away and looked into Eileen's eyes. "Did she say anything to you, ever, that may give you a clue? Was it something... Did she ever say anything to you that would make you think... Jesus Christ, is this my fault?"

Eileen stared into Simon's sorrowful expression; his eyes a

bottomless well of grief and pain. She said the only real truth about her sister she knew. "Clare was complicated and secretive and always so...hard to really know. Even as kids. She was my sister; we shared a *bedroom*, for God's sake, but I've never felt like I really understood Clare."

And when that explanation didn't seem to help ease the pain on Simon's face, Eileen grasped his hands and told him a lie.

"She loved you, Simon."

CHAPTER 16

Clare

Twenty-one years before her death

CLARE STOOD WITH THE AWKWARD CARDBOARD AND CELLOPHANE box open in one hand while she used the plastic tongs to pick up the glazed, jelly-filled doughnut her mother had requested. Careful to keep the box balanced as she placed it next to the other ten assorted sugar bombs she had already selected, all that was left was Eileen's cream-filled éclair. It was Sunday morning, and all of them had slept late. Her mom had promised to make the coffee if Clare would go pick up some doughnuts.

"Fine," Clare had groaned and taken the car keys from her mother's outstretched hand. It wasn't just that her mother wanted her to pick up breakfast. Her mother's frequent requests for Clare to "run to the store" or "drop Eileen off at school" were actually Ella's not-especially-covert attempts at getting Clare past the fear of driving she had developed since the accident.

For months after Clare had come home from the hospital, she

hadn't touched a steering wheel, but none of them really thought anything about it. It wasn't until the following February, eight months after the accident she still couldn't remember, that her mother pulled her car over to the side of the road and unbuckled her seat belt.

"What are you doing?" Clare asked.

"It occurred to me last night that you haven't driven, not once, since…before. I'm getting out so you can drive the rest of the way home." Ella opened her door and was moving around the car to Clare's side before she had a chance to respond.

"Wait—what?" she said, as a panic she hadn't expected clutched at her chest while her hands and feet burned with a surge of adrenaline. Clare watched her mother reach for the passenger door handle, intent on forcing her out of her seat and behind the wheel of the car. On reflex, Clare's hand shot like a bullet from her lap and locked the door. She met her mother's surprised eyes through the closed window and shook her head.

"Clare?" her mother said, a worried frown sprouting between her eyes. "Don't be silly. Unlock the door."

Clare closed her eyes. Her heart thundered in her ears. As surprised as she was by her own behavior and reactions, she was far more terrified that her mom was going to force her to do something she suddenly realized she couldn't. She couldn't move, was barely breathing. Her hands were sweating profusely just from *thinking* about driving. When she opened her eyes, she saw that her mother was still standing outside the car but had taken several steps back. Her arms limp at her sides; she looked shocked.

"I can't," Clare whispered. "I can't." Her eyes welled up with tears that spilled down her cheeks.

Her mom walked back around the front of the car, got in the driver's seat, and closed her door. They sat for a moment, both staring out the windshield, the silence humming in Clare's ears. After several seconds her mom reached for the key, turned the ignition, and shifted the car into Drive.

"We're going to have to fix this, Clare. You know that, right?" She pulled the car back onto the desolate road and accelerated. "I had no idea you were so afraid to drive now."

"Neither did I," Clare whispered.

So her mother started her slow. "Just open the driver's side door." And for the next three days, Clare opened and then closed the driver's side door several times a day. "Today, I want you to open the door and sit in the seat, for as long as you can."

At first, she was only able to sit for a few seconds before the racy, panicked feeling clawed up out of her gut and spread throughout her back and chest. But after a week, Clare was able to sit there for ten minutes, especially if she turned on the radio to distract herself.

"Now," her mother said, standing next to the open door and handing her the keys, "start it up."

Which was how, two months later, Clare was eventually able to drive around their block. By the time summer came, and after the one-year anniversary of that night, Clare was able to make her first short trip, alone, to the store. She had spent the whole summer taking care of small errands for her mother, her mother who was on a mission to help Clare recover, move on—get her life back. So by the fall, Clare could drive again. Short distances only, and she never enjoyed driving. It had now become a necessary evil to be endured, but she could do it. Even if she hadn't really moved on in any other way.

She was nineteen now. She wasn't working or in school and didn't really see a path toward either of those options. Waiting her turn in the checkout line, Clare read the red-and-white Help Wanted sign taped to the wall beneath the customer service desk where they sold lottery tickets and scratchers. There was small, handwritten print, probably detailing exactly what sort of job they were hiring for, in the white space at the bottom of the sign, but it was too far away for Clare to make out.

She inhaled, gathering herself for what she knew she needed to do next. Her mother hadn't mentioned her getting a job, not once, since the accident. But she couldn't spend her every day floating from her bedroom to the kitchen to the bathroom, occupying herself with little more than the words she scribbled down in her journals and daytime soap operas. It was time. She needed to keep moving on with her life, even if that life wore a red smock and a name tag. After she paid for her doughnuts, she would head over to the counter and ask for an application.

Clare felt a tap on her shoulder and jumped. When she turned, she saw Mrs. Cummings standing right behind her. She had pushed to the front of her overflowing grocery cart in order to get closer to Clare.

"It's a shame what almost happened to you," Mrs. Cummings began with a breathless urgency.

Clare stared blankly back at Mrs. Cummings, her face made strange by a heavy hand of makeup that left her eyes ringed with a mix of dark brown and blue, her bouncing cropped perm hacked like a hedge that ended right at her dimpled chin.

"That boy, drinking like that, putting your life at risk. It's simply a miracle you weren't killed as well."

Clare got the impression that this woman had been waiting for exactly a moment like this to express herself on the topic of Adam Collins and the shocking thing that had happened last year.

Mrs. Cummings placed her bloated fingers on Clare's shoulder. "The hand of God. His watchful eye." She nodded. "I just hope you know how much this whole town is grateful that you didn't have to pay the ultimate price for that boy's sins. If ever you need anything…" She nodded her head, the space between her eyes crinkling for emphasis.

Clare couldn't conjure words. They had deserted her, and in this moment when she needed them most. She stared at Mrs. Cummings's foundation-filled pores and remembered that it was her oldest son, Greg Cummings, who had once yelled at her from his lunch table surrounded by his friends, "Hey, Clare? If you ever need some extra cash, I'll let you suck my dick for ten bucks!"

Two tables away, Adam had overheard Greg. He got up out of his seat, strode over with his fists clenched, and punched Greg Cummings in the face. Back then, Adam had only been Adam, recreational basketball player, son of the piano teacher, good student, her best friend. And now he was gone. Her Adam was dead. The realization kept attacking her when she wasn't ready—like now, standing in line at the grocery store, listening to some fat, middle-aged bitch who knew *absolutely nothing* tell her how lucky she was.

"Oh." Mrs. Cummings pointed over Clare's shoulder to the clerk waiting to scan her box of doughnuts. "Your turn, sweetheart."

Clare turned from the woman, paid for her doughnuts with a wad of one-dollar bills pulled from her front pocket, and left the store, forgetting all about Help Wanted signs, red aprons, name tags, and any seedling thought she may have been entertaining about moving on with her life. She rushed through the parking lot and pulled the car keys from her fleece jacket, barely registering what she was even doing until she was sitting behind the wheel of her mother's car, doughnuts still in her lap, the early Sunday morning sun blinding her through the dirty windshield.

In the privacy of the car, Clare gasped, filling her lungs several times. One of her migraines was blooming, right behind her left eye, a storm swirling and gathering speed. Flashing lights began to strobe in her peripheral vision.

"Shit," she whispered, dreading the pain, like a vise on her skull she would now be enduring alone in her darkened bedroom for the rest of the day. She placed the box on the seat next to her and managed to get the key in her shaking hand connected with the ignition slot. Any minute, the waves of pain would blind her, leaving her incapacitated. She considered heading back into the store right now and calling her mother to come pick her up in her patrol car.

She turned the key, cranked the starter, and pumped the gas until the engine turned over and she could back out of her parking space. If she ran back in and called for help, two horrible things were for sure going to happen. One, she'd definitely run back into that bitch Mrs. Cummings. And, two, it would take much longer for her to get to the orange bottles that held an assortment of pills that had been prescribed for her assortment of problems—including her head—that the accident had left broken.

"Ten minutes, please, brain. Just give me ten minutes to get home." All her meds were lined up on the dresser she shared with Eileen in their bedroom. The sooner she got home, the sooner she could try to chemically ward off the seizure starting in her head.

Clare took another deep breath and gripped the steering wheel hard enough to make her hands sweat and her knuckles turn white. She could do this, she told herself as she accelerated out of the parking lot and took a right onto the street.

Ten minutes later, her vision blurred by lightning strikes of pain, tears rolled down her cheeks as she pulled the car onto their driveway. Forgetting everything except her need for the cool dark of her room, Clare managed to at least put the car into park before she pulled herself out of the driver's side door and made her way to the front stoop with her eyes squeezed shut and her temples pressed hard between the heels of her hands.

"Clare?" Eileen's voice broke through the electric currents pulsing across both hemispheres of her brain. Clare heard the screen door open and felt hands on her upper arm and back guiding her up the stairs and into the house. "Mom!" Eileen shouted, sending a fresh shock wave from Clare's ear to the base of her skull.

"What's wrong?" their mom asked from somewhere nearby. Clare kept her eyes squeezed tight.

"Oh! Again? Get her to her room, Eileen. I'll get some water for her pills."

As her sister guided her down the short hallway, Clare dragged her hand along the wall to help keep herself steady. Once they were through the bedroom door, Clare dared to open one eye the thinnest of slivers. Light pouring in from their south-facing window made her clasp one hand over both eyes. "The drapes," she croaked.

Eileen helped lower her onto her bed, and then Clare heard the sound of the plastic drape hooks sliding along their metal runner as her sister pulled the cord until the heavy blackout fabric met in the center of the window and transformed the room into a cocoon of darkness.

"Grab her pills," her mother said as she entered the room with a glass of cool tap water.

"Which one?" Eileen asked, picking up two bottles to inspect the labels.

"Here," their mother said. She placed the water on the side table and took the pill bottles from Eileen. "You go close the car door. I'll do this."

As Eileen left the room, Clare rolled onto her side and pulled her knees to her chest with her head cradled between both her arms. Light, sound, breathing sent a continuous stream of pain radiating out across the interconnected network of neurons throughout her head.

"Clare, here," her mother said as she uncurled one of Clare's clenched fists and placed two pills into her palm. With as little movement as possible, Clare brought the meds to her lips and turned her head enough to allow her mom to get the glass of water to her mouth. After three tiny sips, a thin stream of water ran down her chin, but Clare managed to wash the pills down.

"What else can I do?" her mom asked.

"Nothing," Clare whispered. Even this small sound echoed through her head like a wrecking ball. "Just go."

She felt her mom's cool hand on her neck. It rested there for a moment and then moved to the side of her face. Clare knew she was trying to help her feel better, but even this touch was like a siren screaming across her nervous system. Clare just needed her to leave, close the door, and allow her to wrap herself in silence and darkness until the fireworks exploding in her head stopped. When it didn't seem like that was going to happen any time soon, Clare begged, "Please…go."

On the bed next to her, Clare felt her mother's weight shift and heard her sigh. "Okay," she whispered and stood up. A second later, the door latched closed with the softest of clicks. Clare, finally left alone with her pain, waited for the medication to cut the edge.

She didn't move, barely breathed. Her only concern was keeping a steady pressure on her head and any light from entering her vision. Minutes passed, the drumbeat in her brain an erratic spasm that at first gave no sign of giving way to the drugs meant to keep her from feeling like her brains were exploding all over the inside of her skull. But after a while, the pulse slowed, the intensity softened, and Clare was finally able to pull her arms from her head and open her eyes to the soft gray light in the room created by thin lines of bright midmorning sunshine leaking around the edge of the thick curtains. The flashes of light across her vision had stopped, along with the accompanying swell of nausea that always went hand in hand with these episodes.

Before her accident, Clare had never experienced anything more uncomfortable than a hangover. Now that her body had been ejected thirty feet through the windshield of Adam's truck, and survived, debilitating migraines had become a regular part of life. It was just one more thing about her existence that was awful now.

Clare pushed herself up onto her hands and knees and crawled to the end of her bed, reaching her arm across the narrow space between the bottom of her bed and the dresser. She grabbed the bottle of pain pills and scooted back to the top of her bed. Clare propped herself against her headboard and opened the bottle. It was a recent refill and still mostly full. She tipped the bottle and let all the pills pile into her palm.

She'd thought about it many times over the past year.

Because how hard would it be? A handful of pills. Wash them all down. Lie back and wait. Sleep. Go. Die. Painless.

She didn't know what the point of anything was anymore. She hurt, physically, mentally.

Adam was gone.

She would never get over that. She would never let herself. She loved him, even now. He had been gone over a year, and she still loved him just as much.

More even.

She missed him. All the time. Talking with him, his laugh, listening to him play the piano, watching him play ball, holding his hand, kissing him—making love to him.

Clare let the pills tumble from her hand and onto the bedsheet. She used her finger to spread them out, then pushed them back into a pile. She wished she had been the one to die that night. Why hadn't it been her? What was the point in her surviving? Adam was the one with his whole life, a real life, ahead of him. His talent, his brain, his gifts—if there was a God, like fucking Karen Cummings was so sure of, and that God had spared Clare's life that night instead of Adam's, well then, God had made a huge fucking mistake.

Clare grabbed the water glass off her side table. She picked up a pill between her thumb and index finger, placed it on her tongue, held it there for a moment, then washed it down. She picked up another, placed it on her tongue, then washed it down.

She wanted to die. Her life was useless; she was useless. What was she ever going to do? How could she, Clare Kaczanowski, nobody from nowhere, ever possibly be worth anything without the one good thing, the one amazing person she had lost? What was left? Living with her mom in Casper forever? Red smock and a name tag? Clare picked up another pill, placed it on her tongue, and took another swallow of water.

The handle on the bedroom door turned, and the latch clicked.

Clare pulled her blanket up over her pile of pills.

"Clare?" Eileen whispered as she poked her head through the crack in the door. "Oh." Eileen smiled at her. "You're up. I wanted to check on you but not wake you if you were sleeping."

"I'm not sleeping," Clare said.

"Are you okay now?"

Clare hesitated. For half a second she considered tossing the blanket back and showing Eileen the pile of pills she was planning on slowly making her way through. "I'm okay."

"Does it still hurt?"

"Yes, but not as bad."

Eileen came all the way into the room and sat down on the edge of Clare's bed. "Mom's upset."

Clare looked into her sister's eyes. "About what?" she whispered.

"She's worried about you, I think she's afraid."

Clare stared at the blanket in front of her. "Afraid?"

Eileen shrugged. "I don't know. The migraines…other stuff too, I think. I don't think she realizes they're getting better."

"Better?" Clare raised her eyebrows. "How would you know and how do you figure?"

"Well, before today, it had been two weeks since your last… episode. And before that, ten days. When you first got out of the hospital, they were every week, sometimes two or three. Mom didn't realize that they've been getting less and less over time. I think she was afraid that you'd never stop having them."

Clare looked at her sister. "They've been less?"

Eileen nodded.

"You've been keeping track?"

"Well, it's not like it's hard to notice when you're shut in our shared bedroom in the dark for hours at a time."

"I didn't realize… I didn't know they were getting better."

"I imagine it doesn't seem like it when you're the one dealing with them. Do you think—I mean if you're feeling better enough— that you could come lie on the couch? I think it would make Mom feel better if we were at least all together, even if we're just watching a movie and eating doughnuts in the living room."

"I forgot about the doughnuts," Clare said.

"I brought them in from the car. We're waiting for you."

"The doughnuts are why I ended up with this stupid migraine in the first place today."

Eileen wrinkled her brow.

Clare shook her head. "In line at the store, Greg Cummings's mom said something to me." Clare sighed. "I let it upset me."

"God, that guy was always such an asshole."

"And his mother is horrible."

"Well, at least we know where he gets it from." Eileen smiled. "Will you come out?"

Clare bit her bottom lip and nodded. "Just give me a second. I'll be right there." Clare sat and waited while Eileen got up from her bed and headed back out the door without closing it behind her. She waited a few more seconds, just to make sure she wasn't going to pop back in, then lifted the blanket and scooped all her pills back into their bottle before refastening the cap. She placed it on her bedside table next to the half-empty glass of water.

Clare stared at the bottle, then closed her eyes. "I have to leave," she whispered.

The realization felt so true, the answer to a problem she had not fully understood until this moment. She had been living under a tremendous weight ever since she had woken up in her hospital bed in Cheyenne. The weight of her old life, her old dreams, her old self. Being here, staying here, all she really wanted was that life back, the future she'd lost. That future, that life with Adam, waiting for Adam to come home, marry her, start a life with her. She wasn't ever getting that back. She would never stop loving him, but she wasn't ever getting him back.

"I'm leaving," she said again. She would run from this claustrophobic town and her whole goddamn life. Somewhere it would be impossible for her to ever get tapped on the shoulder and emotionally assaulted by someone who believed they knew the first thing about her, her life…her loss.

Run away from anyone that imagined they could possibly ever know what happened to her the night her life turned completely upside down in the blink of an eye on an old dirt road in the middle of nowhere.

"Clare?" Eileen called from the living room.

"I'm coming," she answered, swinging her legs over the side of her bed.

CHAPTER 17

Eileen

SINCE EILEEN ARRIVED UNSCHEDULED AND UNANNOUNCED TO VISIT with her mother, she needed to wait for half an hour while Ella finished her session with her personal medical assistant and trainer. She was already in the saltwater pool.

"I'm sorry, but changes to her schedule and routines greatly upset her. It's important, for her mental health and well-being, to adhere as much as we can to her schedule."

Eileen nodded. "Of course." If this was any other run-of-the-mill retirement home, she would be suspicious of being kept from seeing her mother right away. Like maybe the woman was spending most of her days alone, in filth and unchanged soiled bed linens, incapable of advocating for herself, due to the fact that she spent half her waking time believing it was 1995. But the sheer opulence of the place, more like a five-star hotel than geriatric home, made Eileen believe it was highly unlikely. After all, Clare wasn't paying fifteen grand a month for their mother to endure daily abuse and neglect. One might assume that in addition to the miles of granite, towering displays of fresh flowers, and tasteful artwork, the community was also able to hire top-notch nurses and caring professionals.

"I'm sorry this is so unexpected," Eileen added, as if she needed to apologize for her sister's untimely and inconvenient suicide. "We've just had…" She took a breath and considered how to word it. "Some unexpected family news."

"I see. Should we have one of our family therapists on hand? To assist with Ms. Kaczanowski with any necessary processing?"

Eileen's mouth fell open slightly. "Processing?"

"Is the news likely to cause Ms. Kaczanowski emotional distress?"

"Oh, well, yes. But I…I don't think that will be necessary."

The woman's mouth flatlined. "Very well. Please let me know as soon as possible should you change your mind. We do advise having a therapist present. Responses, particularly for our patients with Alzheimer's, can be unpredictable and difficult for family members to navigate alone."

Eileen could think of no good way to explain, politely, her mother's long-held views and suspicions about mental-health workers. Perhaps simply letting her know that Ms. Kaczanowski didn't even like her two daughters speaking with the high school counselor when they needed a schedule change, because only walking into the office could potentially land them on a Freudian couch, their minds cracked like fragile eggs, tears spilling down without end for weeks.

Eileen could still remember Ella's instructions, "If they ask you any personal questions, you just tell them it's none of their damn business.

You hear me?" Her mother came from a long line of pull-yourself-up-by-your-bootstrappers, which suddenly made Eileen wonder if that maybe had something to do with Clare's…

"Thank you," Eileen said. "I will."

The woman smiled and nodded. "Please make yourself comfortable in the family lounge area. It's across the foyer, second door on the left." She lifted her hand palm up and used it to direct Eileen's attention to the other side of the room. "I will notify you when your mother's session is complete and she is ready for visitors."

Eileen nodded and did as she was told, crossing over the plush Persian rug and around the taut, cream-colored leather sofas and chairs to the double-doored family lounge. Inside, there was only one other person, an elderly woman with a lap filled with knitting and a steaming cup of something on the coffee table in front of her. At the back of the room, a coffee and tea bar was set up along with dome-covered plates of pastries and bagels. The woman looked up at Eileen, smiled, and then returned her attention to her creation.

Eileen found a sunny seat near the plate-glass window overlooking a lush, well-manicured lawn and geometric flower beds filled with an assortment of bright yellow and orange mums. She placed her tote on the couch next to her and dug through its depths, past her planner, receipts, two hairbrushes, the manila envelope with the photos of her husband fucking Lauren Andrews, half a pack of gum, a wrinkled and yet unsigned parent permission form for a field trip Ryan's class was supposed to be taking to the Museum of Nature and Science—"Shit," she whispered—until she found her phone at the very bottom. She pulled it out to check the clock. She needed to make sure Henry would have enough time to get her back to the house before all the professionals showed up to plan Clare's funeral… and apparently the public relations that would be required. Eileen sighed. She had always known Clare's life was different, but she was only now beginning to realize what an entirely different planet from Eileen's her sister had been living on.

She had missed three calls, one from Eric and two from Paige. Just seeing his name on her screen made her heart beat hard, her palms sweat. She could feel the rage bubble up fast, like roiling lava right at the base of her sternum. Thinking about Eric, what he had done, what he was *still doing*. With all she did for him? Their family? Every goddamn day of her life and he had the audacity to betray her?

She couldn't breathe—the embarrassment, the shame she felt imagining Lauren thinking—what?—that she was *better* than Eileen, that she had *won* something, some goddamn Eric contest that Eileen didn't even know she was competing in?

She felt so fucking stupid.

But why? Why should she feel stupid? When he was the one who… It wasn't like she had *known*.

How could she have fucking known?

Should she have known?

Eileen stared at her phone and considered what would very likely happen, what she wouldn't be able to stop herself from saying, if she called Eric back right now.

She texted her daughter instead.

Everything okay?

Within seconds, Paige responded.

Ya. Just checking on you.

As good as can be expected. Getting ready to see
Grandma and tell her the news.

Paige sent her a tear-faced emoji and:

So sorry, Mom.

I love you. Talk to you later tonight.

K, love you too.

She decided to ignore the call from Eric, for now, and put her
phone away, this time being careful to use the small inside pocket so
she didn't again lose it to her bag's dark abyss. She wouldn't be able to
avoid him forever, obviously, but she had no idea what to say to him.

"Mrs. Greyden?" a woman's voice called to her.

Eileen turned in her seat and saw the woman from behind the
counter peeking her head through the doors. "Yes?"

"Your mother finished early today. She's ready to see you now."

Her mother sat in a low-backed, blue brocade armchair near the
window in her room. Eileen had been here once before, three years

ago at Christmas, but had forgotten how spacious and lovely the accommodations were. Like a small one-bedroom apartment with a separate bedroom, bathroom, and living room area. The only room missing was a kitchen. By the time Clare had moved their mother here, the doctors had determined she was no longer independent enough to be placed in one of the "full amenities" suites. Basically, their mother had no business being near a stove. Almost burning down their old house in Casper was how she ended up here in the first place. But her current cognitive status was functional enough for this, a three-quarter suite with around-the-clock supervision. Eileen looked up and saw the cameras placed strategically in high corners; they were monitored at the nurses' station and were in every room. All her food and beverages were provided either in the restaurant downstairs or delivered to her here if her personal caregiver determined she was not well enough to make it downstairs.

The last time she'd spoken with Clare about their mother, she had said that, for the most part, their mother still made it downstairs to eat with others and would even sometimes play games with the other residents, but she frequently forgot how she'd come to live in this lap of Alzheimer's luxury and couldn't keep hold of anyone's name that she'd met in the last ten years.

Eileen knocked gently on her mother's open door. "Mom?"

Ella Kaczanowski turned slowly from her gaze out the window, a placid smile on her face. She stared at Eileen for several seconds before finally saying, "Hello." Her expression was a question that asked, *Can I help you?*

Eileen blinked, waited a bit longer. Maybe it would come.

"Hello?" her mother repeated again, wrinkling her brow. "Are you lost, dear?"

It wasn't her fault. It wasn't like she could control an overgrowth of plaque and neuron entanglement eating away at the person she once was; but even knowing this, it still hurt to have your mother look at you like she'd never seen you before in her life.

"Have we... Eileen?" her mother suddenly said, sending a wave of relief through Eileen so powerful it nearly brought her to tears.

"Yes, Mom," she answered, coming into the room. She bent down and hugged her mother, who was still sitting in her chair. "Hello. I've missed you."

When she pulled away and looked into her mother's eyes, she was struck by how similar her expression was to her own children when they were much, much younger than they were now. What was it? A wide-eyed innocence? A not-yet knowing? Or in her mother's case, an absence of life's worry and pressure simply because they'd fallen away with the memories of most of her life experiences?

"I almost didn't recognize you," her mother said, patting Eileen's hand between her own. She looked around Eileen and toward the door. "Has Clare come with you? If I'd known you girls were coming, I'd have made some dinner." She looked questioningly around the room, as if wondering what she had on hand that she could offer, her expression darkening when she seemed to realize she was not where she thought she should be.

"That's all right, Mom. I'm not hungry anyway."

Eileen pulled up a chair next to her mother and took her hand. She was smaller, but she was obviously as healthy as could be expected and actually now had a sort of glow about her that Eileen couldn't remember her hard-edged cop mother ever possessing. This place, all Clare's money, was doing a good job of taking care of Ella. Eileen didn't like to think about where she would have probably ended up if she and Eric had had to make the payments every month. For sure there would have been no saltwater pools and personal care assistants. Her mother plastered a smile on her face and stared at Eileen. She may have recognized her own daughter, eventually anyway, but she still had huge holes and questions about who, when, and even what the hell was going on at all times. The smiles were a cover—smiles and waiting for other people to say things that provided her context clues. Ella had been doing that act for years before she and Clare had any real idea that something more serious was going on with their once-sharp mother.

Eileen took a deep breath and regretted the decision to not have a therapist in the room. "Mom, I need to tell you something. Something that is going to upset you."

Ella dropped her smile, her features morphing into an expression of grave seriousness. "Whatever it is, sweetheart, you can tell me anything. Mothers are—well, the good ones anyway—always there for their children, no matter what they've done."

Speechless and completely unsure of how to move forward, Eileen stared into her mother's forgiving expression.

"Is it about the smoking?" Ella leaned forward and whispered. "Well, I'll tell you a little secret, young lady." She held up her arthritic pointer finger to Eileen. "I already know about it." She sat back in her seat and nodded sagely. "I don't approve, and you shouldn't make it a habit. It's very hard to quit. And I shouldn't have to tell you how addiction runs rampant through your father's side of the family."

Stunned, Eileen watched the cognitive train wreck derail before her. In less than half a second, her mother had jumped track and traveled back over twenty years. "No," Eileen said. "It's not about the smoking." She leaned in, uncertain if pushing ahead with her news was really the best decision, but also feeling pressed for time; maybe she could coax her mother back into the present day. "It's about Clare, Mom. She…there's been…an accident."

Ella's gaze hardened. "What would *you* know about that?" She narrowed her eyes at Eileen, as if she'd suddenly become suspicious of a stranger. "Who?" She raised her voice. "Who have you been talking to? What did they tell you?"

"Mom." Eileen tried to reach for her mother's hand, but Ella snatched it away quicker than Eileen would have thought her capable. "I'm sorry, but I need to tell you something about Clare. There's been an accident, and I'm so sorry, but… Clare is dead, Mom."

Ella wrinkled her brow and let out a loud scoff while shaking her head. "You don't know anything." She pointed to the center of her chest. "I was there. I know perfectly well what happened. My daughter is not dead, and whoever is telling you that is wrong. It was that boy, that…" She looked away, out the window, as if the pieces of her mind that were missing might be floating out in the sun beyond the window.

"Mom, please, you're confused. I need you to try to be here with me now. I need you to understand that Clare is gone."

"Adam." She suddenly found what she was looking for and

turned her attention back to Eileen with a triumph. "Not my Clare. It was the Adam boy that died in the accident. You're the one who's confused."

Eileen's shoulders sagged as understanding overtook her. The car wreck. Her mother thought she was talking about the wreck. "I'm not talking about *that* accident."

"And you shouldn't." Ella's face contorted with a sudden rage. "You don't know... I was there! I was there! My daughter—I would do anything for my children. Anything!" Ella shouted at her.

Eileen sat back in her seat. This was a mistake. She should have listened to the woman at the front desk and requested the therapist.

"You don't know!" her mother screamed. "You don't know anything!"

Two attendants in pale-blue scrubs arrived at the door. "Is everything okay?" one of them asked in an alert, but still calm, voice.

Eileen shook her head. "No," she said, watching her mother shake her head violently back and forth as she rocked in her chair. "I've made a mistake."

The attendants came in slowly. "It's okay." They were reassuring Eileen, not her mother. "These things—they happen. It's really hard to predict."

One of the attendants placed a hand at the center of Ella's back. "It's okay, it's okay," she soothed. "Everything is going to be all right."

CHAPTER 18

Eileen

EILEEN PUSHED THROUGH THE REVOLVING MAIN DOOR, PAST THE doormen and beyond the protection of the Regency's entrance awning, and up the public sidewalk. Blinded by the midmorning sun, she tripped on a raised square of concrete, pitching forward, arms cartwheeling. It was only after three huge, embarrassing stumbles that she barely escaped a nasty fall.

"Jesus Christ," she cursed under her breath while she collected herself and attempted to regain her composure.

Looking around, she saw that the doorman behind her and several other passersby had noticed but also had the good grace to pretend not to and quickly glanced away. With a roll of her shoulders and a deep breath, Eileen moved closer to the building to steady her fractured nerves and begin the search for Henry's business card so she could call for a ride back to the house.

After several seconds of frustrated rummaging, followed by new resolutions and promises to both buy a smaller purse and keep it organized, Eileen finally fished out her scratched sunglasses and the small, rectangular card. As she slipped on the glasses, she grabbed her phone from the pocket she'd left it in, *a miracle of organization*, and tapped the call icon. Still distracted by her embarrassment, Eileen dialed the number while continuing to glance at the doorman, who appeared to be keeping a suspicious eye on her.

"Hello?" he answered.

"Henry, it's Eileen." She lowered her head and turned toward the building. "I know you've barely dropped me off, but can you come back now? It didn't go very well. Mom got very upset when I told her about Clare…completely confused. She thinks I'm talking about something that happened over twenty years ago." She waved her free hand in the air above her head as if that could clear away the terrible misunderstanding that had just happened. "Anyway, it's a mess, and I just need to get back to the house before I fall apart right here on the street."

Eileen pressed the phone to her ear and waited for Henry to tell her, *No problem, be right there.*

"Eileen?" he asked. "Greyden?"

Eileen breathed into the phone as an uncomfortable awareness washed over her. Henry didn't sound like Henry. She lifted the business card and inspected it more closely.

"I think you may have dialed the wrong number. This is Samuel Cramer. We…well, bumped into each other in the airport yesterday."

Eileen lifted her gaze from Samuel's card in her hand and stared down the busy street at the press of cars fighting to make their way up the steeply sloping hill. After helping her during her drunken stupor, Samuel had given her his card yesterday. *Shit.* She closed her eyes.

"Is everything all right?" he asked her. "You sound upset. Do you need help?"

"No, I'm so sorry," she whispered. "I meant to call someone else. I grabbed your card by mistake and didn't look... I'm so sorry to bother you."

"It's no bother, really. Actually, I was hoping—"

"I can't begin to imagine—" How could she be so stupid, so careless? She stared at the card in her hand: Samuel Cramer, Vice President, Global Connections. How hard was it to not make a complete and utter ass of herself in front of this man? In a rush of panic, she hung up.

She stared at her phone, acutely aware that she likely just made a merely embarrassing situation horrific by hanging up on a man who she would most certainly be sharing a soccer sideline with in the very near future. There would be no avoiding the man. The shame was tangible, a weighty blanket.

How hard would it have been to simply apologize and end the conversation with a cordial, and humanlike, "So sorry to bother you. Goodbye."

"You are losing it, Eileen," she said out loud to herself, then looked up and noticed the doorman inspecting her. She bit her lip and turned away from his prying eyes.

The card with Henry's number ended up being in her back pocket, not her bag. After two rings, he picked up and promised he could be there to rescue her within fifteen minutes.

Back at the house, Clare's publicist had already arrived with the funeral planner. They sat in the sun-drenched living room looking posh and well prepared, with open laptops, cell phones, and perfectly manicured fingers that flew through screens and schedules. Their expertly lined lips both consoled and explained to Simon, who still looked shell shocked and unwashed, what all the best options were, from the venue for the memorial to the florist talented and capable enough to pull off the large number of enormous, but tasteful, arrangements they would need.

"And we really should get this guest list finalized," Eileen heard the woman with thick black hair spilling down her back say as she entered into their planning session from the mudroom off the garage. When they noticed her, both women turned on sympathetic expressions that fell just shy of genuine emotion. The woman whose flaming red hair was styled into a tight bob stood up first and extended a long, thin arm that ended in graceful fingers with heavy jewels.

"You must be Eileen." She pressed forward and took Eileen's hand between her two cold palms. "I'm Katherine, Clare's publicist." Her brow crease deepened. "I'm so very sorry for your loss."

"Thank you," Eileen managed to whisper.

"We're just getting started. Are you able to join us?"

She didn't want to. She would much rather climb the stairs to her room, strip down, fall into bed, and sleep for the next three days. One look at Simon's blank expression told her she wasn't alone. She wondered if he was actually getting worse as the hours since her sister's suicide added up. With every passing minute, the reality became clearer for Simon, less deniable. His wife was dead; she was never coming back.

"Yes, I'm ready," Eileen said, taking the empty seat on the couch next to her brother-in-law and across from these charged and efficient women being paid to help navigate their grief. "What do you need me to do?"

"Wonderful," the dark-haired funeral planner said, beaming. "I'm Regina," she said as she stood and extended her hand to shake Eileen's as well. Her barely checked exuberance belied her excitement to be working on such a large event. As she gently clasped Eileen's hand, her deep-set brown eyes connected and held Eileen's with a determined sincerity. "Please, as we move through the details, I want you to feel free to ask any question, make any request." She removed her hand from Eileen's and placed it over her heart. "I am here to make this process as simple and pain-free as possible."

Simon stood up suddenly, drawing all attention to himself. For a moment he looked lost, as if he couldn't quite remember where he was or what he was supposed to be doing. He reached out a heavy hand that landed on Eileen's forearm like an anchor. "Can I speak to you? In private?" he whispered near her ear despite the fact that the other two women could clearly hear him.

She nodded and allowed him to lead her away from the white couch to the corner of the room near the large plate-glass window overlooking the lawn and pool. When he stopped and turned, Simon grabbed both Eileen's upper arms in his viselike grip. "Can you handle this?" he asked her, his voice cracking. Eileen watched as he broke. His eyes welled up, and it seemed as if the weight of all his grief was culminating in this very moment. "They asked me... on that table...there is a catalogue of coffins." Tears streamed down his face that now looked wild and—if Eileen didn't understand all he was trying to process—insane. "Please, I'm sorry, but I can't do this. All I want to tell them is no, we're not doing any of this. We're not choosing lacquered boxes to put Clare inside. I can't even think, never mind fucking flowers. I don't give a shit about who is invited. The whole fucking world has ended for me."

"Simon." Eileen took both his hands in hers and shifted her head until he was looking into her eyes. "Go upstairs," she whispered before taking him in her arms. She rubbed Simon's back, like she would to comfort any of her three kids, while he sobbed silently into her hair. When she pulled away, she placed her hands on either side of his rough and stubbly face. "Go upstairs and go to bed. I'll make sure she has only the best of everything. Don't worry about it. I'll do it, okay?"

Simon nodded his head between her hands. "Thank you," he said, his relief at being excused from planning Clare's goodbye from this world was palpable. He turned and left the room without so much as a glance at the other two women waiting patiently and politely for the storm to pass.

Eileen watched Simon leave the room then turned to face the two women waiting to get on with planning the parade that would send the beloved Clare Collins from this world.

Eileen swallowed, took a breath, and headed back to the table. Five hours. That was what it took to shore up the guest list, floral arrangements, memorial location, music, catering, route to the cemetery with police escort, press release, media campaign, and finally, the burial site and specifications for Clare's coffin. When the other two women finally rose from their seats with promises to wrap up the final details, Eileen sat back against the down-filled couch and felt the muscles in her back release as the ache traveled up her spine and radiated out across both her shoulders.

She looked out the window. Time had slipped away, and the sun was now setting. Her sister was dead, her body resting on a slab of cold metal in the basement of the mortuary while the mortician worked to make her appear lifelike. As least, that was what Eileen imagined. The memorial service would be an open casket. Surely someone had determined that this would be appropriate, given Clare's wounds.

Because where had Clare shot herself? Through the temple? Through the heart? Or had her once-vivacious and beautiful older sister wrapped her full lips around the barrel of her 9mm and blown her gifted and intelligent brains out the back of her head? Certainly, their mother never imagined the day might come when her gift meant to protect her daughter would be used in her own hand, against her.

Maybe it was best that her mother not know that Clare was gone. Maybe she need not ever know. In her time warp of dementia, trapped somewhere between now and the 1990s, Clare would always outlive her, as she should have. Maybe, in her brief moments of clarity, she might wonder why her eldest daughter hadn't been to see her, but she would never need to know the abhorrent details.

Eileen stood up and walked out of the room. She was tired. She was sad. She was in need of a full-bodied glass of wine.

She made her way to her sister's kitchen. Past the marble and expensive professional-grade appliances, there was a short, white-washed, plank oak door at the very back of the room. Set in the corner, it would be easy to not notice. The entrance to the wine cellar was an oddity, designed by Clare to be that way, a personal touch that combined the old European styles with a modern flair. Eileen pulled the brushed nickel handle in the center of the door and ran her hand along the wall until she felt the switch for the light. With a flick, the small Italian chandelier reflected an array of light from its every handcrafted crystal and lit the way for Eileen to begin the descent down the tightly wound circular staircase that led to the cellar twenty feet below.

Wines were stored by year and region, and from Eileen's limited knowledge, Clare's collection was impressive. Eileen knew this mostly because Clare herself had told her so. Where Eileen only saw bottle after bottle stacked wide and tall on wooden slat shelves, that Christmas three years ago, Clare had spoken of years, vineyards, grapes, seasons, weather even, as she had toured Eileen and Eric through the cellar with an air of pride. Pride that Eileen had noticed, had found interesting even. Why? Because her sister had accomplished many things. Written scores of novels that were devoured by millions, earning her millions upon millions, allowing her to build this incredible oceanfront home—and yet, the most pride Eileen saw her sister display was while showing off her enormous underground cellar filled with wines from all over the world.

Why not her own library filled with her own books?

Why not every room of her home that she'd carved out for herself?

Why not the cars, the clothes, the international life?

"The skill…" Clare had said. "You can't imagine the work, the toil, the generational knowledge that goes into creating this." She practically beamed while holding a dusty bottle up, like a newly delivered baby, in the dim light for Eileen and Eric to observe. "I want us to share this one, tonight. To celebrate our family being together."

Her sister's gratuitous generosity—the memory made Eileen close her eyes. Eric was so impressed by her sister—starstruck, actually. Her grace, her wealth, her talent... And all of it had made Eileen feel so small.

Now, alone in Clare's cellar, Eileen searched the overhead labels for a region, Burgundy—Clare had declared as her personal favorite—and traced the racks downward for a year, 1975—the year Clare was born. Eileen pulled a dust-coated bottle from the rack and held it up to the light. She had no idea what it was worth. It could be ten dollars or ten thousand, not that either her sister or Simon would have cared, now or ever.

Eileen followed the rows down many more years and pulled a bottle for their mother's birth year as well. Ella was still with them, at least physically, but today Eileen felt her loss just as acutely as Clare's. "For Clare and Mom," Eileen whispered into the stony cellar. She gripped both bottles by their necks and headed back upstairs. She had no business drinking two bottles of wine alone, certainly not in her current frame of mind, but who knew, maybe Simon would venture forth and need a glass or two for himself.

After she had climbed back out of the cellar, the kitchen felt sterile and utilitarian by comparison. Never a cook, Eileen knew for sure that her sister had spent only as much time as absolutely required in this room. After searching through several cupboards, she finally found one with row after row of delicate stemware. Eileen plucked one from the bunch and a wine opener from the utensils drawer before heading upstairs to the one room that would bring her the closest to the sister she had lost.

In Clare's study, Eileen closed the door quietly behind herself and placed both bottles and her glass on the coffee table in front of the couch. The sun was now below the horizon, throwing its last rays of orange and red into the twilight sky. She cut the foil on the 1975 bottle and pulled the cork, leaving it on the screw while she poured herself a glass of the brick-red, aromatic wine. She stood, placed the glass to her lips, and wished like hell Clare was here with her now. She took a small sip, then another larger one as the complex combination of red cherry, hints of cinnamon, and earthy notes of leather promised to help her avoid thoughts, steeped in deep regrets, that she didn't want to allow herself to think.

What if I had reached out to Clare, picked up the phone?

Eileen stopped them all short. She would, eventually, allow herself to nosedive into all the things she should and could have done, all the ways she might have been a better sister; there would be self-inflicted retribution.

But not tonight. After a day spent picking the color and fabric texture of Clare's coffin, tonight was only for remembering and saying goodbye. And the best way she could think to remember her sister was through her own words. With her glass in hand, Eileen turned toward the bookshelves that held Clare's journals.

She took another long drink and considered an entry point into Clare's past.

Today, visiting her mother had been an absolute disaster. She would need to go back and try again. Her mother's misunderstanding had her thinking, about their life in Casper, about the accident, about the time when Adam had died and Clare had survived.

She reached for the journals and pulled several from the shelf and onto the floor, opening random covers and reading first pages until she found exactly what she was looking for. It was an entry from right before Clare moved out of Casper.

My mother gave me her gun today. I'm supposed to take it with me when I move to New York tomorrow.

CHAPTER 19

Clare

Nineteen years before her death

CLARE TAPPED THE MICROPHONE BEFORE HER, HEARD THE AUDIBLE *pop, pop,* and nodded her head once, satisfied the typically temperamental piece of crap was actually functioning tonight—for now. She leaned in and looked out over the small crowd of people scattered throughout the bar, sitting in clusters of two, three. There were a few loners in the group too. Many of the faces Clare recognized as regulars to the Wednesday-night open mic. At the back of the bar, sitting at a table near the door, several of the other students from Donna's MFA program had come to hear her read. They sat huddled, sipping their bottled beers, sharing silent expressions of barely constrained contempt as they sized up the other writers in the room.

Because practically everyone here was a writer, waiting for their own turn at the microphone to share a poem, a piece of micro fiction, or even their inner thoughts spilled in ink onto the trembling page in their hand. Whatever was brought, it needed to occupy less than six minutes of stage time—no exceptions.

Brian, the already balding thirty-something owner of the Blue Spruce Bar and Lounge in the middle of Brooklyn, sat on the corner barstool closest to the stage. With one unsympathetic eye on the reader and one calculating eye on the stopwatch in his hand, the moment that watch read 6:05, he swiped his hand over his throat, and Liz pulled the plug on the microphone power. He didn't care how good, or more often bad, the work or the delivery was; he was a businessman trying to earn a buck. Open-mic Wednesday got business in the door with a five-dollar cover and a two-drink minimum.

"First up tonight," Clare announced, "we have Donna Mehan, who will be reading a selection of new poetry this evening."

To the right of the stage, Clare watched as Donna carefully ascended the sagging plywood steps that had once upon a time been spray-painted black but were now rubbed bare and showed the worn, pressed-together wood particles. As she crossed the tiny stage, she gave Clare a strained smile.

"Thanks, Clare," she mouthed.

Clare had been working at the Blue Spruce for almost a year now, and from almost the day she started, Donna had been showing up to the Wednesday night open mics to read. Donna was good, or at least Clare thought so, which was why she often slated her into the first spot whenever she had anything new to read.

"Thank you," Donna almost whispered into the microphone as she raised her rumpled pages into the light and began to read.

Her voice was low, barely above a breath. Often people in the audience had a hard time hearing Donna. She was a good writer, but the anxiety of sharing her work like this, onstage in public, vulnerable and exposed—Clare wondered if many of the listeners actually even realized how talented Donna really was, or if all they ever noticed was her shaking hands and quavering voice. Her nervousness seemed worse tonight. Clare imagined it was because of her MFA "friends" in the back.

When Donna read her last stanza, well before her six-minute limit, she bowed her head. "Thank you," she finished and turned as the audience clapped politely.

"That was great," Clare whispered as Donna passed by on her way to the stairs.

"It was shit," Donna whispered back and sighed. "I'm going to get a drink."

Clare smiled at her roommate and shook her head. Donna never thought anything she wrote was ever any good. When she'd first met her, she thought it was all just an elaborate attention-seeking act, fishing for the compliments that she must surely know she deserved. But after several tear-soaked, cheap wine–addled evenings, Clare revised her initial impression. Donna Mehan suffered from crippling self-doubt that bordered on loathing. She really and truly had no idea how good her stuff was and lived always in a self-inflicted shadow of judgment.

Clare stepped back to the microphone. "Okay, and next up is David Ramsey. He'll be treating us to the next six minutes of his completed epic fantasy novel, *Ranger's in the Black*. As with every week, he would like me to mention that should there be any agents or editors in the audience, his work is currently available and he would be happy to take business cards, or even speak with interested parties over a cocktail."

There were never, ever, any agents or editors in the audience—but all of them dreamed of discovery anyway. David wasted no time launching back in to where he'd left off last Wednesday.

"Okay, to remind everyone, we are midway through chapter seventy-three and Rangorflet has just escaped the Hand of the Righteous and has entered the tavern at the edge of the Weir Forest."

Clare watched Donna take her bottle of beer from Rachel behind the bar and head over to her friends' table at the back. They were just finishing their drinks and gathering their things, leaving quickly now that they had already heard Donna read. Clare knew Donna would stay the full two hours, out of courtesy for those who had listened to her, all the time silently berating herself. Then she would head back to the apartment and sit on the fire escape, smoking and drinking wine with Sergio and Flynn if they weren't working.

"Liz," she whispered to the spiky blue-haired girl with her hand on the microphone plug, ready to cut David off the moment he went over his time.

Liz looked up at her, her dark-lined, bloodshot eyes already not interested in whatever Clare had to say.

"Can you announce the next few reads? I need to talk with someone."

"Sorry, I'm running the mic."

Clare's shoulders sagged, and she gave Liz her best *are you kidding me* glare.

"Fine," Liz said, sighing. "But you owe me a beer during intermission."

"Whatever. Thanks a lot," Clare snapped and headed down the stairs toward Donna.

"What are friends for?" Liz said, her voice dripping in sarcasm.

"Such a bitch," Clare whispered, careful to keep her voice too low for Liz to actually hear her. She suspected that Liz was all tough show, but she didn't want to take the chance of actually pissing her off and getting her ass kicked.

By the time she made it to Donna's table, the last of her friends were disappearing through the door. Clare pulled out the chair across from Donna and took a seat.

"I've been thinking," Donna started in right away. "I'm going to quit."

"Quit what?"

"Writing," she clarified. "This is such a waste of time. I mean, what am I even doing? *Why*? Why do I do it?"

"Because you're good at it," Clare said.

"I'm not good."

"Can we not start that again?"

"It's true, Clare. I'm not just saying it or blowing smoke or hoping you'll prop me up. If I were good, really good, something would have happened by now. I keep sending pieces out, and nothing comes back but rejection after rejection after rejection. I can't take it anymore. It hurts, physically hurts. Right here." She pointed to the space above her stomach and below her breastbone. "What even is this?" She pressed her finger into the spot on her torso. "Where is your spleen? It seems like this feeling, this sickening sense of failure, should be leaking from my spleen."

"Stop it," Clare told her and reached for Donna's still-full beer. Taking a sip, she pushed the bottle back across the table to her friend.

"That's exactly what I want to do—stop all of this."

"But you don't, not really. You love writing."

"I hate writing."

"No, you hate rejection."

Donna sighed, took a sip from her beer, then raised her eyes to Clare. "Anyway, what about you?"

Clare sat back in her chair. Her gaze wandered to the street scene just over Donna's shoulder through the tinted plate-glass window. People, one after another, rushed by. "What about me?"

"You lecture me about not giving up, but you write too. And you never send anything out."

"I'm not a writer," Clare said flatly.

"What the hell are you talking about? You write every day. You have hundreds of journals stacked up in boxes at the back of your closet."

Clare's gaze suddenly zeroed in on Donna. It was Donna's turn to sit back in her chair. "Yes, I've seen them. Filled to overflowing with words. You are as much a writer as I am. At least I put my work out there."

"You read them?" Clare's voice ratcheted up several octaves.

"No! Of course not," Donna defended herself.

Clare watched her friend for any signs of a lie. She couldn't bear the thought of someone reading her private thoughts.

"I swear!" Donna continued. "I'm not barbaric. But I will say, I wanted to. I want to know what you scribble about in private."

Clare narrowed her eyes. "Nothing, just my life."

"Just journals?" Donna pressed.

"Maybe a short story or two...a couple of poems." Clare shrugged. "I don't know. I don't do it the way you do."

"And what is that supposed to mean?"

"The stuff I write, it's just for me. I don't have the desire."

"Desire?"

"Publication, recognition, for other people to read my stuff. It's mine."

Donna took another sip from her beer and shook her head. "I don't believe you."

Clare laughed. "I don't care if you believe me. It's true."

"Have you ever let anyone read your work?"

Without meaning to, Clare took a sharp intake of breath through flared nostrils.

"Ah ha!" Donna pointed at her across the table. "I knew it! You once upon a time let someone read your work. Or submitted it. Or turned it in for a high school writing assignment and whoever it was fucked you up too early and shot you down."

Clare shook her head. "The only other person I've ever let read my work..." She hesitated. It had been almost three years. She had never even uttered his name to anyone in her new life. And now, it was right there on the tip of her tongue. "He loved everything I ever wrote." She stared out the window, not really seeing beyond the nonsensical blur of this busy city she had so effectively hidden herself away in.

"So why keep it to yourself?" Donna pressed.

Clare returned her attention to the expanse of table between them and shook her head again. "I guess, mostly, it really never occurred to me to do anything with my writing." That was true, sort of. She had occasionally, certainly more recently, considered what it might be like to stand on that stage one night herself, but she never got any farther than imagining the embarrassment, her own hands trembling just like she'd witnessed in so many others. "I'm not sure what the point would be, I guess."

"What do you mean, *what's the point?* The story is the point. The connection, the creation—the rush of knowing someone read your words and *felt* something you *created.* That is the fucking point."

Clare took another, longer, drink from Donna's beer and nodded. Yes, she knew what Donna was getting at. It was just that Donna didn't understand, maybe couldn't understand, that Clare already had that. She'd had it, with Adam. Adam who, for practically their whole lives, would lay his head in her lap and close his eyes. There wasn't any other connection she ever wanted.

She would never feel his head in her lap again. She would never hear his voice. Feel his touch. Look into his eyes.

"Tell me a story, Clare."

"I think you're afraid," Donna finished with a dare.

Clare sighed, not taking the bait but still somewhat intrigued by some new possibility dawning on the horizon of her awareness. "I'll think about it."

"No thinking." Donna smiled. "Do, or do not. There is no try."

"Nice… *Karate Kid?*"

"Actually I think that's from *Star Wars*. Either way, it's high time you dust off some of those journals and let the light of the world's cold hard judgment rock your foundations a bit. Plus, that way we can be miserable together and for the same reason."

Clare smiled. "I better get back to work," she said as she pushed away from the table and stood.

"I'm going to hold you to it."

Clare waved Donna off and headed back to the stage.

"I mean," Donna called after her, "are you really planning on working in this dump for the rest of your life?"

Thrown off by the interruption, the reader onstage lost her place and stumbled over her words while several customers turned to glare at Donna. Brian shot her a dirty look and pointed his index finger at her—*watch it*.

By the time Clare got back to their apartment after her shift, her feet aching and her hair reeking of secondhand smoke, Donna, Sergio, and Flynn were already all the way in the bag. Donna squinted her eyes at Clare as she dropped her purse and kicked off her shoes near the couch.

"Don't think I forgot," Donna warned.

"Forgot what?" Sergio asked.

"Nothing," Clare said as she waved them all off and headed to the bedroom she shared with Donna.

"Come back and have a drink with us," Flynn called after her.

"In a minute." Back in their room, Clare opened the closet door and pushed her clothes to the side. Four square moving boxes stood stacked two by two. They contained all her journals both from her before life, and the after. Earlier, she hadn't been completely honest with Donna. Yes, they were mostly journals, stuff about her day-to-day life. But there was more than a couple short stories in there as well.

Many, many more.

For the first time ever, Clare wondered how many stories she had written over the years. She had never bothered to count. Why would she? Clare pulled one of the top boxes closer. This was the one with the most recent journals, almost all of them from since she had arrived in New York two years ago with a suitcase, her meager life savings, her mother's gun, and absolutely no plan. She had some stories in there. Some of them were maybe not even half bad.

Why didn't she ever consider trying to get one published?

"Wha'cha doin'?" Donna asked from the doorway.

Clare jumped, her hand flying to her chest. "Jesus! Nothing."

"You're thinking about it."

"About what?"

"About what it would feel like to see your very own name in print."

Clare opened the top of the box and stared down at the stacks of journals inside. "My name? Clare Kaczanowski? Yes, it just rolls right off the tongue." She stared at the ring she still wore on her left hand. "I would use a different name."

"Oh ho! We go from not even dreaming of trying to publish to having a pen name picked out in less than five hours," Donna teased. "And you say you're not a writer. So what's this new pseudonym you've already decided on? Tell me and I'll let you know if it makes you sound like an asshole."

Clare took the first five journals from the stack and set them aside. "Clare Collins," she whispered. "If I ever published anything, it would be as Clare Collins."

"Clare Collins?" Donna asked, wrinkling the space between her eyes as she tilted her head back slightly and stared at an empty space of wall behind Clare's head. "Clare Collins...Clare Col-lins." She flattened her lips into a straight line and nodded twice. "Okay, I like it. You can use that."

"Thanks a lot," Clare said.

"On one condition." Donna held up her index finger.

Clare scoffed but still smiled at her friend. "And what is your condition?"

"You let me read something by Clare Collins by the end of next week. And if after reading it I don't think you'll embarrass yourself too much...you'll join my writing critique group."

"With all your MFA friends? No, thanks. I think you're forgetting that some of us didn't even attend their local community college, so there is no way—"

"I'm going to go ahead and stop you right there." Donna held up both her hands. "First, a bachelor's degree in English does not make someone a good writer, and neither does an MFA, for that matter. Second, not everyone in my critique group is from my MFA program. And third..." Donna took a deep breath and let it out before continuing. "Maybe you don't know this yet, but I've seen the look on your face when other writers read their stuff down at the Blue Spruce. You want this. I think you need to give yourself a chance."

Clare dropped her eyes to the stack of journals in front of her. "What if I'm not any good?" she whispered.

Donna smiled. "Now, see, that question right there proves you're a writer. You've already got all the self-doubt, and I see real potential for genuine, clinical-grade self-loathing."

Clare smiled and shook her head.

"One week," Donna said. "Pages, words, in my hands. Got it?"

Clare cleared her throat, swallowed, then sighed. "Okay. One week."

CHAPTER 20

If You Leave

A Short Story by Clare Collins

HE HAD BEEN GROWING MORE AND MORE FRUSTRATED WITH HER ever since the recital. Frustrated and distant. She didn't know what to say to him anymore. All he ever talked about was everything that had to do with him leaving. The date he was leaving, how long the drive out to Indiana would take, what the campus would be like, who his dormmates would be, when basketball practice started, what classes he would be taking in the fall—how over-the-moon excited he was about every single thing that had to do with him leaving Casper and getting on with his life.

Ever since the night of the recital, she hadn't heard very much more about how worried he was to be leaving her behind. There hadn't been any more tears, not out of him anyway, no more sad declarations of how much he would miss her, how impossible it was for him to imagine a life without her in it every day. If fact, lately, all she'd heard was exactly the opposite—how amazing college would be, how he couldn't wait to get on the road. He was starting a whole new life.

She didn't want to talk about it. She didn't want to hear about it. She hated all of it and was incapable of hiding her true feelings; it had become next to impossible for her to even pretend to be happy for him.

The Tuesday before graduation, he had stopped at the mailbox on the way into the house and pulled out yet another large manila envelope. "It's from Indiana!" he said as he smiled at her and held it over his head, the school's distinct red trident-looking logo stamped next to the return address.

She raised her eyebrows, plastered on her weak smile, and nodded. "Great."

Standing in the kitchen, she watched him rip into the envelope like a kid on Christmas. There were several stapled pages of information, more glossy brochures, more details and promises about everything he had to look forward to. She picked up one of the trifolded pieces of marketing card stock. It showed smiling, well-groomed, successful-looking young adults with backpacks sitting under an autumn-colored tree on a well-manicured lawn, the prestigious pale-brick university building looming behind them. The title *Student Life* was bold and centered across the top.

"Why do they keep sending you all this crap? Didn't they get the message? You've already accepted their offer."

Adam furrowed his brow and glared at her. "It's not crap. They're trying to prepare me. It's going to be a huge change."

Clare shrugged and tossed the brochure back onto the table with the others. "They send all of this to everyone, I imagine. Seems like a huge waste if you ask me. I've heard…" she hesitated, but only for a moment, "that thirty percent of college freshmen wash out their first year. If you ask me, they should prepare you for *that*."

Adam stared at her then, a coldness in his eyes that she hadn't seen directed at her before. "Well," he said quietly, "good thing nobody is asking you." He shouldered his backpack, raked all his Indiana papers and pictures, even the torn-up envelope, into his hands, and carried it upstairs to his bedroom.

Still standing in the kitchen, wondering what was happening and what it all meant—why she seemed to insist on making everything between them so much worse—she heard him slam his door. She waited fifteen minutes, paralyzed between hope and rage—hope that he would come downstairs, kiss her, and say he was going to miss her, that he couldn't live without her, and rage that burned brighter with every second that he didn't.

She glanced up the stairs and considered going up to him herself—she could apologize as well. Honestly, she was making this difficult, punishing even. She was punishing him for being happy about all he had accomplished, making him pay for all he had to look forward to by subjecting him to every ounce of her own misery.

On some level, beyond all the hurt, she knew she was wrong.

With one hand on the splintered banister, Clare swallowed her hurt, her fear, somehow even her pride, and started up the stairs to Adam's room. On the wall next to her, the familiar collage of framed school photos of Adam and Kaylee stared back at her—their baby-toothed kindergarten grins all the way through to, up here at the very top of the stairs, their senior portraits. Both of them beautiful, well dressed, posed by a professional photographer outside on a rustic bridge. Not believing anyone in town was capable of capturing this seminal moment to match her exacting expectations, Mrs. Collins had driven Adam and Kaylee down to Cheyenne for the photo session.

On the last step, delaying the mortification of begging Adam for forgiveness, Clare stared at the pictures of them both.

Eileen had taken her senior picture—and actually Clare thought that her sister had done a much better job than Mrs. Collins's professional. Not because of Clare as the subject, no, but because Eileen had an amazing talent, an eye for setting up a shot. Capturing the light, an expression, an exacting tilt of the head, and she always chose the most beautiful locations for her pictures—even if the beauty was not the obvious kind.

Clare's senior picture had been taken in the brick planter in front of the Natrona County Library with the bronze statue of an upside down Prometheus giving the gift of fire to humans. Despite the architectural attempt to spice up the front with a concave cement facade, the library would be nobody's obvious choice for a senior photo. Except it made perfect sense to Eileen when thinking of where to pose her sister. Aside from school and their own house, the public library had been the setting for their childhood. It was always safe, warm in the winter and cool in the summer, and so long as they kept their voices down and didn't mess around, the librarians would let them stay as long as they wanted. When they had been little, and their mother was on duty, and their father too unpredictably frightening to be around, the library was their first choice whenever it was open. Probably other people wouldn't understand Clare's senior picture, but to Clare and her sister, it was the perfect spot.

Eileen had taken several photos of Clare in typical poses, a variety of smiles, but the one they both thought was the best, and the one Clare submitted to the yearbook, was one Eileen had captured when Clare wasn't paying attention. Clare was in profile, staring up at Prometheus, her hand resting gently on the one part of the statue she could reach, the ball of flames. Her face was relaxed, curious, and much more natural than any of the poses. But the coolest part had been how their reflections, Prometheus's and Clare's, had been captured in the library's half circle of windows behind them, reflecting their image from every angle that the photo did not.

"I think that is the best picture I have ever taken of anyone or anything," Eileen had said after they got the prints back from the One-Hour Photo.

"The best one yet, anyway," Clare had said, staring down at the picture of herself in her hands. She felt almost the same way looking at the picture as she did looking at the art itself. It was beautiful, yes, but there was something more to it, a deeper meaning, and even though she was part of the art's subject, being the art didn't give her any instant insight. "Thank you," she had said to Eileen.

In her personal opinion, it was much more special than standing on a bridge in a town you didn't even grow up in.

Clare placed her hand on Adam's doorknob and took a breath, preparing to humble herself before him and apologize. When she heard his voice, low and muffled on the other side of the door, she paused, then leaned in closer and strained to hear better through the hollow core wooden door.

He was on the phone—and he was obviously trying to be quiet.

She stood there, her heart beating hard, adrenaline leaking into her bloodstream as her mind raced. Something was going on. She could feel it—her body knew, even if her brain couldn't formulate a logical reason for the storm of panic brewing in her chest. She should open the door, walk in, see how he reacted—but her body wouldn't move. What would she say if he looked even a little bit guilty? *Guilty of what?* she wondered. Speaking with someone privately on the phone? Yes…but why? And more importantly, who? Who would Adam have called right now, because she hadn't heard the kitchen phone ring, so he was the one who made the call from the extension in his room.

Clare took a breath and opened the door.

Adam was lying on his back on his bed, his left arm behind his head while his right cradled the phone to his ear. His eyes met hers. "I have to go," he said in a now-normal voice, removed the phone from his ear, and placed it on the cradle on his nightstand. When he sat up, he swung his long legs over the side of his bed and stood up to face her, but he didn't say anything.

"Who was that?" she asked, the accusation clear in her tone, even though she had wanted to act like nothing was wrong.

"My mom," Adam said, his tone flat as his eyes shifted to the floor.

He was lying. She could hear it, she could feel it, but she had no basis for accusing him. Clare licked her lips and glanced at the phone, wishing there was some sane way for her to pick up his extension and hit redial. "What is going on with us?" she asked him.

"Why don't you tell me?" he snapped back. "You're the one that's been pissed off with me for weeks. Everything I do, everything I say," he continued, "all I ever get from you is dirty looks and shitty comments. So why don't you clue me in on what's going on with us."

She stared at him, her arms feeling tingly and weak at her sides. She was at a loss for words. She had been shitty; she knew that. That was why she was coming up here—to apologize. But…she couldn't shake the suspicion that there was something else too. Something she was not in the wrong about.

"Are you leaving me?" she blurted.

Adam pulled his head back, as if in shock. "What are you talking about? Of course I'm leaving. You know I'm leaving. I don't get to Indiana without leaving."

He didn't answer her question. Clare set her jaw, uncertain of where she was heading with this. "That's not what I meant," she said.

"Then what do you mean?" He turned away and busied himself with organizing the mail from the school that was spread all over his comforter.

"It just…I feel like…" Her eyes focused on the window behind him. The late afternoon glare made it difficult to see his face clearly.

"What?" he commanded as he tossed the pages and pictures onto his already messy desk. He turned back to face her. "You just feel like what, Clare?" His tone was nasty, impatient.

He was making this so much harder. She didn't want to fight

with him. How had they ended up here? "I feel like…it's over," she managed to get out.

"What's over?"

She shook her head, overwhelmed and uncertain. Instead of reassuring her, it felt like he was being intentionally difficult and distant, like he wanted this to escalate and get worse. "Us! I feel like we're ending. You're leaving, I'm staying…it feels like you're already gone!"

He took a step toward her. Out of the shadow from the bright window light behind him, she could see his features clearly. With his brow furrowed and his mouth set into a hard line, Clare knew he had no interest in moving past this argument right now. "If you remember correctly, you're the one that said *no* to me. Do you remember that, Clare? Me asking you to marry me, you telling me no?"

She had never heard him speak to her like this before. It felt like he hated her. "I remember," she whispered.

"And how do you suppose *that* made *me* feel?"

She didn't know, not exactly, but if the way he was acting now was any indication, she could guess. He was hurt and pissed and maybe scared—but for the first time in their lives, she felt like she couldn't ask him any of that. Long before Adam had ever become her boyfriend, he had been her best friend. Now, right when she needed him most, a wall had come up between them.

Everything was changing, right before her eyes, but to her it felt like Adam was changing the most and the fastest. Without thinking, her thumb reached for his ring still on her finger—did it mean anything anymore? She was too afraid to ask him, too afraid he would hang his head and say no.

"I'm sorry we're fighting," was all she could manage to say. "I'm going to go…home." Her voice was soft, careful, unsure of everything.

When he didn't answer and only continued to glare at the floor between them, she turned from him, his room, and all the tension and unanswered questions she had about what was happening to him, to them. She headed down the stairs, past the framed lifetime of Adam and Kaylee, every single year that had brought them all to this moment right now. Kaylee would always have her brother. They were bound by blood, family. No matter how far apart they grew from each other, their lives would eventually spring back together.

When Clare reached the bottom stair, a sense of utter loss opened up inside her. She was not Kaylee, and despite the lifetime she had spent inside it, the childhood acted out between these walls, it was not Clare's home. Her picture didn't hang on any wall here, and her connection to this place, these people, that boy upstairs that she loved too much—the intangible fragility of those bonds was suddenly crystal clear to her now that they were breaking.

"Clare," Adam's voice called down to her.

She turned and looked up at him on the landing, a hope opening up inside her that he was calling her back. He would take her in his arms. They would lie on his bed like they had done a thousand times before. He would hold her and kiss her, make love to her—because he felt the loss too and wanted to hang on to her for as long as they had, every second that was left.

"I'll call you later, okay?" he said. His face now softer. She could see the concern around his eyes—but it was not an invitation for her to come back to him.

"Okay," she said as she forced a small smile and turned to leave.

On the front porch, she closed the Collinses' front door behind her. Her hand lingered on the brass handle, and Adam's ring caught her eye. That night. Adam's unexpected proposal, and her *yes*.

Then, the suffocating rush of fear the next morning.

She loved him, more than anything, more than anyone, but there was a message. She remembered her mother's own words, filled with regret, and often repeated to both her and Eileen whenever the opportunity presented itself.

I was too young when I married your father. I loved him too much, and it made me blind to all his flaws. I couldn't see the path he was on. With a little more age, a little more experience, I would have known exactly where he was headed. Instead, I let him take me with him.

The morning after Adam's proposal—waking up to him in his tent, naked between the piles of sleeping bags and blankets he'd brought—the small ring he'd given her felt like the weight of an entire lifetime pressing down on her.

"Adam?" she whispered.

He opened his eyes and smiled when he saw her on the pillow beside him. "I'm going to love waking up next to you every day of my life."

She took a shaky breath. "I'm only eighteen," she finally managed to say.

His eyes searched hers for a moment, but the shift in his expression told her he sensed what was coming. "I know that." He sat up, gathering one of the blankets into his lap. "So am I."

"I'm not ready," she breathed and closed her eyes. "I'm sorry. I love you, but I'm not ready to get married."

He turned away from her. It was impossible to make out the expression on his face.

"Are you angry?" she asked.

He sat there, motionless for several more seconds before he turned back to face her. "No...mostly, I feel stupid."

Clare sat up too and shook her head. "You shouldn't feel stupid," she whispered.

"I'm scared, Clare."

"So am I."

"What are we going to do? I'll be so far away. I can't even..."

She didn't have any answers.

He reached for her hand. "You don't have to marry me—not now." He touched his ring on her finger. "But this is still for you. Maybe someday you'll decide to be my Clare Collins."

It changed everything. She didn't realize it at the time, but those two little events, his, "Will you marry me?" and her no had plucked her from the life she had always known and placed her onto this unknown and unfamiliar path that felt like it was heading, hard and fast, toward a life that didn't include Adam in it. Which was impossible to even imagine. Would she be standing here, feeling this way, the canyon between her and Adam growing larger every day if she had simply stuck with her yes?

Could she still give him a different answer? What would he do if she told him she changed her mind—again? Yes, yes, Adam, I will marry you. Also, I think we should go through with it before you leave for school.

It was desperate...and exactly how she felt.

Clare watched Donna set the last page facedown onto the coffee table between them. She had been burning with embarrassment since she'd first handed the pages over, certain she'd made a huge mistake agreeing to any of this. Oh well, lesson learned. Now she would calmly sit here and take it as Donna broke the news: Clare sucked, obviously, as a writer and frankly shouldn't bother wasting another second on creating drivel.

"It's not bad, Clare," Donna said, sounding sincere. "I mean, it needs some editing, some tightening up, and obviously you need to change the names of your characters unless you *want* everyone to assume this is about you and that it actually happened."

Clare nodded, trying to keep her facial expression neutral and not let on just how much Donna's small praise had filled her heart with a joy she hadn't felt in a very long time.

"Is it true?" Donna asked.

For a few seconds, Clare considered lying, but Donna was her friend, and she trusted her with the truth. "Basically." Clare shrugged.

Donna raised her eyebrows while she considered this confession. "Well then, you'll for sure want to change those names before our meeting with the rest of the group on Wednesday. Also, don't tell them. Let them think it's just fiction. Trust me. This way you won't feel so exposed when they rip it to shreds."

CHAPTER 21

Eileen

THE GRASS WAS COOL, SOFT, AND A SOGGY SQUELCH OF WET EARTH rose up between her toes with every step Eileen took. In one hand, she had a half-finished bottle of wine gripped by its neck while her other reached for the weathered wooden handrail that ran the length of the steps leading from Clare's backyard to the beach below. In the dark, with only the half-moon high in the sky to light her way, she took her time descending the splintery and steep stairs. The last thing any of them needed right now was a drunk Eileen found dead with a broken neck.

Remembering exactly how Clare had come to receive the gift of protection from their mother all those years ago, Eileen didn't have the stomach or the strength to read any more about her sister's life tonight. She left Clare's words spread open but facedown on the glass coffee table and wandered with her wine through the dark house and out the back door. The sound and smell of the ocean pulsing just below called to her.

The last step was half-buried by sand, and then her feet sank, one step after another, into the cold and shifting beach as she made her way toward the water's edge. She walked until the sand solidified, like cool concrete spread even and smooth by the waves' relentless grooming, then stood and faced the dark swell and rush of power before her, its salty winds blowing through her hair and making her eyes water.

Her legs folded beneath her, crisscross like her children, and she raised the bottle's lip to hers and took a long swallow. The crash of the waves filled her ears and was nearly loud enough to drown out her own thoughts entirely.

Nearly.

She looked down at her left hand. Because of all the traveling, stress, and drinking she'd been doing over the last few days, her fingers were horribly swollen, which made her wedding set cut painfully into her ring finger. Eileen screwed the wine bottle down into the sand, then began working her wedding band and engagement ring off her finger until she held them in the palm of her right hand. She considered, briefly, walking to the water's edge and tossing them into the rushing waves before her. The thought was simultaneously liberating and terrifying, but she couldn't help but wonder if essentially that in effect was what had already happened to her marriage. Because, no matter what happened next, how could she ever expect to feel the same way about these tokens of the trust and promises Eric had made and then betrayed?

"Mind if I join you?" a voice suddenly asked.

Eileen jumped and turned toward a pair of hairy man legs. Leaning back, she quickly shoved her rings into her pants pocket as her eyes rose up past a pair of wet board shorts and a large striped beach towel wrapped around Simon's shoulders and arms. "Jesus Christ!"

"Sorry...sorry," he added quickly as he crouched before her and shook his wet head of hair. "I didn't mean to scare you." He turned slightly and indicated with his head the place on the darkened beach farther down where he'd come from. "I saw you come down. I tried calling to you, but the surf was too loud."

Eileen lowered her shoulders and took another drink from her bottle as Simon plopped down onto the damp sand beside her. "You scared the crap out of me." She handed him her bottle without him asking and watched as he inspected the label then took a long drink himself. "You're swimming?" she asked, unable to keep the incredulous tone from her voice. "At night?"

Simon shrugged and handed the bottle back to her. "Not really."

She turned her head sideways and watched his profile, uncertain about whether or not she knew her brother-in-law well enough to ask what she was now thinking.

"And no." He turned and met her gaze. "I wasn't trying to drown myself, if that's what you were thinking. But I can't sleep, eat, even drinking hurts. It's like I don't even know what to do with myself, how to function...if I even should be functioning." He took a breath, held it for a moment, then let it go. "I wanted to stand in the waves. Let them roll over me, crash on top of my head, fill my ears. I don't why. I guess I just needed to feel the ocean beating against my body."

Eileen nodded, not needing any further explanation. She

wondered if maybe she could use the same sort of beating right now. "Are you cold?" she asked him.

"Yes, but it's hard to care. Like all my nerves are numb. I hardly feel anything."

Eileen handed him the bottle for another drink, watched him swallow, and then settle the base of the glass bottle into the sand between them. "Can I ask you something?"

He didn't look at her but nodded, like he was waiting and bracing himself for something horrible.

"Where was she?" Eileen asked.

Simon lifted his head and gazed out at the water before them. "Right there," he said. "In the water. Her body was found on the beach the next morning, but the investigators said she shot herself in the ocean. It was the only way to explain…" His voice caught on his words, and he stopped for a moment.

As he picked up the bottle and finished off the last several drinks, Eileen stared out at the ocean and tried to imagine her sister standing before her. The waves rocking her slender frame, the silky pale-blue dress from her premiere that night clinging to her skin, the 9mm in her hand.

"There wasn't very much blood." Simon said, finally able to continue. "The gun was found in the water by the forensic search-and-recovery divers partially buried twenty feet from the shore. Plus, there would have been more blood in the sand if she'd shot herself on the beach…or so they told me."

"I'm sorry, truly, Simon, for making you talk about this…but I have to know. Was it…did she…?"

"Through her heart," he said, already knowing exactly what it was Eileen couldn't bring herself to ask him. "She shot herself in the chest, through her heart. They promised me…they didn't think she would have suffered very long. They thought it would have ended quickly."

Eileen stared into her brother-in-law's eyes, her fingers covering her lips, her mind working through the images it conjured of her beautiful and talented older sister, standing in the waves before them, squaring the gun between her breasts with both hands, and pulling the trigger on her own seemingly perfect life.

"Why?" she asked Simon. "Why would she do it? Do you know? Or have any idea? I go over it and over it, but I just can't make any sense as to why she would do it."

Simon pulled the beach towel tighter across his back. His arms resting on his knees propped up in front of him, he let his head hang between his shoulders. "Maybe…" he said so low Eileen could barely hear him. "I don't know…but maybe."

Eileen dug her toes into the smooth sand, cracking the surface while she waited several seconds for him to go on, but when he didn't she prodded. "Well, what? Why? What are you thinking?"

She watched him struggle to say whatever it was, his expression contorting into a mask of pain, then fear. Eventually, Simon squeezed his eyes tight shut, then opened them wide and turned to face her directly. "I was seeing someone else—another woman. And I think Clare may have found out." He broke completely on his last word, all his obvious guilt washing up and out of him. Eileen watched his confession pour out of him like a dam breaking. "I loved her, Eileen.

Clare, I mean!" he added, obviously worrying that she may have thought he meant the other woman. "God, I loved her. Ever since the day I met her, from almost that first second, watching her up on that stage in that shitty little bar in Brooklyn. You have to believe me. I'm so sorry for what I did… I was just so fucking lonely all the time. But you have to believe me, I love Clare more than anything. More than everything."

He continued to sob long after his words stopped, turning away from her, staring at the space between his feet. If the information had come from anyone other than Simon himself, she would never have believed it.

Eileen filled her lungs with the cool sea air, then let it out in a rush. She didn't know what to say to him. Her thoughts were suddenly on a hundred different crisscrossing paths. Everything that had happened, her own current marital nightmare, the past, her sister, Simon's confession—it was all so overwhelming she didn't know if she was supposed to berate Simon or confide in him. The clearest thought she could grasp was this—*Clare never loved you, Simon, not ever the way you thought or hoped she did.* Which then led her to the realization that could both save Simon from his plague of guilt and possibly make him hurt so much more.

"Even if she had known, there isn't any way that was the reason."

Simon snapped his head sideways to look at her, his surprise obvious. He had been expecting Eileen, Clare's sister, to rip him apart after admitting something so awful. "How do you know? Did you *speak* to her? Do you know something?" His desperate need for absolution was obvious.

"No, not recently."

"Then how can you be so sure? I've been over it a thousand times in my head, trying to figure out if there was any way she might have found out. I just don't see how it was possible. I was so careful."

This did make her mad, but not for the reasons it should. "Oh, because that's the most worrisome and important part? That there was no way you could have been stupid enough to get caught?" She was imagining her own husband now—a husband that was loved by his wife—a wife that was devastated by the betrayal.

"Eileen...no, I—"

"No, of course not." Her voice dripped with sarcasm. "Because you *loved* her, right? Clare, that is, not whoever your fucking piece of side ass was?" She was on a runaway collision with the truth now. She couldn't even feel the brakes.

"You want to know the truth, Simon? How do I know Clare didn't kill herself over you? Because she never fucking loved you in the first place. Not the first day she met you, not the second she saw you in that crappy bar in Brooklyn, not the day she moved in with you, not the moment she fucking married you, not even on the day she stood on this goddamn beach and blew her own heart out of her chest. So that's how I know, for sure, that even if she had been handed an envelope filled with pictures of you fucking Lauren Andrews, it wouldn't have made one damn bit of difference to her!"

Eileen stood up, grabbed the empty bottle from the sand, pulled her arm back, and flung it as far as she could into the approaching surf before storming through the loose sand to the stairs leading back up the cliff to her sister's mansion above.

Her bare foot had barely touched the third stair when she felt a tight grip on her forearm. "Eileen!" Simon said. "Stop."

Still seething, but already realizing it wasn't Simon she was enraged with but her own husband, she turned and faced him.

"What are you talking about?" he begged her. "Please," he sobbed. "Please talk to me. I feel like I'm losing my mind. What do you mean—she never loved me?"

Simon stared up at her, waiting for some answers.

"I'm sorry. I shouldn't have said all that. A lot of that was not even about you, or Clare. I'm sorry, Simon."

"But what you said, about how she felt…what about that?"

She considered lying to him, or rather, allowing him to continue to believe whatever it was he had always believed about her sister and the relationship he had with her. It might have been kinder—except now Simon also believed that it was possible that Clare would ever take her own life because of something he had done. Whatever he had done, no matter how many women Simon slept with—Eileen knew Simon didn't deserve to lug around the degree of guilt he was so obviously floundering under.

"Let's go upstairs," she said, pulling her arm from his desperate grasp. "Let's talk up at the house."

"But you know something? You think you know why she did it?" he questioned her as they climbed the stairs together.

"No, but Clare was complex, often hard to understand. It occurs to me that we both knew things about my sister, maybe very different things. We should talk about her, together, and see if there is some way to make sense of all this."

They climbed several more steps in silence, the exertion making Eileen's heart pound uncomfortably in her chest.

"Who is Lauren Andrews?" Simon suddenly asked.

Eileen's shoulders sagged, but she managed to keep marching up the seemingly endless stairs. "She's nothing to do with Clare, but maybe that's something else we can talk about." For several more steps, she considered exposing that very hurtful and embarrassing information to her brother-in-law. "In fact, I think I might really need to."

Back inside the house, Simon went to his room first and changed into dry clothes before he met her in Clare's study. Eileen watched Simon stand near the door and take in Clare's presence, her style, her things, her work, her memories. "It hurts to even be in here," he said before moving closer and joining Eileen on the couch.

She opened the other bottle of wine, her mother's birth year, and filled both glasses she'd grabbed from the kitchen on her way. Simon noticed the open journal she had been reading earlier and raised his eyebrows.

Eileen took a sip from her glass and explained her reasoning for not feeling guilty. "If my sister is going to take her life with zero explanation, then I figure that gives me the right to search for one."

Simon turned to the first page and read a few lines before looking up at Eileen. "It feels wrong. Like a violation of her trust."

"I felt that too, at first. You'll get over it. Look, she spent her whole life filling those books. There has to be an answer in there… somewhere."

"You've read more than this?" He held the slim volume up like evidence.

Eileen nodded.

Simon reached for his glass and took a drink. "So what do we do? Just go through all her things? All her work? All her private thoughts?" He sounded incredulous, like he expected her to confirm how wrong that would be.

"We could start there," Eileen said, ignoring the uneasy expression on Simon's face. "But first, maybe we could just talk about her, about the Clare each of us knew. Fill each other in?"

"She would lose her mind if she knew we were even in here without her. Going through her things."

"Simon." Eileen reached across the couch and placed her hand on his. "She's gone. And maybe you don't need this, but I do. And if the only way is by raking through every word she left behind, then that's exactly what I'm going to do."

He looked down at the journal on his lap, then nodded. "What did you mean, when you said Clare never loved me?"

Eileen took a sip and considered how best to proceed. "I understand this may be hurtful, and that is not my intention, not even close. But..." She sighed and gathered the will to continue. "Clare cared for you, and even told me once that if she were capable of experiencing love like that again, she believed you would be exactly the sort of person she would love. Which is why she married you. But something died in Clare..." Clare's recent book, *A Perfect Life*, was sitting on the table in front of them. Eileen leaned forward, grabbed it, and quickly flipped to the dedication page. She pointed to the words on the page.

For the love of my life.
Finally, our painful truth.

"This right here," she said and looked up into Simon's eyes. "Do you know what this means? What is the painful truth in this book that she's referring to?"

He stared at the words for several seconds. Eileen watched him closely, his eyes moving through Clare's dedication several times. "When the book released, that surprised me," he admitted. "It wasn't what was in the final draft sent to her editor. When I called them and asked about it, they said Clare had made the last-minute change and requested they not loop me in. Honestly, I've read that book probably ten times through all the revisions, and again since her death... I can't figure out what she's pointing to." He raised his eyes to Eileen's. "If I'm being completely honest, I don't recognize that story as having anything at all to do with our life. I see Clare in it, clearly, but if this book is supposed to be about us, our life, our marriage?" He shrugged. "I can't piece it together."

Eileen closed the cover of the book and held it in her lap. "I don't think it's about you."

"But I'm her husband," he protested.

"But you weren't the love of her life."

Simon's face darkened as several thoughts and hurtful possibilities competed for attention in his head. "You think she was also having an affair?"

Eileen shook her head. "No. I don't think Clare would do that.

I don't think there would have been any point in something like that for her."

"Well, what then? Or rather, who?" He pulled the book from Eileen and opened it back up to Clare's final dedication. "If it's not about me, her husband, who was the love of her life?"

"Adam Collins."

Simon looked confused. "Her friend…from high school?"

Eileen sat back, wide-eyed and stunned. She stared at her brother-in-law and considered exactly what his question meant. "What do you mean?" she asked.

"I mean exactly that. You think she dedicated this book to her dead friend?"

Eileen shook her head. It wasn't possible. Was it? Had Clare seriously never told Simon? Hidden it from him all these years? "He was her boyfriend," Eileen breathed.

"She never mentioned that."

Eileen felt the blood drain from her face. "He died in the accident…in high school?"

"Yes, I remember she said something about that. They were good friends, and he had died in a car accident, or something. That was why she got that tattoo on her back. She said she got it done at a hole-in-the-wall place in Cheyenne, right after he died. She said they didn't do a very good job. The whole thing was blurry, bleeding at the edges. I always assumed it was one of those impulsive things you do when you're younger and end up regretting later."

He remembered *something* about that? "The car accident?"

Eileen tried again. "She never told you…they were both in it, Adam and Clare."

Simon shook his head. "She never said that."

Eileen wracked her brain, trying to imagine how her sister had spent a life with this man and never shared any information about the most traumatic event in her life.

Simon got up from the couch and walked to the plate-glass windows that reflected the light and images of the room back at them. He turned and looked around Clare's office, from the ceiling to the floor. He stared at her bookcase, her artwork, and finally his eyes landed on her desk. In a few strides, Simon stood before Clare's desk and reached behind her monitor. He held something in his hands, but with his back to her, Eileen couldn't see what it was. He turned around and came back to the couch, holding the object in his hand out for Eileen to take. "Who is that with her?" he asked.

Eileen took the small picture frame and looked at the young faces, smiling, so obviously in love. "It's Adam."

"She took his last name."

"She did."

He sat back down on the couch and laced his fingers on top of his head, like he was trying to hold it together, his thoughts, everything he thought he knew, everything he now realized he didn't know.

"I'm sorry, Simon."

"No, don't be sorry. I'm the one who didn't…and she…how could I not know?" He unlaced his hands and reached for his glass on the table. He took a drink as he picked up Clare's journal from the couch. "I want to know," he said. "I don't care what she would think. I need to know. Everything."

"I don't know everything," Eileen admitted. "Clare was mostly a mystery to me."

"To us both," he corrected. "But we can piece together as much as we can."

"Yes," she agreed. "I started already. Several of her old journals are in my room."

"What is this one about?" he asked, opening it back up to the first pages.

"Brooklyn, when she first moved there, and her roommate, Donna Mehan. Who was Donna? That name is familiar for some reason. Maybe Clare mentioned her to me back then."

"Maybe, or maybe you remember her name from the *New York Times* bestseller list. She had a book a few years back, won the National Book Award. Everyone was reading it. Donna and Clare were roommates once upon a time. When I first met them, they were living in a cramped one-bedroom apartment with two other people."

"You knew Donna?"

Simon nodded. "Technically, I still *know* her. I met both of them in a crappy little bar, the Blue Spruce, during an open mic night."

CHAPTER 22

Clare

Sixteen years before her death

WHAT DID IT MEAN? SHE COULDN'T SAY FOR SURE. EVERYTHING? Nothing at all? It was possible in this moment to believe both versions could be equally true. The *Atlantic Monthly*, it was no small thing and yet still utterly meaningless in the grander scope of worldwide accomplishments happening to thousands of other people right now. She hadn't saved anyone's life, crested Mount Everest, or even dug a well for an impoverished village somewhere in the middle of Africa. She had published a short story. That was all.

But standing here, in the living room of the third-floor apartment she shared with Donna, Flynn, and Sergio, her two free copies still hidden inside the thin mailer, Clare allowed herself to feel the thrill, momentarily permitted a balloon of pride to swell in her chest. She had done it. She was now "published," for God's sake. It was real; the proof was in her hands.

She kept her now-sweating hands from ripping the package

open. She wanted to wait, take her time, savor this moment—absorb it fully. Because, even though she was right in the middle of it, on the swell of the accomplishment, the downslope from here was already cresting on her mental horizon.

What if this was it? What if it never happened again? She could plainly see that was the emotion that immediately followed this wonderful moment, and because of that, in spite of it already casting an early shadow, she needed to draw this out a bit. Really taste it.

No one else was home today, and that was a relief. She wanted this for herself, seeing the cover, opening to the table of contents, seeing her name and story title listed there. What would that feel like? After three years of trying, and almost a hundred rejections from editors all over the city, letters which she had piled up in three shoeboxes at the back of her closet, now, finally, one of her stories had found an editor who loved it at a publication she could be proud of.

Donna would, quite simply, shit a brick when she found out. Never quite believing that it would ever actually happen, Clare hadn't told Donna she'd finally landed an acceptance. She would show her tonight, the proof in her hands. All four of them would drink a good ten-dollar bottle of wine to celebrate. She would run down to their usual corner liquor store as soon as she had digested this realization for herself.

She perched on the edge of their ripped and badly beaten couch. Someone, probably Flynn, had left their dirty plate and silverware on the coffee table. She reached for the knife, slid it through the envelope's top crease, and pulled two copies out along with a hand-written note from the editor.

Congratulations, Clare! Your first story. I'm confident it will eventually be only one of many! I will forever get to brag that I found you first. You have a beautiful and raw talent, and I hope to one day have the opportunity to work with you again.

Sincerely, Emma

She placed the letter carefully to the side and considered whether or not she should have it framed, decided that was silly, but then changed her mind yet again. She would want to remember this day, this feeling, this utter and complete sense of accomplishment in the very likely event that she never received a letter like this one again.

The leading story in this month's issue was something about fame and fantasy, the cost of it. It was written by the daughter of the famous psychologist Erik Erickson. Clare would read it—she would read everything in this issue, even every single advertisement. She wanted to digest every page of this magazine that had done something for her, to her—even if she wasn't exactly sure what that something was yet. The cover for this issue was a cartoon of three famous men drawn large in a too-small boat. Clare pushed past this to the table of contents page. There near the bottom, second from the last, was her title: *Lost on the North Platte, Clare Collins.*

She turned to page sixty-two and spread the periodical open to her story, printed, being sold—being read. A sense of exposure, a raw vulnerability swept through her on a wave of embarrassment. She was grateful that she would never know what other people thought of her story after having read it. She considered not showing Donna after all, hiding this likely accident of luck from her. She was Clare's harshest critic.

"You need to toughen up," Donna would say, often smiling while tossing Clare's red-soaked pages back at her. "Do you think an editor is going to write you a love note? Should either one of us ever get published it will be after nearly drowning in a sea of red ink."

Clare looked down at the magazine in her hand, her story, her words. Anyone who really knew her would see through the fiction printed here to the truth—the truth that she obviously had not kept hidden. Beneath the changed names and slightly different plot events, this story was undeniably about her and Adam. How many people would be able to see that? Her mother and Eileen, yes. And maybe any one of her closer high school friends—Kaylee would know. Of course, how many of those people actually read the *Atlantic Monthly*? How many people in all of Casper? In all of Wyoming? The library might, *might*, have a subscription. Also, there was the fact that she published under her pseudonym—although taking Adam's last name was hardly a Sherlock case to work out. Still, it was most likely that if she simply did not share, with anyone, that she had published this story, no one would ever know.

Not even the people here in her New York life.

Would I really prefer obscurity? Because *what if* she kept it secret? What if there was no celebration, no frame, no acknowledgment beyond this small moment here. Just her, her story, and two free copies. She would keep writing, like always. Having spent almost her whole life with a pen in her hand, stopping wasn't something she could even imagine. But the publishing, this new thing, the exposure—she could stop that right now if she wanted. It was as simple as keeping all her words in her own journals. She didn't have to share any of it, she realized.

Clare stopped short. Something about those thoughts filled her with regret.

Clare laid the magazine on the table and stood up with her keys in hand, ready to head down to the corner liquor store. She grabbed her purse off the stool, where she'd absently tossed it yesterday, and opened the front door. Her feet moved rapid-fire, like a quick-step dancer, down the three stories of stairs that led to the building's front entrance.

Outside her building, on the sidewalk at the bottom of the concrete steps, her hand gripped the cold metal handrail. All around her people went about their own business, walking, crossing the street, getting out of a cab, carrying their dog, begging for change, running, drinking coffee, buying a sandwich, holding hands. Right in front of her, a woman rummaged through her purse looking for something. Three stoops over, a small child with a head full of black curls was crying in her father's arm.

They were nobody to Clare.

She was nobody to them.

She was nobody to anybody who bought this month's copy of the *Atlantic Monthly*. But every person that read "Lost on the North Platte" by Clare Collins, those faceless people—what did she become to them after that? Her words, her life, pieces of her very being. Could she really still be nobody and still have some form of existence in their minds?

The woman with the purse dropped her keys on the sidewalk and bent over to pick them up.

Clare kept moving toward the liquor store. If she did end up telling Donna, Sergio, and Flynn about this latest development, she would remember to bring up these questions with them. She smiled and picked up her pace, dodging a guy with a buzz cut and ten multisized dogs radiating out from him on a fan of leashes taking up the whole sidewalk. It was exactly this sort of philosophical bullshit that would keep them up and drinking well into the night.

At the liquor store, Clare pushed aside worries over her rent that month and pulled three bottles of wine off the second-to-bottom shelf. If she didn't decide to tell her roommates, she wasn't sure how she would explain the out-of-character expense. At the register, Murphy raised his eyebrows when she lifted the bottles onto the counter. "Well." He smiled at her with tobacco-stained teeth. "Looks like someone's moving up in the world." He gave her a sidelong look and punched the prices from the small orange labels into the keypad on his register. "One shelf at a time, that's what I say. Nice and steady." He chuckled.

"Very funny," Clare said and nodded. "I just have a little bit of good news that I'm considering celebrating."

"I should say," Murphy said as he totaled her purchase. "That'll be thirty-two twenty-one?" he asked, clearly wanting to know if Clare was sure she wanted to spend that much considering her usual max spend was something near nine dollars.

She nodded and added, "Can I also get a pack of Marlboro Lights."

"No refunds," he clarified.

"Jesus, Murphy. I have the money." Clare pulled three tens and a five out of her wallet to prove it.

He held up his wrinkled palms. "Okay. All right. I just don't want you waking up tomorrow in an apartment where the water's been turned off and you suddenly realize, you know, that the bottom shelf coulda sufficed." He took her money and counted out the change.

"Thanks for the concern. If you see me next week begging on the corner, you can tell me 'I told you so.'"

He winked at her. "That's a deal," he said as he pointed at her then handed her the cigarettes before he bagged her bottles.

"Don't you have some kids of your own to worry about?"

Murphy nodded. "Six of 'em. All older than you and your friends." He handed her the paper sack. "So how about you just indulge an old man who never learned how to mind his own business?"

Clare gave him a dramatic sigh. "Fine, I guess. But does this mean I get to run to you every time I need—"

"Next!" Murphy called over her shoulder.

She stuck out her tongue at him and smiled when the old man laughed.

By the time she had reached her building, she felt good. Buoyant. Successful even. She was ready to share this enormous feeling of accomplishment with her roommates. Because how could she hide it? Clare started to shuffle through her keys and match each one with the appropriate lock.

When she reached the fifth and final lock, the door flew open in front of her, ripped her keys from her hand, and made her gasp. Clare stumbled back a step and suppressed a scream right as her brain processed Sergio standing in the doorway in front of her, arms flung wide, face beaming.

"Clare!" he tilted his head back and exclaimed before reaching for her and her paper bag at the same time. "You'll never, ever, ever guess what has happened!" he said as he pulled her into both the apartment and his arms. "My every *wish* has come true today!"

Stunned, Clare fell into Sergio's arms and only avoided dropping the wine and herself to the floor because he was quick and had a strong grip on her. Still beaming, he helped her steady herself, then whisked the wine into the kitchen as he launched into the explanation for his radical exuberance.

"So, you already know that I had that huge audition today…"

Clare nodded absently, although Sergio was always going on about one audition or another. If he had decided to quiz her about exactly what he had going on today, she would have been forced to offer up nothing but vague guesses. *Commercial? Off-Broadway musical? Print ad?*

"Well," he said, then paused and grinned at her—dramatic effect. "Guess who just landed the role of Second Male Dancer?"

Clare's attention was pulled from Sergio already working to uncork one of her celebratory wines, to the living room. He wasn't the only one who had come home while she was at the store. "Um…" she stalled, processing both his question and the sight of Donna standing in front of the couch. Her back was to them, and she hadn't said anything since Clare had walked in the door. "You?" Clare answered, barely even registering exactly what she and Sergio were talking about.

"Yes!" he yelled at the ceiling and pulled the cork in one triumphant climax.

Even this didn't pull Donna from whatever she was focused on, because Clare could now see she was clearly and intently focused on something in her hands.

"Congratulations," Clare offered up, distracted by Donna, already knowing what she was so intent on, and wondering what she would say.

"Congratulations?" Sergio pulled his head back in mock shock, his hand flying to his chest. "Congratulations, she says." He shook his head. "Clare, honey, this is Coke! Coca-Cola! And I…" He pointed emphatically at himself. "Am mother-fucking Second Male Dancer in the highest-budget commercial they are filming this year! They are shutting down Times Square! Times. Square." He took a breath and shook his head. "This is it."

Clare stared at him, flabbergasted between the need to respond with an appropriate level of enthusiasm for Sergio and Donna's silence in the living room. She started with a huge pasted-on smile. "That's amazing!" she threw her hands into a wide V. "Pour the wine!"

Finally satisfied, Sergio pointed directly at her and narrowed his eyes. "That's right, baby. We're pouring the wine!" He turned to grab glasses out of the dishwasher.

In the living room, Donna turned around to face them. Clare's *Atlantic Monthly* was splayed open across both her palms. "Sorry to burst your bubble, Serg, but it looks like you don't get to solo on the celebration center stage tonight." She was smiling, closed mouth with her eyebrows raised into two high-pointed arches. The resulting expression was confusing, something like sorrow masquerading as happiness—Donna looked like the victim of an accident who was in shock.

Clare met Donna's eyes and saw the fear, raw, bottomless, and framed in self-doubt. But the revelation was swept away in less time than it took Clare's heart to beat because Donna forced her face into a manic wide smile, all teeth. "This. Is. Amazing!" she suddenly proclaimed, shaking the magazine with a violence. She sounded nothing at all like the deeply critical, borderline cynical Donna Mehan Clare had lived with for the past four years and everything like a crazed, super-pumped sorority sister.

Clare stared at her, mouth slack, wondering if she should just roll with this fake congratulations or pull Donna into their shared bedroom and try to have a real conversation with her. "Donna, I—"

"What's this, now?" Sergio emerged from their tiny kitchen holding two mismatched tumblers of Clare's wine. "I'm not the only one with news?" He placed one glass in Clare's hand and held the other out to Donna, waiting for her to free one of her hands from the magazine. Donna handed the magazine to Sergio to see the evidence for himself, then took the glass and immediately raised it to her lips as she nodded to Clare.

Sergio turned to her, his face a question mark waiting for an answer.

Clare looked from him to Donna, then back to him as his eyes dropped to the pages in his hands. "My story got published," she whispered.

Sergio's eyes scanned the page, then he flipped to the magazine's cover.

"The *Atlantic Monthly*," Donna helped him. "Very, very impressive."

"Clare!" Sergio said, looking up and smiling. "That's fantastic!"

Despite the fact that she knew Donna was struggling to digest all this, Clare couldn't help the smile that cracked open across her face. She nodded. "Thank you," she managed to say.

He threw his head back and let out a howl as he threw his arms wide. "We are the luckiest bitches in the whole world today!"

Behind him, Donna raised her glass and nodded, her eyes connecting with Clare's. "To the luckiest *bitches* on the planet."

CHAPTER 23

Eileen

IT WAS THE SOUND OF THE OCEAN CRASHING. EILEEN KNEW IT BEFORE she opened her eyes. Despite the raw throb of the hangover she was waking up to, this time there was no mistaking her sister's guest bedroom for her own. She remembered where she was right away.

Her phone buzzed against the dresser on the other side of the room; that was what had pulled her from the depths of her booze-induced coma. Her swimming head reminding her that she, and Simon, drank way too much last night.

She also remembered…

A slick swell of guilt rose up inside her. "Oh my God," she whispered as she forced her bloodshot eyes to open to the blinding glare of fresh morning light streaming through the open sliding glass door.

Her phone buzzed again. She knew it was someone from home. One of her kids, or Eric, and this knowing turned the sound into an accusation. The vibration erupting from her phone seemed both louder and harder against the wood.

Eileen turned her head, already knowing what she would see—or rather, who. There he was, still deep and far away in his own alcohol-soaked stupor. Simon, with his mouth slightly open and the faint rasp of his breath moving past the back of his throat, was still asleep on the pillow inches from her face. This close to him, in the intimacy of her sister's guest bed, she stared at the smattering of dark brown hair on his naked chest. The breeze from the open door behind him picked up the scent of him, woodsy and unfamiliar—not Eric's scent, not her own husband.

Eileen covered her mouth with her hand and turned her gaze back to the bright white ceiling above them. What had happened last night? What had they done? Eileen pulled her hand from her mouth and placed it between her legs to see if there was some hor-rifying and irrefutable clue as to what happened and why she ended up in bed with her sister's husband. There was nothing so obvious as a used condom down there. She was wearing underwear, not her pajama pants, and had on the same T-shirt from last night—no bra. She forced her brain to focus on anything she could remember—the beach, wine, Clare's study, sitting on the couch and talking about when Simon first met Clare. A slick swell of shame rolled in and settled in Eileen's gut.

Sometime later in the night, after they had finished the second bottle *and maybe there had even been a third*, she had a memory of Simon holding her. They were both crying, both drunk; Simon opened his arms and she had fallen into them.

He kissed her. On the top of her head at first, and then she had lifted her face to his—*shit, shit, shit*. What the hell was wrong with her?

Eileen shifted the white sheet and duvet off her and slid her legs over the edge of the mattress, willing the bed to not move or make a sound. *Please, God, do not let him wake up.* She simply could not deal with looking her sister's husband in the eye while they were both still half naked in the same bed. Thankfully, this was not her bed at home, the eighteen-year-old, sagging sack of squeaking springs on a rickety metal bed frame that shifted and shimmied any time she or Eric took a deep breath or rolled over. No, her sister had only the best. Eileen's bare feet met the rug, and she transitioned out of the bed without a single tremor to announce her departure. She collected the pants she'd worn yesterday and her bra from the floor and clutched them to her stomach as she dared to turn and face Simon's still-sleeping and slack expression. *God, what had they done?*

Eileen backed toward the door, trying not to imagine Simon's eyes flying open at any moment and catching her awkward, shame-riddled escape, but stopped dead.

Strewn across the floor at the end of the bed, there were the large photos of her husband and Lauren Andrews and the note from Dave threatening Eric. Eileen held her breath—*why were these out?* She glanced again at Simon, still sound asleep, before kneeling down and raking together the pictures as quickly and quietly as she could, scooping them up into her pants and bra bundle. She grabbed her phone off the dresser and backed out of the bedroom, careful to close the door so the latch wouldn't click.

In the hallway, hoping there wasn't a housekeeper anywhere near to witness her quick steps into the next nearest bathroom, Eileen tried to piece together what had happened after she and Simon had kissed on the couch. With the door shut behind her, she wiggled into her black capri pants, and sand from the night before spilled from the wide cuff and onto the gray tiled floor. She turned on the faucet and gazed at her reflection in the silver-framed mirror, scanning her bloodshot eyes for some memory that would send her running from this house in embarrassment.

There was nothing, a black hole where the end of last night should be stored. "You have to stop drinking so much."

Downstairs in the expansive kitchen, ready to kill for a cup of coffee, Eileen stared down the complicated espresso machine. She reached out and pressed a random button, but the hulking box of stainless steel didn't blink.

"Goddammit, you piece of shit," she whispered. "I would throw you off the balcony for a fifteen-dollar Mr. Coffee and a package of Folgers right now."

"Do you want some help with that?"

Eileen gasped and turned around; Simon, looking haggard and hungover, held up his hand in apology.

"Sorry," he said. "Sorry. I didn't mean to startle you."

"Christ," Eileen exhaled as her shoulders sagged.

She shook her head and closed her eyes. The rush of adrenaline drove a headache like an ice pick through her temples. Eileen pressed the soft spots on either side of her head and nodded at her brother-in-law. "Yes, please," she said and stepped out of the way so he could bring life to the complicated machine holding the caffeine hostage.

Simon nodded. "But first," he said as he opened one of the drawers on the far side of the enormous island. He pulled out a small bottle and shook it. The pills it contained rattled with the promise of pain relief. He popped the lid and shook out several brown pills into his palm. He walked over to her, pinched two between his fingers and thumb, and held them out for her.

"Thank you," she whispered, scanning his eyes for any hints of guilt, regret, soul-crushing levels of mortification—but there was only his same dark-ringed grief. She took the pills and popped them in her mouth, swallowing hard and wishing she'd waited for the glass of water he was now getting them both from the fridge.

"I suppose it's safe to say we both had way too much to drink last night," Simon said as he handed her the icy cold glass and took a long swig from his own. "I'm sorry, by the way."

She tried to decipher what his apology might be for. For getting drunk? For crying on her shoulder? For having sex with his dead wife's sister?

Feeling the two pills stubbornly lodged halfway down her throat, Eileen coughed twice and took several large swallows of water. She placed the glass on the counter in front of her and gathered the nerve she needed to actually talk out loud about her potential shame. "Sorry?" she asked, forcing herself to look up, if not exactly into Simon's eyes then at least at his chin. "I don't remember what happened last night," she admitted.

"No, I imagine not," he said as he began pushing buttons and twisting handles on the espresso machine. "Just coffee? Or I could make you a cappuccino, if you like. Or anything really, espresso, macchiato, latte. We even have some flavored syrups," he offered as he opened the cupboard above the machine. He turned and looked at her, waiting for her order.

Eileen tried to figure out how bad this was. Was Simon really feeling this casual because nothing had happened? Or was this his way of sidestepping the avalanche of personal disgust and shame they both should feel because they had crossed the worst line ever last night?

"Just coffee, please."

He gave her a quick closed-mouth smile and then turned to begin the task. She watched him, the way the fabric of the same short sleeved T-shirt he'd worn yesterday stretched and pulled across his muscled back, his bare arms, the hands that had no trouble getting the espresso machine to grind coffee beans and begin percolating her a perfect cup of aromatic caffeine. His hands had touched that back. His hands had held her face. Their lips had—

"So, again," he said, turning to face her while the machine hissed and gurgled behind him, "I'm really sorry about last night." He looked at the floor before raising his eyes to hers and waiting for her response.

Eileen bit her lip, wishing he would say more, wishing she could remember more. God, she didn't even know how horrible she should be feeling. "I'm sorry too," she said.

Simon blew a fast stream of air out through his lips. "You?" He shook his head. "You're a saint. Seriously, Eileen, I don't know what I would have done. Thank you, for everything."

She raised her eyebrows, envisioning all the ways this *thank you* could be so completely inappropriate. Had she slept with him? Done other equally unfathomable sexual things with him? She couldn't bear to think she was capable of such a betrayal, to her sister, to Eric—but she also couldn't be sure that she wouldn't do it given the amount of alcohol she had been applying to her utterly dysfunctional life lately. She was going to have to say it, the question, out loud right now. She pressed the pads of her fingers to her closed eyes.

"Simon…what exactly happened last night? I woke up in bed next to you…half dressed. And I can't remember anything except that…" God, this was awful. "Except that, we kissed. I *do* remember that." With her hands still covering her eyes, she forced herself to go on. "But I don't remember much else, and if we…if we…" She dropped her hands from her face and hung her head. "Please tell me we didn't."

"Wait…you think, we…?"

"I don't know *what* to think, Simon. All I know is that I remember kissing you in Clare's office, and then, I'm waking up next to you in bed." Eileen's phone vibrated in her back pocket. She pulled it out to look at who was calling, and her already racing heart leapt into overdrive. "Shit, it's Eric," she said to herself.

"That asshole. You want me to talk to him?" Simon said.

Eileen looked at him like he was insane. "What? Why would I…and I thought…you and Eric liked each other." She declined the call and saw that it was one of seven calls she had missed since last night.

"Wow, you really don't remember *anything* from last night?" He pulled one full cup of coffee from the machine and replaced it with an empty one. "First off, no, and I kinda can't believe I have to say this, we did not sleep together. Not like that." He handed her a cup of coffee and pointed to the fridge. "Would you grab the cream?"

Nothing had happened. The relief of it swept away her

embarrassment in an instant. She pulled open the fridge door and searched the shelves until she found the small carton of half-and-half on the inside of the door.

"To give you the short version, you showed me those last night." He pointed to the pictures of Eric and Lauren, laid facedown on the island. "You told me about what was happening with Eric, how you found out about it, and what you planned to do about it. You cried, which made me cry, and also tell you about...my own affair." Simon paused and reached for the cream, hesitating. "Which led to the whole discussion that sent me into a mental health nosedive and, along with also being incredibly drunk but apparently not quite as drunk as you, led me to telling you that I had been thinking about—"

"You asked me if I thought Clare had killed herself because of what you did," she suddenly remembered. "Because you had cheated on her."

Simon nodded.

"And you wanted to die too," she whispered. "That's what you said. I remember that now. You said you wanted to take Clare's gun and shoot yourself." Eileen's forehead furrowed as she watched Simon take a drink from his coffee cup, then give her the barest of nods. "Simon..."

He swallowed and placed his cup on the island between them. "Which is why I apologized, and thanked you. You made me stay with you last night. Not because anything happened between us, but so you could make sure I didn't do anything to myself. You wanted to keep me safe—even after I told you what I had done."

He had been serious last night, emphatic about not wanting to live without Clare or with his own guilt. He did seem better this morning, but would that last? What about tonight, when he was alone again in their shared bedroom? Or after the funeral? What about when Eileen got on her flight and headed back to Colorado, leaving him completely alone in this architectural mammoth her sister had built, where every scrap of furniture, every linen, every piece of art, the very location was all Clare's doing?

"Where is Clare's gun now?"

Simon placed his cup on the island between them. "I wouldn't do it," he whispered. "Last night, everything...the realization that she was gone...forever. It hit me. And that feeling, of being... somehow responsible." He shook his head. "But I don't really want to die."

Eileen nodded. "Where's the gun?"

"The police still have it."

"And will they return it?" she pressed.

"I don't remember everything they said. That whole morning they were here; it's just a blur in my head."

"Okay, so if and when they do return it...what are you going to do with it?"

He was hesitating, staring at his cup. She watched him take a deep breath like he was trying to think of the *right* thing to say. Eventually he let out a fast sigh instead.

"I don't know," he whispered.

His answer made Eileen all the more positive she would need to make sure Clare's gun never came back to this house. Not that she didn't believe him; Simon really didn't want to die right now, and he was obviously relieved that Eileen had been here to keep him from making an impulsive and irrevocable decision last night. But he was reluctant to let the entire possibility, the potential exit strategy, go altogether. Because what if he changed his mind later?

"I'm going to need you to give me the number for the lead investigator," she said, sounding more like her cop mother than she realized she was capable of. "I know there are a hundred other ways you could kill yourself, but the most statistically successful way will not be coming back through this front door." The raw certainty of what needed to happen, and her own sense of authority to make it happen—it surprised her. She was drawing a line for Simon, a man she barely knew, and she felt a swell of righteousness that she was prepared to argue with him about. He needed to be kept safe.

Simon nodded. His sudden surrender, because she had insisted on something, put her foot down—Eileen wasn't sure how to handle it. She wasn't used to being so…demanding. Instead of saying anything else, she nodded once and took a sip of her coffee.

Her phone buzzed in her pocket and broke the heavy silence. She pulled it out. "It's Eric again," she said more to herself than Simon. "He's called eight times since last night."

"You should probably take it then," Simon said.

Eileen met his eyes over the rim of his cup. "You said I told you last night how I planned to handle this situation with him." She placed her palm flat on top of the upside-down pictures next to her. "What did I say?"

"You said you'd probably forgive him. Or maybe just act like you'd never even seen those. You talked a lot about the kids, how it would affect them. You said you were worried about all that change, if you left him, and how it would ruin everything."

"Yes," Eileen said. "That sounds just like me." She held up her phone. "I'm going to take this."

"I'll be in my office if you need me."

"Thank you."

As Simon picked up his cup and left the kitchen, Eileen swiped her phone and held it to her ear. "Hello?"

"Eileen." Eric sounded surprised she answered. "Jesus, I've been trying to call you since yesterday. Is everything...okay? I mean, of course it's not. I know that, Clare, obviously. But, well I guess I thought you'd still be reachable. Are you all right? Is there... Are you all right?"

His tone was higher-pitched than usual, and he was fumbling around for words. It was so unlike him. Eric, always so steadfast and self-assured; normally he possessed a self-confidence that she sometimes felt came off as a little arrogant.

"I'm fine," she said, not at all sure where this conversation could possibly lead. Now alone in the kitchen, she turned the photos on the counter faceup and fanned them out. It all depended on whether she decided to say anything. "There's been a lot to process," she said as she shifted through the photos of Eric and Lauren until the one of them spooning, Eric's face nuzzled at Lauren's neck, was clearly visible.

"I can imagine," Eric said. "It's such a shock. I'm sorry you're having to deal with all this."

"Deal with all *what*?" she snapped.

He didn't say anything, and an uncomfortable silence stretched out on the line between them. Eileen closed her eyes. She hadn't meant to lose her temper—she didn't want to, not now, not when she wasn't yet sure how she wanted to handle this situation. If she started an argument with him now, there would be no turning back. She wasn't ready for that.

"I'm sorry," she forced herself to say. "I'm tired, and there has been a lot to deal with."

"Of course, and you don't have to apologize. The kids and I, we were just worried…about you."

"Are they okay?"

"Yes and no, I guess. I mean, in truth, they hardly knew Clare. But then again, she was so famous, and their aunt. I think it's a little weird for them to process too. Grieving for someone the whole world knows *of*, if not *well*. They've been getting calls from their friends, saying how sorry they are about their aunt dying. I think it's just hard for them to know how to feel, never mind how to respond. Mostly I think they just want you to come home."

"Me too," Eileen whispered into the phone.

"When is your flight back again? Everything happened so fast, and you left in such a rush I don't even know when your flight home is."

"The funeral is tomorrow; I'm flying out the day after."

"We'll pick you up. What time?"

"I have your car at the airport," Eileen reminded him.

"Oh, that's right…" For several seconds, silence stretched out again between them. Eileen knew her husband well enough to know something else was going on with him. "Hey," he finally said, his voice again pitchy and uncertain. "Completely off topic, but did you happen to save that paperwork from Carl about the insurance? You said he left it on my car?"

That was it, she suddenly realized. Under normal circumstances, there was absolutely no reason Eric would bring up insurance paperwork neither of them wanted or needed right now. Something had happened, and Eric was scared. Eileen touched the photos on the counter, shifting them again across the white marble.

"Yes, I have them," she said.

"Good. That's good. We should look into that," he said, but Eileen could hear that his mind was somewhere else. "I don't suppose you've had a chance to look at them?"

"Not really." She pushed the photos together into a pile. "I've been busy."

"God, of course. Such a stupid question."

"Yes," she answered like a blunt instrument. "It was stupid." She could hardly believe she said that. They had never spoken to each other like that.

The silence settled between them again, like they were both trying to figure out some new reality. "Eileen, when you get home, we should talk."

"About what?" she dared him.

He knew she knew. Or at least, he suspected that she might know about him and Lauren. Something had happened since she last spoke with him. Either Lauren's husband, Dave, not receiving an answer to his first threat, had approached Eric again, or Eric had spoken with Carl and learned there was no insurance paperwork. For

Eric to sound this scared and uncharacteristically unsure, Eileen was guessing it was Dave again.

"I just want to make sure you're okay."

Liar. "Yes, we'll talk. But I have to go now; tell the kids I love them and I'll call them later this afternoon."

"Okay. Hang in there. I love you, Eileen."

"Goodbye," she said, and hung up.

CHAPTER 24

Clare

Sixteen years before her death

"I'M SWEATING," DONNA SAID, FANNING HER FACE WITH HER LIMP page. "I think I am, no shit, going to pass out. Clare, I'm serious. I can't do this."

Clare pulled Donna's paper from her hand and grasped her shoulders. "Donna, look at me." Only when Donna's eyes stopped spiraling around the packed room beyond the stage and zeroed in on her own did Clare continue. "You *can* do this, and you *will* do it. Do you hear me? You're going to be fine, better than fine; you're going to be great. He obviously is interested in you, your work…otherwise he wouldn't have agreed to come."

Donna stared at Clare and nodded, but her terror was still apparent. "I wish I hadn't ever mentioned the open mic. What was I thinking? I just wanted to keep the conversation going, and I didn't know what to say. I was just babbling. Why did I have to babble about this place?"

Last week in Donna's writing class, her professor had invited a literary agent to come and speak with them all about all things publishing. Afterward, the guy had hung around to chat with the students and even invited a few of them to submit work to him. It was then that Donna, for whatever reason, had mentioned that she regularly read at an open mic on Wednesday nights in Brooklyn.

"Really!" the agent had said. "I live in Brooklyn. Where is it?"

And so, Donna had told him, and he'd said, "I really enjoyed what you shared in class today. Maybe I'll stop by. What was it? The Blue Spruce? Next Wednesday?"

So now, today, the Blue Spruce was packed beyond capacity because Donna told Clare that this lit agent might be coming, and Clare might have mentioned it to Liz, who told Dave, who told everyone, and now Brian, the owner, was pissing himself over the extra money he was pulling in off his standard door cover alone.

"Do you think I should have raised the price?" he'd asked Clare earlier in the evening when he saw the line of hopeful writers forming outside his door. "Damn, I should raise the cover."

So now, the bar was packed, Donna was freaking out, and Clare seriously wondered if this agent guy had any idea how much chaos and panic and outright racketeering his "stopping by" was the genesis of.

"Wait." Clare turned to Donna, who looked like she might now be holding her breath. "Is this guy even here? Do you see him in the crowd?"

Donna shook her head. "I'm too afraid to look."

"Jesus, all this circus and the guy probably didn't even show."

"No," Donna said. "He'll be here. He's a really great guy."

Clare sighed. "Okay, well, keep breathing, for God's sake. Otherwise you really will pass out. I have to check the numbers, but I'll be back in like three minutes to announce you. I think you should scan the crowd and see if you can at least see the guy. What if he's late?"

Donna grabbed Clare's hand and pulled her back. "Thank you, Clare, seriously, for everything. Our friendship, the support…you always believe in me. I sometimes think, if you hadn't come out here when you did and we hadn't moved in together, I for sure would have given up and gone home years ago."

"No you wouldn't. You forget all your fancy MFA friends."

"Those judgmental piranhas? Sure, I have them. But not a single one of them, despite all their *many* charms, has yet to publish in a major way. *You* did that! And sure, I was jealous, but when I eventually got over that, I realized that I have totally been selling myself short—something you've always said, for years now. And seeing your story in print, I finally knew it was true because if one of *your* stories can find a place at a major publication, mine can for sure. Once I realized that…honestly, I think it was why I had the courage to even speak to Simon Reamer last week."

Clare blinked as her mind worked to unpack exactly what her friend had just implied.

"Anyway, I don't want to keep you. But I wanted you to know how much your success has totally lit a fire under my own ass. Now, if I can manage to get through this reading without completely losing my shit…" Donna smiled. "I think this could actually be it for me, the night when my career really comes together."

Clare swallowed, then turned and continued down the rickety plywood stairs. What the hell? Was she hearing her right? Donna basically thought that if someone like Clare could manage to fall ass-backward into a publishing deal, certainly she, Donna Mehan, could. Donna Mehan, who was more talented, more deserving, the much more obvious success story.

Because Clare wasn't.

Was she reading too much into this? She didn't think so. In fact, she was pretty sure Donna had just backhanded her while smiling to her face. And part of Clare felt like Donna knew exactly what she was doing.

Like she wanted to tear Clare down a little.

The bar was packed, and Clare had to squeeze through bodies and dodge filled glasses of low-quality wine and bottles of beer to make her way back to the door, where Brian was practically giddy with greed.

"I'm going to get started with the first read," she shouted near his ear. "I have no idea how we're going to get to everyone on the list who's waiting to read. I just checked and it's over fifty people. At six minutes, were looking at five hours!"

Brian paused for half a second before his brain calculated a solution. "Three minutes tonight. Three minutes, then pull the plug."

"Seriously? You gouge them at the door, overcharge them for drinks, then barely give them half a second on the stage."

Brian grinned and turned his attention back to calculating the current door totals. "I told you, not a charity."

Clare shook her head and headed back to the stage. She sure

as hell hoped at least one of these writers had their wish come true tonight. She scanned the crowd as she pushed her way back through it. What if this Simon Reamer wasn't even here?

She climbed back up the stairs, still processing Donna's shitty remarks but deciding to let them go—for now—and switched on the microphone.

"Ready?" she asked Donna, who was waiting at the back of the stage and nodded. "Have you seen your guy?" Clare asked.

"Yes. He's sitting at the bar. Jeans, black T-shirt, and a highball in his hand."

Clare looked out into the crowd and saw the agent sipping his drink and waiting for the readings to begin. She wondered if he'd just leave as soon as he heard Donna read or if he'd stick around for at least a little while. All these people here just because they heard he would be—and he likely had no idea.

She tapped the mic a few times and listened to the audible *pop, pop*, then lowered her head to begin her introductions for the night. "Excuse me," she spoke into the mic, but her voice was completely drowned out by the hustle and chatter of the room. Clare cleared her voice and prepared herself to speak louder. She opened her mouth, but right then, a large hand reached in and grabbed the mic from the stand in front of her.

"You stay right here," Brian said to her before raising the mic to his own fleshy lips. "Okay, listen up," he said exactly once, and the room fell silent within seconds. "I know you're all anxious to get started, so just a few things beforehand. One, for those that are new to the Blue Spruce, we do this open mic every Wednesday night. I am a huge supporter of writers and books and artists in general, so remember, Wednesday nights. Two, despite my great love for the work you all do, a man still needs to be able to keep the doors open. With that in mind, tonight we have a three-drink minimum." He held up his three fingers once again for anyone who might need the visual aid. "And finally." He raised up some rolled pages he had in his left hand. "Before we get started tonight, I think that it's worth mentioning that one of our very own employees here at the Spruce has recently been discovered by the literary community and had one of her stories published."

With a growing sense of horror, Clare stood several feet behind Brian just left of his spotlight.

Donna leaned forward. "What is he doing?" Donna whispered into Clare's ear.

Too worried about what Brian would do or say next, Clare could only shake her head.

"It bears mentioning that this little lady launched the start of her sure-to-be-successful writing career right here." He pointed the rolled pages to the stage below his feet. Clare was now almost certain that it was the latest issue of the *Atlantic Monthly* in his hand. "And just goes to show that if you keep at it, keep showing up here, Wednesday nights"—he threw in another reminder—"then one day you too could find yourself a huge success, just like our little Clare. Now." He turned from the mic, grabbed Clare's wrist, and pulled her back into the light as he replaced the microphone into its stand.

"What are you doing?" she whispered as far away from the mic as she could.

"It's good for business." He leaned back into the mic. "Ladies and gentlemen, the Blue Spruce's very own Clare Kaczanowski."

A smattering of polite applause broke out throughout the bar and then stopped. From the spotlight, Clare gazed out at the people staring back at her.

She sighed. She hated Brian. Really, truly, hated him.

Clare licked her lips and leaned into the mic. "Ummm, thank you." She glanced up toward the bar. Donna's agent friend made direct eye contact with her, and a cold chill ran across her back.

"And now it's time for me to introduce our first reader. Up first tonight we have Donna Mehan. She will be reading a selection from her current, presently untitled, novel."

When Clare turned away from the mic, Donna stepped forward and avoided making eye contact with Clare.

"Good luck," Clare said and meant it despite Donna's earlier remarks. Clare decided to let it go. Donna was probably just stressed about this moment. After all, Donna felt this could be her big chance to really break out. All that pressure would make anyone act a little crazy.

"Thanks," Donna said and stepped into the light.

Clare figured one of two things would happen. Either the agent would speak with Donna later and tell her everything she most wanted to hear—in which case it wouldn't matter how jealous she'd been over Clare's publication because Donna would be living on joy planet. Or nothing would come of it, and it wouldn't matter how upset she'd been with Clare because Donna would dive into a depression of epic proportions. Clare sighed and headed down the stairs to wait in the wings while Donna began her reading.

In the dim light of the side stage, Clare stood near Liz, who was timing the reads with the microphone plug in her hand, and reviewed the reader list so she could prepare to announce the next writer.

"Excuse me?"

Clare looked up from her list. A man was standing by the speaker trying to get her attention. It took her half a second to place his face. It was the agent who was sitting at the bar with his highball, the agent who was supposed to be listening most attentively to Donna, who was onstage and barely through her first paragraph.

"Yes?" she asked, glancing up to see if Donna had noticed he wasn't sitting in the audience.

"Clare?" he asked her and smiled.

Clare nodded at him. If he was standing here talking to her, he obviously wasn't listening to Donna onstage. "Is there something I can help you with?" She glanced again up at Donna, hoping he would take the hint.

"Hello." He thrust his hand out toward her. When she took it in her own, he continued. "I'm Simon Reamer, and I'm a literary agent. I read your story in this month's *Atlantic*. Congratulations, by the way. I didn't realize you'd be here, but then I heard that guy's announcement and saw you onstage. I thought about waiting until the end of the evening, but it's pretty busy in here and I didn't want to miss the opportunity to meet you in person."

Clare pulled her hand from his and tried to process what this guy was saying to her while also trying to work out the response that would get him back to his seat and attending to Donna's reading the fastest. "I work here, so I'll be here all night," she said.

"Oh, yeah right. Of course." He gave her a nervous smile and dropped his eyes to his shoes. "So do you think, you know, maybe after, you'd have time to chat?"

Jesus, they were running out of time and this guy hadn't heard a single word Donna had read. "Yes, sure." Impatient now, she waved her hands, trying to usher him from the side stage and back to his seat in the audience. "Whatever you want," she finished, and when he still didn't make any move to leave, she took a step toward him to more physically encourage him back out front.

"Great! That's great." He reached into the back pocket of his jeans, pulled out a business card, and handed it to her. "But just in case." He pointed to the linen-colored card. "It is really busy in here, so just in case we don't connect after. Please call me. I'm really interested in you... I mean, in your work... I'd like to read more of your work, for sure."

Clare blinked at him. "Okay," she said, hoping he was leaving now.

"Okay." He smiled at her again and, finally, turned to go. Just when Clare thought it might be possible for him to at least hear Donna's last page, he turned back around. "You swear," he joked. "I mean, I know talent when I read it. Promise you'll find me, or call me. There might be other agents here." He looked over his shoulder, like it was possible someone else could be waiting to muscle in on him at any moment.

"I swear," Clare said, and shooed him with her hand while turning fully away from him and directing all her attention up at Donna on the stage, hoping this would give him the clue he needed to pay attention.

"Great!" he said.

Clare didn't dare turn and look or acknowledge him any further until she felt certain he had left. After a few seconds, she leaned back and checked to see if he had made it back to his seat. He was just settling back onto his stool and taking hold of his drink, turning toward the stage…

Right as Donna's voice dropped away at the end of a sentence, paused, then concluded with, "Thank you very much."

Clare closed her eyes. "Shit," she whispered, then headed up the stage stairs to announce the next reader.

Halfway across the stage, out of the spotlight but still in full view of the audience, Donna walked right up to Clare until their faces were only inches apart. "Did you have a nice chat?" Donna seethed, careful to keep her voice low enough so that no one else would hear.

Intimidated by Donna's obvious fury, Clare fell back a step. "I didn't…" She glanced quickly out at the audience, who maybe couldn't hear them, but they obviously could see. She looked back into Donna's fiery glare.

"You didn't what?" Donna snapped, her eyes glistening from the tears beginning to form along her bottom lid. She shouldered past Clare and fled down the stairs.

"Donna," Clare called after her, wishing she could chase her friend.

While she was still trying to process what she should do next, Brian rounded the side of the stage, his face pinched and pissed off. "What the hell are you doing?" He threw his hand in the air. "Get the fuck on with it already. We don't have all night."

Feeling trapped, Clare took a breath and turned back to the stage and the spotlight. As she stepped up to the microphone with the list in hand, she scanned the audience, who didn't appear to be in any particular rush as they sipped drinks, talked, and in general appeared to be having a good time. At the bar, Simon Reamer was turned toward her, his face alert and his body leaning slightly forward in his stool as he waited attentively for what was to come next.

Toward the front of the bar, someone was pushing through the crowd, parting couples and groups, creating momentary gaps of space in the overstuffed room. It was Donna, her ratty messenger bag slung over her shoulder, head down, scurrying for the exit as fast as the sea of human bodies would allow.

Clare leaned into the mic and, for the briefest of moments, considered calling Donna's name, telling her stop, come back, wait…it's not too late. Instead she watched as Donna yanked the right half of the double doors toward herself, then disappeared into the flow of the Brooklyn sidewalk at rush hour.

Clare raised her list to eye level. "Okay, folks, up next we have…"
It was nearly two in the morning when Clare finally announced the last reader on her list. Most of the bar had cleared out, and her eyes were scratchy and raw from hours spent in a cloud of cigarette smoke. She walked down the stairs for the last time of the night and headed for the bar to collect her purse from Rachel, still washing glasses behind the bar.

When she saw Clare, Rachel tilted her head sideways toward the single booth, where the agent now sat along the opposite wall. He was one of only a handful of people still in the room. "What's his name?" Rachel asked. "Simon? He wanted me to tell you he'd like to *talk* to you." She raised her eyebrows suggestively.

"It's not like that," Clare said. "It's just business."

"Sure it is. But I was standing right here watching that guy lose his shit every single time you got up onstage to just read a name and title. I also fielded no end of questions from him about your own literary pursuits, of which I know not, and after several highballs, your personal, ahem, commitments, of which I know a little." She smiled.

"The only reason he's even here is because of Donna," Clare added.

"Maybe. But as far as I can tell, you're the only reason he stayed." Rachel winked at her and plunged her hands back into her soapy sink.

Clare sighed and slung the long leather strap of her purse over her shoulder. She turned from the bar toward the booths and met the man's still expectant gaze.

When he waved her over, Clare inhaled, gently rapped her knuckles on the bar once, then began walking over to his table.

The moment he realized she was coming to see him, Simon Reamer stood up from his seat. He looked her in the eye, smiled, glanced away, smoothed his shirt, squared his shoulders, and looked her in the eye again, lost his smile, found it again, and finally reached out his hand when she was within striking distance.

"Clare," he said, sounding more breathless than she knew he would like.

She took his hand, shook it twice, then slipped into the seat across from him. "Mr. Reamer, it's nice to meet you…again, I guess," she said, trying to lighten the mood.

He laughed, a forced chortle that was too loud for the now-quiet space. He sat back in his seat. "I've been thinking about that," he said, sounding so sheepish Clare felt a small bloom of sympathy crack open inside her. "I would love to have a really cool, smooth reason to explain myself. But if I'm being honest?" He took a breath and sighed before letting his shoulders droop a few inches. "I really, really loved your story."

Clare sat, silent. He was sending her signals that confused her. His words were about her story, her work. But his body language, facial expressions, and stumbling word choice communicated a different message. This was a guy who was into her. Just another one of the many New York men who flirted, flattered, and tried to figure their way into her bed and between her legs.

The end result was both: This was not *that*; and yet, not entirely *not that*.

"You're interested…in my *work?*"

He sat back in his seat and cocked his head to one side. Clare had the distinct impression he was hesitating. "Yes." He nodded. "God, yes. I'm interested."

It was not lost on her that he failed to add *in your work* to the end of his emphatic declaration.

She took a breath; a nervous excitement like an electric pulse radiated through her. What the hell was happening here? Something major, some Big Deal, something she knew For. A. Fact. Donna had hoped and planned would be happening for her tonight. Now here it was, unfolding for Clare. Clare who had no—zero—expectations about landing an agent and had barely wrapped her Casper, Wyoming, ambitions around the idea that she had been published in a major magazine. A happenstance that was, quite frankly, eating her best friend and roommate alive.

She had spent most of the evening worrying over Donna. What she was thinking? How mad would she be when Clare got home? How catastrophically disappointed she probably was that her hopes about Simon Reamer, and advancing her career to the next step, hadn't panned out the way she hoped tonight?

Then again, Donna was the one who stormed out of the bar early. Simon was still here, had been available for her to speak with for hours after he missed her reading. She might have still made something of the opportunity if she had kept her fucking cool and tried to salvage the situation instead of rushing back home to tantrum to Sergio and Flynn—which was undoubtedly happening right now, along with a large bottle of wine.

"So, what exactly did you want to speak to me about?"

Simon put his beer bottle down, sat back in his seat, and folded his hands on the table. "Well, like I said, I'm a huge fan of what you have here. And having seen you up onstage…and hopefully I didn't sound too weird earlier…" He shook his head and sighed. "I'm just going to say this… I think, have this feeling really, that you've got some real potential, Clare. And having that feeling, about your talent, I want to be the one to sign you—bring you to market."

Clare laughed. "Like a cow."

Simon's brow furrowed. "No…I mean…I didn't—"

"I'm kidding. You were saying…"

Her comment had rattled him, thrown him off his track for a few seconds. When he started back up, he got right to the point. "I want to be your agent."

It was Clare's turn to sit back in her seat. "Based on one story?"

Simon bit his bottom lip for a moment. "Do you have other work? Stories? Essays? Maybe a novel? And it's okay if you don't," he quickly clarified. "I can wait, but well, I guess I assumed…I mean, this is something you want, right? I find it hard to believe you simply conjured that singular story out of the gates the first time. You have written other things?"

"Yes, I have other things. Not a novel, but some stories."

Simon's face lit up. "Great! How many?"

"Ever?" Clare considered the four moving boxes in her closet filled with journals. "Countless? I mean"—she smiled so he wouldn't think she was taking herself too seriously—"I've been writing in journals since I was twelve. I've filled tons of notebooks. But believe me, they're nothing you'd be interested in."

"So that answers my other question. You *do* want to be a writer."

"What makes you—"

"You've been doing it your whole life. Practicing, getting good, even if you never realized that's what was happening. You're like those kids that spend their childhood in front of a piano and then end up at Carnegie Hall." He took a sip from his beer, his eyes never leaving hers, then lowered his bottle back to the table. "Clare, let me be the one that gets you to Carnegie."

CHAPTER 25

Simon

IF HE WANTED TO, HE COULD PRETEND SHE WAS UPSTAIRS RIGHT now. Locked away in her study; either buried, as she almost always had been, in her journals or sequestered behind her keyboard—writing, writing, writing. He had known Clare for sixteen years, been married to her for eight, and all that time, most of it had been spent exiled from her presence while she worked.

He sat on the edge of his mahogany desk, his bare feet on the seat of his black leather desk chair, staring at his bookshelves from a perspective of his office he'd never taken before. The three enormous bookshelves held the collective works of all his author-clients. Clare had been only one of twenty-three writers he represented, and yet, her books and their foreign translations filled up over half of the shelf space. Before she started writing *A Perfect Life*, she had averaged between five and six books a year. Ever since he found a publisher for her first book and opened the door to editors for her, Clare had basically taken over, stampeded the gates, and flooded the world over with her words.

He stared at all those spines on his shelf: sixty-six. It was like seeing them all for the first time. All those hours, days, weeks—they were all right here in front of him. This was the physical manifestation of his marriage to Clare, the evidence of it. Not photographs, not mementos or trinkets from trips, not memories of a life spent together. It was sixty-six books.

Of fiction.

He looked down at the book he held in his hands, her last book, number sixty-seven. "Which of these things is not like the other?" he whispered to himself.

"Simon?"

He turned and saw Eileen, looking exhausted and life blown, standing in his doorway. "Come in," he said, turning back to his shelf. "I've just been contemplating the meaning of my existence. Not in the ways I was contemplating it last night, so don't worry." When she didn't immediately respond, he turned to look at her. She was just standing there, staring into the void. "Eileen?" he asked. "Everything okay?"

Her eyes shifted and met his. "Yes…no. I guess I'm doing the same…contemplating the meaning of my existence."

"How'd the call go?"

She shrugged and walked into the room. "Fine. Weird. I don't really have any idea, but I think he knows I know. Or at least, he suspects I might. He wants to *talk* when I get home." She lowered herself into one of the armchairs in front of his desk.

"Do you know what you'll do? Do you think you'll really forgive him?"

She shook her head. "I don't have any idea. I don't even know if that would be possible."

He lowered his feet to the hardwood floor and came down off the top of his desk, moving around to the front so he could sit in the armchair next to hers. He handed her Clare's book. "There is something about this book. I feel like the answers I'm looking for are here, but I'm not seeing it clearly."

She turned the book over in her hands, ran her fingers over the book's description and quoted praise. Halfway down, her fingers stopped. "Donna Mehan?" Eileen looked up at Simon with questions in her eyes. "She wrote a blurb for *A Perfect Life?*" she asked, pointing to the quoted text. "I thought, after what happened in Brooklyn, they hated each other now?"

He knit his brows. He hadn't ever understood how the praise from Donna had come to be for this book. "As far as I know, they did. When the finished book released, and I saw that…I never got a straight answer from either Clare or her editor. Only that Clare had reached out to Donna personally with an advanced copy of the book. Apparently Donna read the book and well…" He shrugged. "As you can see, she had nothing but gushing praise for the work."

"Her old roommate?"

"The same."

"Did they make up or something?"

"I don't really know. Actually, that's what I've been sitting here thinking about. She is my wife, my most successful client. I've lived with her for sixteen years. Her whole life, as far as I know it—" He pointed to the shelves in front of them. "That's it. Right there. It's what we talked about. It's what we planned about. It's what we ate, slept, breathed. For the most part, anyway." He turned and met Eileen's eyes. "I have no idea if she made up with the one person on the planet I would have said was her mortal enemy. But now that I think about it, I'm not sure that how they felt about each other would really have anything to do with Donna's reviews. Was she mad at Clare way back? Absolutely. But did Donna hold that grudge all these years and use her literary platform to take a public dig at Clare's work every so often? I don't think so. I think Donna really did hate all this." He swept his hand across the span of shelves in front of them. "But having read her response to this book"—he nodded at *A Perfect Life* in Eileen's hand—"it makes me believe that her criticism was always her honest opinion about the work, not Clare."

"And this book is really so different from Clare's others?"

"Completely. From the premise to the point of view, thematic elements, pacing, character development…it's just an altogether different sort of book from her others. There are elements to Clare's other works that her fans have come to love and expect, their commercial appeal, heroes and heroines to root for, tears that lead to happy endings. These are the reasons Clare topped the *Forbes* highest-earning author charts for the last six years. People all over the world loved to escape into her worlds, safe in the knowledge that they would emerge from the other side feeling like they had just lived a life that is more exciting, more colorful, more emotionally terrifying and uplifting than anything they ever find between their nine-to-five and doing the dishes after dinner."

Eileen smiled and nodded. "I remember that much about them. Back when I used to read them, they were a great escape."

Simon nodded. "But this?" He put his finger on the book. "Her typical fans are mostly hating it, or feeling ambivalent at best. Too depressing. Too real. Too literary." He scoffed. "So she pleased the Donna Mehans of the world and alienated all her bread and butter."

Eileen opened the book to the first page of the first chapter. "Why do you think she wrote it?" she asked him.

Simon thought about her question for several seconds. "I'm not sure. To prove she could? To shut Donna up, or impress her? Maybe she just got tired of what she was writing and wanted to do something different. Any of that could be true."

"But you think it's something else."

He stood up and walked over to the shelves that held all Clare's other books. He studied their spines, as if some obvious clue could be deciphered from those sideways titles. "It's just a feeling. Like, everything changed for Clare when she started working on that book. And I don't just mean her writing, although that was completely different as well."

"Different how?"

"Well, the pace for one. Like I said, she typically churned out five or six books a year. But when she started working on that one, it took her over a year to get even the first draft finished enough to send to her editor. Then she agonized for months on end over revisions. They almost didn't make her deadline date because Clare kept insisting on changes—minor stuff too. And the movie? Jesus, the script writer was working off one of the earliest drafts, and the whole production got the green light early so the movie release could coincide with the book release. She was pissed with me for weeks for allowing the movie rights to be sold off so quickly. She had always been indifferent about all the Hollywood stuff before. So, things had been tense between us for a long time, but when I think back…it all started right around the time she first began working on it."

He turned and faced his sister-in-law. "Which makes me wonder, What was the trigger for that book? For the change?"

"Can you remember what was happening for her then? Anything unusual? Does she have any friends you could ask?"

He scoffed and shook his head. "Friends? Not that I'm aware of anyway. She has people who work for her. I'm not sure she'd have called them friends. The only other living thing that was close to Clare…" He stopped.

"What is it?" Eileen stood up from her chair.

"I didn't even think about…but surely that wouldn't have been it. Right around the time she started writing *A Perfect Life*, I'm almost certain it was before, Clare came home from visiting your mother in the city, and she found Charlie dead in the road, right in front of the house. Clare, she was a mess, and I was in New York for editor meetings. She blamed herself because in a rush she forgot to close the garage door. She was convinced she ran him over herself."

"Oh, God! I remember him from Christmas, such a sweet dog. And Clare was so crazy about him. She must have been heartbroken."

"It was horrible. I don't think she ever really got over that. Finding him that way. Henry told me later that he couldn't pull her away. She just knelt out there in the road, staring down at his little body. Henry said it was like she was in shock. He almost called 911, he was so worried about her. But she eventually snapped out of it, picked Charlie up herself, and carried him to the backyard. Henry offered to take care of it, but she insisted she would handle it herself and sent him home for the day."

"What did she do?"

"She got a shovel out of the shed and dug a little grave for him, right near the blackberry bushes on the south side of the lawn. The next day she ordered a small, custom headstone made for him. It's still out there."

Eileen sighed and looked like she was thinking all this over. "I know it's very sad, but do you really think...I mean, honestly, that how she felt about her dog would be enough...?"

"To send her over the edge? No, not really. But it is the most obvious thing I can think of that was a very big deal to her at the time. When I got home from New York two days later, she still hadn't left her study. She slept on the couch in there and ate what little food there was in her mini fridge until I got home. And she stayed in there for the whole next week. It made me practically crazy. She wouldn't listen to anything I said. I even went and got another puppy, from the exact same breeder Charlie had come from. She was furious with me, wouldn't even look at it. Told me she didn't ever want another dog again. So yes, it was traumatic, but I don't believe Clare, even with all her eccentricities, would be driven to suicidal thoughts simply because her dog had died...even if she really thought it was her fault."

"But?" Eileen asked. "Something was different."

"Yes. I mean, she was always reclusive, but she completely withdrew. From me, from her editors, from her fans. She holed herself up in that room and wrote that book in the span she would normally take to write ten. I don't understand it. Any of it. And I *need* to. I can't shake this feeling, like somehow I missed something, something that could have saved her if I'd just been able to see it."

"Simon, you can't possibly think—"

"Can't I? With all that change in her…and she writes a fucking book where the main character kills herself in the end? I am her agent, her husband…" He shook his head and felt the hot ball of grief building at the back of his throat again. "Why didn't I see it?"

Eileen looked down at the book in her hands. "You said she didn't have any real friends. But she used to."

He didn't follow what she was saying.

"Donna Mehan," Eileen said. "She lived with Clare for over five years, and whatever may have happened to drive them apart, they were once friends. And now, Donna did this for Clare." She held up the book. "She might know something. If Clare was in contact with her, she might be able to help us figure this out."

"What? You think I should email her?"

"No," Eileen said, reaching for the phone on his desk. "I think you should call her. Right now." She lifted the receiver off its cradle and held it out to him.

He didn't move. *Call Donna Mehan?* "I can't do that," he blurted.

"Why not?"

He scoffed. "She's…*Donna Mehan.*"

"And my sister, your wife, was *Clare Collins*. You want to get closer to your why? Start with what small clues we have."

"Even if I wanted to, it's not like I just have her num—"

"What?" she asked him, still holding the receiver.

"I don't have *her* number, but I do know her agent."

In two quick steps, he stood at his desk and was taking the phone from Eileen before he had a chance to think this through or change his mind. Eileen was right. What the hell was he thinking? Everything was turned to chaos in his world. The old rules of professional etiquette did not apply here. He didn't care if he needed to hunt down the Queen of England to get the answers he wanted; he would find a way and do it. He put the hardline receiver down and pulled his cell phone from his pocket. In ten seconds he was scrolling through his hundreds of contacts until he landed on Susan Gomes, Donna's agent. He had both her office and cell numbers. He touched the cell and switched his phone to speaker so Eileen could listen in.

"What should I say?" he asked Eileen as the phone began to ring.

Eileen shrugged. "Just ask if—"

"This is Susan Gomes," the voice from his cell phone suddenly announced.

"Susan, hi," he jumped in, still not sure of exactly how he was going to approach this call, explain why he needed what he wanted. "It's Simon Reamer."

"Simon?" Susan asked, her shock evident. "Oh, God…I'm *so* sorry."

He closed his eyes. Everyone already knew everything. The whole publishing world would be in shock over what Clare had done.

There was no need to explain anything to anyone. "Thank you," he whispered. "I'm calling because I need to get hold of Donna. Clare recently reached out to her."

"For the blurb request—I remember."

"I'd like to speak to her. See if she knows anything."

There was a silence on the other end of the line, and Simon imagined Susan was weighing this request, determining the appropriateness of it and how she would go about meeting it. "I'll call her cell right now. Is this a good number for you?"

"Yes."

"I'll let her know you want to speak with her about Clare and give her your number."

"Of course." Even in a situation like this, there was no way Susan was going to violate the privacy of her biggest client. "Just please... let her know...I really need to speak to her." His desperation and vulnerability colored his every word.

"I will. And again, my deepest condolences," she finished and hung up.

He laid his phone down on the desk, ignoring the streams of text message and email alerts that had been pouring in since the news broke about Clare. He couldn't imagine ever dealing with any of it. He would ask his assistant to go through it all and make the appropriate responses later in the week.

"Do you think she'll call back?"

He shrugged. "I have no idea. The last time I saw Donna was at that big release party for Clare's fifth book."

"I was there," Eileen said. "I wonder if I met her."

"Maybe. Things were pretty ugly between—"

His phone rang loudly, echoing off the solid wood desk. It was a New York number but not someone from his contacts. He tapped the answer and speaker icons. "Hello, this is Simon."

"It's Donna. How can I help?" she asked.

Her sincerity and urgency were obvious. Whatever harsh words and flaming reviews had been exchanged between Donna and his wife in the past, he could tell Donna wasn't giving any of it a moment's thought right now.

"Thank you," he said, "for calling us back so quickly."

"Us?" she asked.

"Yes, I hope you don't mind, but I have you on speaker. Clare's sister, Eileen, is here too."

"Eileen? Yes, I remember you from that release party Clare had." Her sigh came through the speaker. "I really am so sorry, for your whole family. I still can't believe this has happened."

It was a nice way of putting it, he thought. Clare's suicide was something that *has happened*. Like Clare had only suffered an avoidable accident instead of willingly pointing a 9mm handgun at her chest and blowing her heart out.

"Simon? Did I lose you?" Donna asked.

"No, I'm sorry…I'm just…"

"We were hoping you might be able to help us." Eileen leaned closer to the phone on the desk between them.

"I can try," Donna said. "What do you need?"

Eileen looked at him, unsure of what to say. He didn't know either.

"Well, this might sound strange, so bear with us. We've been trying to figure out, well, to be frank, why Clare would do this. And nothing makes any sense, but we can't ignore how different her last book was, especially the ending." His voice cracked a little. He took a breath to steady himself. "And I know you're familiar with some of her work—"

"All of it," Donna interrupted.

"I'm sorry?" he asked.

"I'm very familiar with all of Clare's books. I've read every one. And the ones I reviewed, I read at least twice."

He and Eileen met each other's eyes. "What?" she mouthed.

"Um…okay, I guess that really surprises me," Simon finally said. He could add that, given the mostly negative reviews over the years, he didn't really think Donna Mehan was a fan of Clare's books, but figured he should leave that out since he was asking for her help now. "But I know she spoke with you about the blurb, and we were wondering if you could let us know if you had any insights into… I don't really know how to put this, but basically into what Clare might have been thinking lately? I know that sounds—"

"It doesn't sound weird. Obviously something big happened for her, I mean for her to… I'm sorry, are you okay if I just speak plainly? And by plainly I really mean blunt like a hammer? Because I actually do have some thoughts, but given the current situation, and also how the both of you are likely feeling right now, what I have to say will probably come off as indelicate at best."

A panic of nerves broke loose inside him. When he had called, he half expected for Donna to either not respond at all or give him a verbal shrug. *Sorry, I have no idea.* She knew something, something that would maybe confirm his worst fears—he was a shitty husband and should have done more to save his wife from herself.

"Please just tell us what you think. Mostly, we are wondering about her latest book. Did she mention to you why she decided to do something so different?"

Donna cleared her throat on the other end of the line. "So, to start off, and please forgive me now because I think this is where I say something that you may find offensive, but I guess I'll start off by saying, I disagree with your foundational premise for starters."

"I'm sorry, what?" Eileen chimed in.

"Meaning, you're telling me that you think there was something significantly different about Clare's last book, when in actual fact it is very much like every other book she has ever written. She just finally was able to successfully tell the story she has been trying and failing to tell for her whole career. Clare was finally brave enough to look at the truth, and tell it. Unfortunately…I think that truth broke her."

Simon stared out the door to his office. The large birds-of-paradise arrangement was beginning to droop. "How?" he managed to ask. "I'm not seeing it."

Although he would be lying if what Donna was saying wasn't hitting a nerve with him, a suspicion he had never looked at head-on. It was only ever a whisper, tucked somewhere deep down in the dark corner of his awareness. Like a trapped little bird that would flap its wings, just to let him know it was there every time he first read one of Clare's new manuscripts. It had always been easy enough for him to ignore before.

Donna paused for a moment before answering. "Every happy ending Clare ever wrote was her own. It was hers…and it was Adam's. I assume you both know about Adam?"

Simon met Eileen's eyes. "Yes," he said and swallowed. "Yes, I know."

"Every book, every short story, they were, every one of them, really about her and Adam. The multitude of fantastically fictional lives they might have had if he had lived. She gave them different names, different jobs; they lived in different cities, experienced different conflicts, but it was always Clare and Adam happy and together at the end of every book. Until…well, until she told herself the truth."

"What truth?" Eileen asked.

"That before Adam died, he stopped loving Clare. Even if he had lived, she couldn't have him. Not the way she wanted. Do you remember that first short story she published, in the *Atlantic Monthly*? 'Lost on the North Platte'?"

"Yes," Eileen blurted. "I remember it. She sent me a copy. I remember thinking it was so obviously—"

"About her and Adam," Donna finished Eileen's sentence. "She changed the names in the published version, but like so many of her short stories back then, I read the original with all the real names still in them. Everything after that story, she spent her career pretending she would have had a happy ever after, when really she and Adam were always going to have a tragedy. With *A Perfect Life*, she finally wrote it."

Of all the things he had feared Donna might tell him, this was not it. He knew it was true, now that he saw all Clare's work in the proper light. With the appropriate thematic framework that Donna had so helpfully painted, it was undeniable. He was in awe of his wife, worshiped her talents, respected her work ethic, longed always to be near her, in her extraordinary presence. He loved her.

He had loved her too much.

But he had never known her.

CHAPTER 26

Lost on the North Platte

By Clare Kaczanowski

SITTING NEXT TO HIM, BOUNCING GENTLY ON HIS TRUCK'S OLD SEAT, Clare racked her brains for a way to turn the hostile mood in the truck's cab around before they reached the party. It had been her idea to go, because she thought he would like it. That he would have fun and would enjoy hanging with their friends and celebrating the end of their senior year. But just thinking about showing up at Heather's, and having to endure her and the bitchy posse of friends, it had soured her mood and made her regret suggesting they go.

"Do you want me to take you home?" he asked her again.

Clare looked sideways across the seat at his profile. "I thought you wanted to go," she said.

"Oh, *I am* going." He glanced at her for a second before returning his eyes to the rutted dirt road in front of them. "I asked if you want me to take *you* home."

Her breath stopped in her chest. If she needed any further

evidence that she and Adam were shifting into completely unknown territory, here it was. His words, his tone, his utter lack of emotion recently—it felt almost like a slap. She had no idea how to change the atmosphere between them, but she needed to figure it out, and fast, if she had any hope of following through on what she wanted to get accomplished tonight.

She had changed her mind, and she needed to let Adam know as soon as possible, but with their relationship teetering on the brink of near-constant conflict, there didn't seem to ever be a good time to bring up what she wanted to say. *Adam, I was wrong. Yes, please, I want to marry you. I want to be your wife. I want us to be together now and forever, just like it's always been.*

"No, I'm good." Her tone was light and sounded fake in her own ears. "I've just never really gotten on with Heather and her friends, but there's no reason why we can't still go and have a good time with our friends."

"You never gave Heather a chance," Adam suddenly said. "Just because she was homecoming queen—is that really a reason to hate someone?"

Clare stared out the windshield in front of them, her breath shallow sips of the dusty air seeping through the vents, the truck's headlight illuminating the rough road before them. Yes, because Heather was homecoming queen...and Adam was homecoming king. It bothered Clare; it bothered her a lot. That night, watching the two of them up onstage together, voted together by the majority. The majority of people at their school had voted her Adam into the arms of Heather. Clare stood and watched them dance their king and queen dance together. But it wasn't just because of that, although yes, that had been incredibly painful to endure. It was also because Heather so obviously *wanted* Adam. She wanted him and didn't even bother to hide it. That was why Clare hated her. She was blatant competition, and even though Adam had always been Clare's boyfriend, she still somehow felt like the underdog in the match.

"It's not a reason," Clare forced herself to say. "It was nice of her to invite us."

Adam nodded. "It was nice of her."

Clare took a very deep breath and said nothing more. She had one objective tonight: to win her boyfriend's affection back and tell him she had changed her mind. That was not going to happen if she allowed them to delve into a stupid fight over the true intentions of Heather fucking Roberts.

Clare reached across the seat and put her hand on Adam's thigh.

He kept both his hands on the wheel.

Rumor had it that Heather's parents and her little sister had left earlier that morning for Denver. She had their whole hundred acres and sprawling million-dollar ranch to herself. Two kegs were being delivered, and the entire graduating class was invited to celebrate the end of high school.

It annoyed Clare, Heather's magnanimity with her guest list. Heather could have been selective, inviting only her closest, most popular friends, but she had flung her doors open to everyone, including Clare. It put a serious dent in Clare's *Heather is a selfish, insecure bitch* statements and did the double duty of making Clare look like the one who was in the wrong.

Adam pulled the truck past the open, large wrought-iron gates anchored into stone pillars that marked the entrance to the Robertses' property. High over their heads was the arched metal sign: Four Roberts Ranch, flanked on either side with two metal-cut, rearing stallions. Heather's family had money—lots of money. It was just one more reason for Clare to hate her. A snide comment about Heather and her great good fortune of being born into a family that owned half of Casper rose in her mind but died on her lips. Adam, ever the perfect person, had always chastised her about her habit of saying gossipy things about people, but lately, as the connections between them seemed to pull thinner and become less sure, his tolerance for her laser-point critical accuracy was nonexistent.

A coldness shifted into her chest as a loneliness she had never really known swept in. The person she loved most in this world had become a stranger. Someone she didn't know anymore—someone who didn't know her. They had grown up together, had been the first of everything to each other. She had assumed it would always be that way. Now it was like everything she had ever known was wrong. If she didn't have Adam, who did she have?

No one. Not one person who really, really knew her. He knew her and loved her because of that knowing—or even in spite of it.

Adam drove his truck up the paved, tree-lined lane that led to the Robertses' ranch. She hated Heather, was afraid and jealous of Heather—but she couldn't say any of that to Adam. Not anymore. She was terrified of pushing him any further away than he already was.

Before they could even see the house, two parallel rows of parked cars were stacked up on either side of the lane.

"Jesus," Adam said as he braked and shifted the truck into reverse so he could pull in behind the last car on the right. "It's like the whole world is already here." Once he had set the parking brake and put his keys in his usual place, folded into the sun visor above his steering wheel, they got out so they could walk the rest of the way to the party.

It was warm, with the scent of late spring carried on the gentle breeze that was rustling the leaves of the giant cottonwoods that stood like ancient sentinels along the road. Clare met Adam where he was waiting for her next to the blue Jeep they had parked behind. They turned in the direction of the house and could hear the music and voices of the party in the distance. She reached for his hand, and he took it in a limp grasp.

"This will be fun," she said and turned to check his profile.

"Yeah." He took a deep breath and sighed it out.

Clare refocused her attention back to the road, on keeping her low-heeled sandals away from any of the larger rocks on the dirt road. She didn't want to think too hard about the way Adam was acting.

They could see the house, its expansive front porch lit up in a multitude of colors. Their classmates were everywhere: the porch swing, lounging on the wide steps, spread out across the front lawn. Two enormous speakers flanked either side of the porch, and people danced and drank and sang along with the bass-heavy song thumping into the night.

Someone in the center of the chaos saw them approaching hand in hand on the road. They were still too far away and it was too dark for Clare to see clearly who it was, but the person raised their arm and pointed at them right before they broke away from the pack and staggered out to greet them. It was Kaylee, with a huge, goofy grin, a slopping red Silo cup in her hand, and a crooked, clumsy walk that gave away the fact that she'd been drinking.

"You guys!" she exclaimed, holding her arms wide and spilling half her drink onto the dirt road. "You came!"

Adam shook his head at his sister. "You're already drunk." He laughed.

"You're right." She pointed at his nose. "Here." She handed Clare her drink. "You have to try this. It's delicious."

Clare took the wet, sticky plastic cup from Kaylee and took a sip of the sweet-smelling drink. It had a warm, tropical flavor. Pineapples and coconuts. Clare could see an orange slice floating on top of the ice in the cup.

"What is this?" She took another sip. "It tastes like a vacation."

"Right?" Kaylee said. "Ryan Edwards is making them inside. Has a whole bowl full of it." Kaylee linked her arm through Clare's and pulled her away from Adam. "Let's get you one of your own. This one's mine." She smiled and took back her cup before having another huge swallow. Both girls looked back over their shoulders at Adam, who didn't appear to be following them.

"You coming?" Kaylee asked her brother.

Adam raised his chin at them. "You go ahead. I'm going to hit the keg instead." He gestured to the group of guys standing around the metal cylinder in a rubber trash can filled with ice next to the porch.

Kaylee waved off her brother. "Neanderthals and their beer. Come on." She dragged Clare forward by their linked elbows. "It's only the good stuff for us."

Clare called over to Adam, who was already heading for the keg. "I'll come find you in a minute?"

He shrugged at her. "Sure. No worries."

Clare watched from over Kaylee's shoulders as Adam turned and walked away. "Do you think your brother has been acting strange lately?"

"Yes, absolutely," Kaylee said right away. "He's a complete lunatic about leaving for college. I mean, don't get me wrong, I'm totally excited to be going too…but it's all he ever talks about anymore. I think it's making my mother depressed."

"Huh, never would I have ever thought your mom and I would have something in common."

"Oh come on, she has always loved you. It's just that now she probably has a mental image of you getting it on with her one and only golden child under her very own roof."

"Kaylee!" Clare gently hip checked her. "That's not funny."

"But it is true." She held up her pointer finger for emphasis.

Inside the Robertses' house, they squeezed through the growing swell of people to the dining room, where Ryan Edwards manned a makeshift bar. Half-empty liquor bottles, juice cartons, and cut-up oranges and limes littered and spilled all over the shiny surface of the mahogany dining table. A sticky-looking wet dish cloth sat piled with a wad of used paper towels off to the side in an obviously failed attempt to keep this disastrous bar in check.

"Heyyyy!" Ryan called out in a slurry welcome and waved them closer. "Back for some more of my magic juice." Ryan raised his eyebrows and leered at Kaylee suggestively, letting her clearly know that he'd be up for abandoning his drinks post if she wanted to slip away into one of the nearby bedrooms.

"Keep it professional, Edwards," she told him. "We're just here for the drinks. Clare here is as dry as a bone."

Ryan clutched his heart. Whether it was because Kaylee wasn't taking the bait or because Clare was stone cold sober was hard to tell. Ryan pulled a fresh Solo cup off the stack next to him, spooned ice straight from the plastic bag in the cooler beneath the table, and then ladled several servings of red booze from the swimming pool–sized punch bowl into the cup. Once he added a slice of orange and a wedge of lime, he started to hand the cup to Clare before changing his mind.

"Wait," he explained and placed the cup back in front of him. "Since you're late and thusly behind…" Clare watched as he grabbed the vodka bottle to his left and added an additional hearty dose to her cup. "There you go." He slid the almost-overflowing cup toward her. "That should get you right up to speed."

Clare dipped her finger into the cup and attempted to stir some of the vodka floating on the top into the rest of the drink. She dipped her head to the cup and sipped the too-full drink away from the edge. "Agh." She made a face and then smiled at Ryan. "I guess that'll catch me up or kill me," she said, now at least able to pick the cup up.

She waited, sipping her drink while Ryan filled Kaylee back up and winked at her. "We could still have our moment, Kaylee Collins.

I don't leave for UW for another three weeks. Summer fling?" He held his arms wide in a final bid to get Kaylee to jump into them.

"Stick to making the drinks," Kaylee said and blew him a kiss.

Ryan's head fell back like he'd been shot. "You're killing me," he said as the girls both shook their heads and headed back toward the front door.

Ryan Edwards had been trying since their freshman year to get into Kaylee's pants. "That guy's still got it bad for you," Clare said.

"Please. He'll give the exact same song and dance to the very next girl who walks up to his table with two boobs and a pulse."

Clare laughed. "Come on." She took Kaylee's free hand in hers so she wouldn't lose her in the now even more crowded house as they wormed their way toward the exit. "Let's go find your brother," she called over the voices and music.

Outside, the music and lights filled the warm night as people danced, drank, smoked, laughed, and made out with each other all over the Robertses' front porch and steps. In the front yard, Clare and Kaylee still held hands as they made their way over to the now-larger group of people standing around one of the kegs. Someone had brought their beer bong, and a separate circle had formed to the right of mostly guys chanting, "Chug it! Chug it!" to Steven Channing, a junior on the football team, on his knees with a clear plastic hose coming out of his mouth. The other end was held high over his head by Blain Dixon, the captain of the football team, who was helpfully pouring a beer into the blue funnel on the other end. Clare didn't see Adam anywhere around—not that beer bongs were exactly his thing.

"What'd I say?" Kaylee asked as she lifted her drink toward the chanting group of guys. "Neanderthals."

Clare laughed, and they both drank their drinks and watched to see if he could get the whole beer down in one swallow. When Steven's throat seized and beer sprayed from his mouth onto half the guys standing and watching, everyone laughed.

"You suck, man!" Blain shouted. "Who's next?"

Kaylee put her arm around Clare's waist and her boozy head on Clare's shoulder. "Cheers, girl," she said and lifted her cup.

"Cheers." Clare tapped her cup with Kaylee's.

"Here's to finally being finished with high school and this one-horse town."

Clare hesitated for only a second. Kaylee was drunk and not thinking clearly. In this moment, with everyone celebrating, Kaylee wasn't considering that Clare wasn't actually going anywhere. "Yes," Clare recovered, not wanting to spoil the good time by being depressed over her own circumstances. "Here's to all that," she added and took a huge swallow from her drink, which now mostly tasted like juice. Her head felt soft, her limbs loose. The night was warm, and people were having fun. Adam had been right to make her come. So what if it was Heather Roberts's house? Clare hadn't even seen her once since she'd been here.

A new song started up over the speakers. A familiar, heavy beat that the whole party recognized wove through the crowd of people outside and in. A collective roar went up into the night as they all hollered their joy into the air and began chanting the verses every single one of them knew by heart.

With one long swallow, Clare finished her drink and allowed herself to get pulled by Kaylee into the fray of a group dance forming at the bottom of the porch steps. With a wide stance, her spine swayed and her hips rocked—Clare's body loosened more with every verse. Arms were in the air. People jumped, while others screamed the lyrics; in front of her, Kaylee had the biggest open-mouth smile, her perfect white teeth framed by her deep coral lips that flashed various shades of blue under the colored strobe lights. Clare felt Kaylee grab the empty cup from her hand and watched as she shook it in front of Clare's face; she was going to go get them some more drinks.

That first drink was so strong that Clare was already fuzzy headed and just over the line of drunk, but she didn't care. She grinned and nodded at Kaylee, who gave her a silly face and a thumbs-up before turning toward the wide porch steps.

Clare loved Kaylee—just like a sister. Maybe even more than her actual sister. After Adam, she was the closest person to a best friend Clare had. It was easy, so easy, to see how their lives would eventually play out. Clare and Adam, Kaylee and someone she married. Weddings and homes. Christmases and Easters. Kids of their own. Always a big family, always together.

When Clare and Adam did get married, Kaylee would be Clare's maid of honor. She would be the godmother of all their kids.

Behind her, someone placed their hands at Clare's waist, their body rocking and matching the rhythm and sway of her own. Someone dancing next to her—*was it Denise?*—handed her the remains of a small joint. She pinched the hot pill between the nails of her thumb and index finger, placed it to her lips, and inhaled as the paper and pot burned the tips of her fingers. She handed it back. Alive, free, feeling the pulse of this very moment, Clare tilted her head back against the person's shoulder and let go as the music moved through her. With her arms crossed over her head, she smiled with an intoxicated sensuality, an acute sense of collective freedom that she couldn't ever recall experiencing before, made doubly poignant by the realization that nearly every other person here felt the same. They were done. The daily obligation of school, attendance, attention, assignments, homework—it was all over. They were adults now, and their lives were finally their own. If she wanted, Clare could go anywhere, do anything, experience it all. The world was literally hers to do with as she wished. She had never even considered, until this very moment, that she was completely and totally obligation free. Yes, she was expected to turn up Monday morning to her little desk at Carter's Moving and Storage—but what if she didn't? What would it matter—really?

Clare's every cell released in a collective sigh of relief. She was not only a little drunk, she realized, she was flying. The song ended and shifted into the next high-energy beat right as Kaylee returned with their refreshed and filled plastic cups. She handed Clare her drink and made a disgusted face at the person grinding on Clare from behind. With a flick of her hand, she shooed away whatever hanger-on Clare had been dancing with. When the guy ignored Kaylee and instead slipped his hand around Clare's stomach, she turned around and faced what turned out to be a baby blonde sophomore. Clare placed her palm on one of his smooth cheeks.

"Time to go, now," she said in his ear before turning back to

Kaylee. Both girls toasted, took huge gulps from their cups, and again found the bump and sway of the beat in the collective mob of bodies filling the lawn.

Clare couldn't even taste the alcohol in her drink, but by the time she noticed her cup was again empty, it was difficult for her to focus her eyes. She had been dancing so long a sheen of sweat had formed between her skin and clothes.

Kaylee took her cup again. "Gonna get some," she slurred into Clare's ear.

Clare nodded, her lids heavy, her smile lopsided and slack. "'K!" she shouted back over the music. She watched, trying to force her eyes to focus as Kaylee gripped the porch railing but tripped on the stairs anyway. "You're drunk, you bitch!" she shouted out to her friend, who didn't hear a word she said because of the blaring music and noise of voices. Clare laughed and returned to her dance.

They had been dancing for a pretty long time—and she hadn't seen Adam since they arrived. Not that she would expect to ever see him dancing. It was totally not something he would ever be caught dead doing. She should look for him, she thought. He was probably inside somewhere, playing darts or pool, maybe even sharing a bowl with someone out in the backyard. Adam usually gravitated toward the smaller, quieter groups during parties.

"'S'cuse me," Clare said as she pressed past several globs of dancing bodies toward the stairs Kaylee had just tripped up. "Sorry, just trying to…'s'cuse me."

She grabbed the white-painted porch banister as soon as she reached it and used it to guide her uncooperative legs upward. The image of the stairs and the people sitting on them blurred before her. God, she was totally wasted. If she passed through the kitchen, she should get a drink of water.

Inside the house, it was just as loud as outside but also hot from the collective press of bodies and lack of fresh air. To her left, she could see Kaylee now leaning on the dining room table with one arm and smiling at Ryan Edwards over his nearly empty punch bowl. She tried her best to scan the room for Adam, but her eyes refused to align and cooperate.

She sighed deep and asked the nearest person to her left, "Have you seen Adam Collins?"

The girl was Becca Mack, and if Clare had realized that before opening her mouth, she never would have asked the question. Becca was one of Heather's crew, one of her admiring hangers on, forever competing for position within Heather's closest circle. Clare was pretty sure she had been one of the girls leaving the auditorium with Heather the night of the Cleaver High talent show.

Becca's eyes widened into two large white ovals as her lips disappeared between her teeth. She stared at Clare, having clearly heard the question, but didn't say anything as she shook her head and took a sip from her own cup. When she turned away from Clare, she immediately whispered into the ear of the guy sitting on the couch in front of her.

Whatever.

Adam obviously wasn't anywhere in the living or dining room. Clare walked, as carefully as she could, through the crowd and deeper into the Robertses' house. Out back, there were even more people hanging out around and splashing in the illuminated in-ground pool. The watery turquoise light shimmered, and steam lifted off the surface, obscuring the exact identities of the few people who floated, played chicken on shoulders, or were making out against the tiled walls. Clare wandered from group to group, scanning the backyard for Adam, but he didn't seem to be here either.

"Hey, Clare!"

She turned. Carl stood behind her, smoking pot from a blown-glass pipe and drinking with a few juniors who had crashed the party. "Hey," she said. When Carl offered her the pipe and his lighter, she took it and lit the already charred bud while she inhaled deeply. She held on to it for several seconds before tilting her head back and releasing the rich-smelling smoke into the air above her. "Thanks," she said, handing the pipe and lighter back to him. "Hey, have you seen Adam anywhere?"

Carl nodded and passed the pipe to a short blond girl in a bikini top and cutoff jeans to his right. "Yeah, maybe ten minutes ago? Or maybe it was longer? Shit, I don't know. What time is it anyway?" He laughed. "He was coming out of one of the bathrooms."

"Oh, thanks. Do you happen to know where?"

Carl shook his head. "This fucking place is huge—a goddamned mansion compared to my house. Maybe somewhere in that wing?" He laughed again and pointed toward the far end of the house. It was dark, far away from all the lights and noise emanating from the living and dining rooms.

"Thanks," Clare said again and headed for a small patio area that had a sliding glass door that led back into the house.

Inside, Clare slid the heavy glass closed behind her and entered what was most likely Heather's parents' master bedroom. The large, king-sized bed was expertly made up with an expensive-looking comforter set and matching pillows piled against the sturdy oak headboard. A matching armoire and dresser flanked opposite walls and supported porcelain figurines and silver-framed photos of Heather and her little sister.

Feeling like an intruder in this personal and private space, Clare rushed for the wood door on the opposite side of the room, careful to close the bedroom door behind her. The hallway on this side of the house was dark and quiet compared to the thump and grind in full swing on the opposite side. There were several doors down here, probably the other bedrooms and bathrooms, but it didn't sound like anyone else was here. If Adam had been here to use the bathroom, he had probably already rejoined the party.

Clare took a right, ready to head back into the noise and chaos—but stopped. She heard someone's voice, low and trying to be quiet, behind one of the doors farther down the hall. Clare turned back around; it was probably just someone getting together in one of the dark bedrooms, but for some reason, her heart beat a little faster and her arms felt weak. She took a step into the darkness, the sound of the whispers becoming clearer.

"Are you sure?" someone asked.

"Yes," another voice answered.

Clare stood right outside the door, her hands on the frame, bracing herself. She shouldn't be eavesdropping, but in the moment, some morbid pull she couldn't explain held her there. *Just someone else's gossip*, she rationalized. Except her body, already picking up alerts of the imminent crash, sent a flood of panic to warn her.

The sounds of the two people on the other side of the door, kissing, their bodies shifting in the dark, the unmistakable sound of a zipper being pulled. Clare wished one of them would at least give away a name. That way she'd have some substantial dirt for Kaylee. When she heard the rhythmic, repetitive sound of what could only be the sex the two people were now having, and then the hard crash of a headboard hitting the wall behind it, Clare decided enough was enough—time to go.

"Adam," the girl said.

Clare froze. Her chest felt like a vise squeezing her lungs, holding her breath tight. She shook her head once, as if to clear it of some horrific impossibility forming at the brink of her consciousness.

She turned back to the door, her hand on the brass knob turning, turning, turning, until she pushed the door, slow, uncertain, wishing she could just walk away. Standing in the doorway, she could see them now, in the dark, their bodies moving together beneath the blankets on the bed. Her right hand slipped up the wall, found the switch, and pushed.

In an instant, the room was washed in the bright, incandescent glow from the ceiling light above. Clare saw the last thrust beneath the blanket before the couple scrambled to move apart, stay covered, and figure out what the hell was going on.

Adam turned over and stared directly into Clare's eyes.

Beside him, Heather Roberts's face peered over the arm he'd placed protectively to shield her from discovery.

Her heart beat, once, twice, three times. Clare swallowed, her throat dry and tight.

"Clare," Adam said. "I'm sorry…" He sat up, his naked legs falling over the side of the bed so he could get up.

She backed out of the doorway as Adam scanned the floor for his pants. They were crumpled at the end of the bed, out of his immediate sight. For half a second, she almost moved to pick them up and hand them to him.

"What the hell am I doing?" she whispered, backing farther away.

"Clare," Adam said. "Wait…just—just wait a second."

"No," she said, suddenly finding her voice and the ability to move. "No." She turned back toward the party and walked away. She made quick, long strides that turned into a jog until she reached the crowded living room, where she shoved her way past and between the other people.

"Hey! Watch it!" someone yelled after her.

She ignored them, raced out the door, down the front steps, through the still-crowded group of people dancing to the music that now blared from the enormous speakers, breaking into a sprint as soon as she was free of the tangled web of people. Her sandals slipped on the gravel road, but she kept the pace up as best she could.

Halfway back to the truck, she heard Adam's voice. "Clare!" he shouted. "Stop!"

But she didn't listen to him; she didn't stop. She ran as fast as she could for the truck—and Adam, athletic and much, much faster than her, ran after her.

CHAPTER 27

Eileen

CLARE'S FUNERAL WAS ELEGANT, WELL ATTENDED, AND EILEEN thought it a fitting way to honor the regal and talented woman her sister had become throughout her life. Regina and Katherine, as promised, had taken great care to ensure that both she and Simon could spend their time remembering and saying goodbye to Clare instead of being consumed by a multitude of minutia—like making sure there would be enough parking available for the two hundred attendees.

Eileen sat next to Simon in the front row, her mother in a wheelchair beside her. She worried about the potential reaction should a lightning bolt of understanding strike through the dense neural web of plaque most likely protecting her mother from comprehending what was happening here. Eileen was playing it smart this time, and when the Regency offered to send along both a nurse and a mental health counselor to help out, she reined in her *She's my mother and I can do this myself* pride and said, "Yes, please. That would be a wonderful help." Both the nurse and the counselor sat right behind

Eileen, just like family, waiting for any sign that they might need to unlock the wheels on Ella's chair and exit right back up the aisle.

It allowed Eileen the mental space to relax, just a little, and focus on exactly what was happening. Most people, actually everyone except Simon and her mother, were here to witness the burial of one of the most successful and well-loved authors in the world

Eileen stared at her older sister's profile, surrounded by the white silk coffin liner she had picked out herself. Her big sister, Clare Eleanor Kaczanowski, was dead. The girl she had grown up with, fought with, played with, run from in fear, and toward for protection.

Her mother shifted slightly in her wheelchair, and Eileen checked on her from the corner of her eye, nervous about disturbing the quiet, blank expression Ella currently wore. She had seen first-hand just how distraught her mother could become when she was confused. But Ella only stared straight ahead at the sleek mahogany casket and the six poster-sized glossy photos of Clare throughout her life, as if she were attending the funeral of a stranger.

One of the photos was Clare's senior class picture—the picture Eileen had taken of her reaching up to touch Prometheus's flame outside the Natrona County Library.

After hearing Donna's theory about Clare's work, Eileen had spent the rest of the day and into the night up in her guest room reading *A Perfect Life* from cover to cover. When she'd finished that last sentence just before midnight, it was impossible not to believe that Donna was right. To Eileen, who had grown up with Clare, it read like a thinly veiled memoir. Only in this version of Clare's life, Adam survived their car accident. He married Clare right out of high school, eventually became disillusioned with her, cheated on her, and was about to leave her—until she killed him, and then herself.

It was dark and sad, full of complexity and depth, and very, very different from any other book of Clare's Eileen had ever read. It was not at all surprising that many of her most devoted fans disliked it. If Donna's assumption was correct, and Clare had been using her fiction to create one fantasy life after another for her and Adam, this one stripped all the romance and illusion off the page and left readers with a clear sightline of two flawed characters navigating a failing marriage under a florescent glare of reality.

Many of her readers called it depressing.

Donna had labeled it a worthy and triumphant accomplishment.

Eileen thought both were equally true.

Ella squirmed again in her seat, and Eileen turned toward her, wondering if maybe her slouch was growing uncomfortable in her wheeled perch. She was surprised to find her mother sitting erect, staring straight ahead at the mourners lined up and passing by Clare's casket. Ella narrowed her eyes.

A single pearl of sweat ran down Eileen's back. She felt it coming, like a shift in the atmosphere around Ella, her confusion coalescing into a narrowed, focused misunderstanding of what her eyes were seeing. She had her feet planted on the grass and stood up from her chair with a strength and speed Eileen would never have bet on.

"Mom," she hissed, reaching her arm behind her to signal the nurse for help.

"There's been a mistake!" Ella shouted, with an officious

authority she'd not actually possessed in decades. As if she'd been called upon to clear an unruly mob, Ella's right hand moved to her arthritic hip, where it rested on her now-invisible sidearm. "Folks!" she called out.

"What the hell is happening?" Simon asked, leaning into Eileen's left side.

"I'm going to have to ask you to leave the premises in a calm and orderly fashion." Ella held up her sagging left arm, calling for the attention of everyone at the funeral. "There has been a terrible misunderstanding. I was there myself."

Both the nurse and counselor approached Ella with hands raised and heads crouched, like she was a silverback gorilla that had escaped its zoo habitat and they were afraid of startling her into a rampage.

"Ella?" the nurse soothed. "Everything's okay. We're here to help you."

Eileen watched her mother turn toward the two women, her face set in an expression of stony command. "Ladies," she said, taking a step toward them to establish her jurisdiction over them and this situation. "I'm going to ask you one more time to disperse. Now please collect your belongings and exit the premises with the others in a timely and orderly fashion."

The two women looked momentarily shocked, like they were suddenly questioning if they should, in fact, be listening to what Officer Kaczanowski was ordering them to do.

The entire funeral had stopped. The guests standing next to the coffin turned away from Clare, their curiosity getting the better of them. Others who were still seated either craned their necks or turned in their chairs, obviously unsure of what was happening and what they should do.

"Do we need to leave?" one woman a few rows back asked out loud. "Is there a problem?"

"Eileen," Simon begged, grasping her forearm. "Please, do something."

Yes, but what exactly? She felt like a limp rag in her seat. "Mom?" she tried, her voice thin and childlike in her own ears. She was not at all sure her mother would even recognize her.

Hearing her, a look of surprise washed over Ella's face, and she turned to Eileen. Seconds ticked as Ella stared down at her, the contaminated cogs of her mind working through the sight of her younger daughter at the funeral for her older. What year was it for Ella? What state were they in? How old did she believe Eileen was, and did that number make sense in relation to the middle-aged woman she saw in front of her?

Some mental consensus was reached. Ella's face softened, and she motioned to Eileen to come here, come quick, as she once again scanned the crowd.

Eileen rose from her seat. Both uncertain and embarrassed, she glanced at the nurse and counselor, who were still standing by. They gave her encouraging smiles and nods while they made no expert moves to de-escalate the situation. "Mom?" Eileen asked again, without any real hope that she would get her mother back into her chair and up the aisle of gawkers without further incident.

Out of the corner of her eye, she saw a man in a gray suit

surreptitiously angle the camera in his lap in their direction. How many media people would have been invited to Clare Collins's funeral?

"Eileen?" Two arching vertical lines formed in her mother's forehead as she grasped Eileen's shoulders and pulled her close with a strength Eileen wouldn't have guessed possible. "Honey, what are you doing here?" She placed both her hands on either side of Eileen's face, like she had done when Eileen was eleven and she wanted her full attention. "This isn't what it seems, okay?"

Over Ella's shoulder, the counselor moved into Eileen's view and gave her an exaggerated nod. "Go along with it," she mouthed.

"Okay, Mom," Eileen said.

Ella gave her a soft smile. Her right hand pushed Eileen's hair back as she brought her lips close to her ear. "Your sister," she whispered. "She's okay, you hear me. These people don't seem to know that." She shook her head once. "But that doesn't matter. I was there; I know. I don't want you to worry. I took care of it." She pulled back until she could again look directly into Eileen's eyes. "It was a horrible accident," she whispered. "But we're family, and we're all we have. Do you understand, Eileen? They will come after Clare, but she still has her whole life ahead of her. We need to protect your sister now."

Eileen's mouth felt dry. Her mother was talking again about Clare's car accident—but also something else. She glanced again over Ella's shoulder, and the counselor gave her a thumbs-up and then made a single rolling hand motion. *Keep it going.*

Eileen took a breath and swallowed. "Mom? Can we go now?"

Ella placed both her hands on Eileen's face again. "First, I need you to promise to help me."

"Help you what?" she asked.

"Keep this one secret." Ella closed her eyes, as if she were sorry to have to do this. "I know it might *feel* wrong. But I need you to trust me right now. I know what's best. Can you do that for me? For your sister?"

With her face still between her mother's hands, Eileen nodded.

"Good girl," her mom whispered, kissed Eileen's cheek, and then released her.

She gave Eileen another smile, so full of love and motherly devotion, and then shifted her gaze to the space all around them. Eileen watched as the confidence and self-assured authority drained away from her mother and confusion rushed onto her expression to fill the void. Her shoulders dropped two inches, and her mouth fell open. Her eyes raked back over Eileen without a spark of recognition. Eileen took a step forward and grabbed Ella's hand, afraid that her mother might flail or fall. The nurse and the counselor took some cue that now was the time to act and moved in behind Ella, gentle and careful to not startle her as they guided her backward and into her chair.

"She's exhausted. We'll take her out now," the nurse said.

Eileen nodded and watched as they released the brake, turned the chair around, and rushed Ella back up the aisle.

"Jesus," Simon whispered as they both returned to their seats. "Is she okay? Are you? How did you get her to calm down?"

Eileen stared ahead at Clare's frozen profile as the momentum of mourners returned and then began filing past to say goodbye. "I promised to keep her secret."

"What secret?" Simon glanced over their shoulders, as if checking to make sure Ella was truly gone.

"I'm not sure." She turned her head and faced him. "But it has something to do with Clare…and I think maybe Adam too."

CHAPTER 28

Clare

Two years before her death

THE WORK WAS AFFECTING HER IN WAYS SHE HADN'T ANTICIPATED. Largely because, when she had first decided to dig deep and write *A Perfect Life*, she hadn't envisioned the story the way it was turning out. She was only a few chapters in, and already she was wondering if she should abandon the project altogether.

There was a darkness to them, like her mind and creative energy were being dragged down into some backwater of her subconscious. The words were crafted behind some gauzy neurological filter that she couldn't see beyond. She only felt them. And all the words felt like loss, betrayal, regrets, and grief. For the first time in her career, she was beginning to avoid writing. Instead of marching upstairs with coffee in hand ready to jump in every morning, Clare found herself spending more time sifting through her old journals and pictures and the memories they dredged up. She would spend hours just sitting on her couch, staring out at the Pacific and thinking about her life, about her family, about Adam—about the girl she had been and the woman she had become. The beliefs she had about that woman. The beliefs she had about the events that shaped her life—this work was making her question all of it.

The questions were somehow tied up with the book, and she was beginning to think that maybe the book was formulating an answer to these questions. It was beginning to frighten her because she realized she had no idea what would happen next. She sat down every day and picked up the thread from where she'd left off the day before with no plan or plot or even forethought, if she was being completely honest.

It was most like writing in her journals, the free flow that was never meant to be seen by anyone other than herself. Did she realize that millions of people all over the world would eventually read this book? What would all those people think? Since beginning this new project, she herself rarely liked what she wrote—and she was pretty sure she hated her largely unsympathetic characters. A long suffering and childless couple, whose withered ambitions, broken promises, and marital betrayals had left them both bitter and prone to engaging in verbal jousts and petty slights. Would two such people even stay married to each other? And if so, why would they do it? Maybe she should guide them to some redemption—some reconciliation. If that was the case, she couldn't see any ladder up from the pit she had flung these two characters into.

Curled on her couch with her feet beneath her, Clare sighed in frustration. She wasn't *probably* making a mistake with this project; she knew she was.

What are you so afraid of, Clare? It was like she could actually *hear* Donna, all these years later.

Charlie, tired of lying in the sun at the edge of her shag rug, jumped up onto her lap, stretched his paws high onto her chest, arched his back, and extended his mouth up for a quick lick of her face. He stood there, squirming and wagging his tail, insisting she come back to the room, back to this present, back to the sun and the view and the life that was right here. She smiled at him, and his tail picked up the pace.

"How can I love you so much? You silly dog." She held his long ears in both her hands and kissed his head.

Her phone rang on the coffee table in front of her. It was the Regency, her mother's care facility. Clare's back tensed. It was the third call this week. She had Henry drive her out there every Thursday for a visit, and those visits were typically pleasant. Her mother was, mostly, cogent, relaxed, and well cared for. During their visits, Ella would tell Clare about all the activities she had participated in over the week. Then last month, something had changed. Her mother had been less lucid during their visits, more confused, and would often speak to Clare as if she were still a child. Last Thursday her mother had launched into a conversation about Clare's upcoming high school graduation as if it were 1993. Without the doctors having to tell her so, she knew her mother's condition was getting worse.

She picked up her phone. "Hello, this is Clare."

"Ms. Collins, hello. This is Winston Crane, director here at the Regency."

Clare sat up straighter. It was always hard to tell from the onset of a phone call if the reason why the top dog was contacting her directly was because the situation was really *that serious* or if it was simply because she was *Clare Collins.* "Yes. Hello, Winston." She worked to keep the edge of panic from her voice. Maybe it wasn't even about her mother. Maybe her assistant had simply forgotten to pay their enormous bill. She stood up and walked to the plate-glass wall. "I hope everything is okay?" she asked as she gazed out at the ocean, which was reflecting sharp shards of sunlight. A lone person in a kayak paddled far out beyond the breaks.

"Yes, well…I am sorry to be calling you again…"

Clare closed her eyes.

"But I'm afraid that Mrs. Kaczanowski—well, two members of our staff needed to restrain her. I know this is distressing to hear, but it was a safety measure we needed to deploy as your mother was physically attacking another resident. I assure you, it was only done in strict accordance with our policies on restraint and as a last resort to protect the other resident."

Clare tilted her head back and closed her eyes again. She wasn't sure what to say next: *Is she okay? Is the other person okay? Why did she attack another person? Are you kicking my mother out?*

"We are going to need you to come down and sign some paper-work. It's part of our policies and procedures when restraint has been used."

"Legal," Clare blurted, returning her head to its upright position.

Winston cleared his throat. "Yes, but we also take the opportunity to fully explain the event and response to the family—to answer their questions fully and hopefully reassure them that their loved one is being cared for by only the best and most thoroughly trained individuals at all times. Is there any possibility that you can come in today?"

"Yes, of course. I will come right now."

"And," Winston said, hesitating, "will you be bringing legal counsel with you?"

She could almost hear him wincing on the other end of the line.

"No," Clare said, sighing. "I doubt that's necessary." She knew as well as anybody her mother's physical capacity. She had been a cop for forty years. Coupled with her worsening confusion—"Do you know why she attacked the other woman?"

"Ah, a man, actually," Winston corrected her. "And after interviewing the staff and other residents who were present when it occurred, I'm sorry to say we have been unable to identify a plausible antecedent. Several people did report that she was yelling and calling the other resident Jim. She seemed to believe that he was about to hurt someone named Eileen? I'm not sure if that helps, but we can certainly discuss it further when you—"

"I'll be there as soon as I can," Clare blurted and hung up her phone. Jesus Christ. Ella thought the man was Jim, her long-dead, abusive husband.

She rushed from her study and down the stairs. Her bare feet quick stepped on the cold marble as Charlie kept an excited pace beside her. "Simon!" she shouted, her voice echoing throughout the empty house before she remembered he had left on a flight for New York that morning. "Damn it!" Also, she realized it was Sunday and Henry had the day off. "Shit!"

She would have to drive herself. Which she *could* do, thanks to her mother's insistence and homespun amateur behavior therapy two decades ago—but she still didn't *like* to. "Shit, shit, shit," she whispered to herself as she pulled the car key off the hook in the mudroom, slipped on a pair of sandals by the door, and snatched her purse off the bench.

She rushed out, hit the button to open the double garage door, and slid onto the driver's seat of her Bentley—not noticing how the airflow between the open garage and the open windows in the living room prevented the house door from closing behind her. Pushing the ignition, she pointedly ignored the flood of adrenaline and the deep recesses of her brain that were forever hardwired to be afraid of driving. She backed out of the garage, her neck craned so she could see over her shoulder, down the drive, onto their street. Then she cranked the wheel left and pointed the car toward the city, silently cursing Simon and Henry, her mother and the Regency, even though she knew that none of this was anyone's fault.

When she pulled up, the Regency valet opened her door, and Winston was at her side within moments. "Ms. Collins—"

"Just take me to her," Clare said, cutting him off as they entered the double doors being held open for them by two uniformed doormen. "I promise to sign all your paperwork after. But I want to speak with her first."

"Of course. Her personal therapist is in speaking with her now."

Clare nodded, wondering if her mother, in one of her mental time travel episodes, ever went into an apoplectic fit over the idea that she now saw a *mind meddler*—and twice a week at that.

"Here we are," Winston said as they arrived at Ella's private rooms. "She is calmer now, but would you like the therapist to stay? Just in case."

"No," Clare said and opened the door herself. "I think we'll be fine."

"Very well. If you change your mind—"

Clare waved off the rest of his sentence with her hand. When the door opened, the therapist rose from her chair in the corner with a smile. "We've just been—"

"Thank you," Clare said. "I know how to call if I need you."

"Yes, um…of course. I'll be…it's just that…"

"Thank you, Doctor Keen." Winston cued the woman to wrap it up and leave. "Ms. Collins will let us know, should she need us."

Without any more broken sentences, they both left the room, closing the door without a sound behind them. Clare had half expected to find her mother lying flat on her back in bed, wrists and ankles secured at her sides by two-inch leather straps. Or in wilder thoughts incited by asylum scenes in old movies, her mother may have been forced into a dingy, once-white straightjacket of some kind.

Instead, Ella Kaczanowski sat quiet, in full possession of all four of her limbs, sipping what was possibly hot tea from a small blue china cup. She turned and smiled at Clare without a trace of recognition. "Hello," she said, sounding a little surprised but not necessarily unhappy to have her private afternoon suddenly interrupted by a strange visit. As if remembering her manners, she asked, "Have you come for a cup of tea?"

Clare licked her lips. She was tempted to ask her mother, in the shittiest tone she could conjure, if she had bothered to offer the poor elderly man she had *assaulted* a fucking cup of tea before she attacked him. *It's not her fault*, she reminded herself. *It's the disease advancing throughout her brain more and more every day, cleaning house and shutting off the lights.* She took a breath; what would Eileen do? She had watched her sister barely break a sweat while dealing with her own three children fighting like cats. Jesus, she wished her sister was here right now.

"Mom?" she finally asked and took a step forward. "It's me, Clare."

Ella's smile faltered, but only for a second before Clare saw the awareness move into her eyes. "Of course you are, silly girl. Who else would you be? Come, sit down. Someone made us tea."

Clare could tell this thought tripped Ella up again, because *who* had made them tea? As she sat down, she watched her mother gaze around her bedroom—*and for that matter, where were they...exactly?* Her mother may have realized that she was Clare, her daughter, but other than that, she was still not in the here and now.

"Mom, do you remember what happened?"

"Course I do. I was there."

This could mean anything, really, but Clare decided to press on anyway, just in case her mother was more lucid than she appeared to be. "Can you tell me what happened? Why did you do it? I'm going to have to go and sign some paperwork, legal stuff, and I want to make sure—"

Ella dropped her teacup into her lap. "No!" She reached forward, grabbing Clare's leg.

"It's okay," Clare said, taking her mother's hand and looking around the room for something she could use to mop the mess up. She stood up. "I'll just go get a towel from the bathroom. We'll get you cleaned up."

Her mother tightened her grip on her hand, keeping Clare from leaving. "Listen to me," her mother hissed, looking around the room as if there were some danger of being found out. "Sit down." She pulled hard at Clare's arm, her bony finger digging painfully into her flesh. "Sit down right now."

Oh shit. She shouldn't have pushed. It was always a mistake. Not wanting to upset Ella further, Clare did as she was told. If she went along, sometimes her mother would stay calm and the episode might pass quicker. "Okay, Mom. I'm sitting. And I'm sorry."

"Listen to me." Ella leaned in close. "You are not to sign anything. Do you hear me? Nothing legal, nothing confessional. They don't have anything. I know it. I was so careful, Clare." Her mother shook her head and looked like she might start crying. "So careful. I have no idea how they suspect…unless someone from the party saw you leaving? Did someone else see you?" She squeezed Clare's hands tighter. "Think, Clare. Could someone have seen you get in the truck?"

Time stopped. Clare stared back into her mother's aged and frantic expression. Her heart beat hard and heavy in her head. Her mother was lost in time, and she'd dragged Clare along with her. "What are you talking about?" she whispered.

"I know you didn't mean it, honey. It was a horrible accident. But you have to listen to me now because they're not going to see it that way. Because you were drinking and that poor boy—"

Clare pulled her hands away from her mother's and stood up. Her mother reached for her again. Clare took a step back.

"Who approached you? Was it Joe? Teddy? Did Adam's parents come to you? We have to consider that they may not have any evidence. They may only be trying to get you to slip up."

"What do you mean, you were *so careful*? What did you *do*?" Clare asked her.

"I found you. I thank God every night that it was me. And I saw Adam's truck turned over in the ditch and—" Ella choked on her own words. "I just knew you'd be in there. And I prayed for you to please, please don't be dead." Tears ran down Ella's face. "You can't know—"

"What did you do!" Clare screamed at her mother.

"I moved you…"

Clare waited for her mother to finish saying it, out loud.

"From the driver's side, so nobody else would know—"

"That I was driving," Clare whispered.

"It was an accident," Ella cried.

Clare turned around and faced the wall. Her hands clutched fistfuls of hair on either side of her head. She stared into the oil painting in front of her, a mahogany framed replica of Monet's *The Japanese Footbridge*. She reached out and placed her palm flat against the painting's center, barely keeping herself from grabbing it and ripping it from the wall.

"Clare, I know this is upsetting, but you need to listen to me now. We need to be smart."

Clare turned back around. A gummy white paste had formed at the corners of her mother's mouth. Clare couldn't deal with Ella or her disease right now. She needed to leave. "It's not 1993," she stated. "No one is coming for me. No one knows what I've done…or what you have done." She picked up her purse from the floor. "I'll let them know you need to change your clothes."

"But the legal paperwork," her mother hissed.

Clare resisted the very strong urge to scream. "It's not about the accident. It's not about anything. You don't have to worry."

Her mother's shoulders slumped several inches. "You're sure? It could be a trick. Always read the document first." She raised a single arthritic finger. "The whole document."

"Goodbye, Mother."

Ella nodded. "I'll be home in a bit. Just a few things to finish up around here." She gazed around herself at nonexistent piles of work that didn't need doing.

Speechless, Clare watched her mother scan the room for several seconds, then closed the door behind her.

She left the Regency in a haze. Barely registering anything on her way to the door, she scrawled her name on some papers for Winston and declined to sit through a lengthy explanation of what exactly happened in the game room between Ella and the other resident who "must remain nameless for confidentiality purposes."

"I'm sure your staff handled it appropriately. Please have the valet bring my car right away."

The director sputtered a few words, but when Clare turned away from him midsentence, dug her sunglasses out of her purse, and proceeded to leave, he picked up his phone and called for her car. "Ms. Collins's Bentley. Straight away, James…run."

She pulled out of the Regency's drive too fast, her tires squealing against the concrete. She barely missed sideswiping a white Prius with the right of way. Clare's heart thundered in her chest as the driver of the small car laid into their horn and rolled down their window to yell at her.

"I'm sorry." She raised one hand, the other shaking on the wheel in front of her. "I'm sorry." She felt the tears, hot and wanting to tear loose from the back of her throat. "I'm sorry," she said again, even though the Prius had sped away in front of her. "I'm sorry, I'm sorry…I'm so sorry."

The drive out of the city and over the bridge was a blur, her mind filled with her mother's confession.

It was her fault. All of it. Everything. That night, twenty years ago, she remembered. She was so afraid of losing him, to school, another girl, his extraordinary life. Everything about Adam was so big, so bright, so seemingly beyond her. She was so afraid that what everyone thought was true; Adam was too good for her. Throwing away his life with a bit of white trash who had come from nothing and was going to be nothing. And then, seeing Adam with Heather, it was happening, had happened, her worst fear right there in front of her. She ran away, through the party, out the door, her whole world collapsing and the pain of it splitting her in half. She saw his truck. She was almost there.

"Clare!" Adam shouted. "Stop!"

She heard him. She could still hear him, years later, an echo in her head begging her to stop.

But she didn't listen; she didn't stop.

Her memory ran out right where it always did, like blank frames at the end of a movie reel. There was nothing again until those painful days in the hospital when she first woke up.

Only now, she knew the truth. Adam was dead because of her. She killed him, and her mother had covered it up.

Clare turned left on their road and saw something in the distance, right at the end of her driveway. It looked like an animal, a rabbit? She slowed down, pressing the Bentley's brakes until her car stopped completely fifteen feet away.

No, she was wrong. Had to be. It was something else—anything else. "Please," she begged. "Oh, please...no."

Every second she stared at him, the more certain she became. Her vision blurred; she was dizzy and might pass out. Clare gripped her steering wheel, not wanting to move or breathe or think. "Please, not Charlie," she sobbed. "I'm so sorry."

Clare opened her door and walked to where he lay, her eyes taking in his bright white fur and blood and stillness. When she looked up her driveway, she saw her garage door was up and the door to the house gaping. The interior of her home was exposed. She could see right through to the naked white glare of the living room.

I didn't close the doors.

Her legs buckled beneath her until she sat slumped at the edge of the road. She placed one hand on top of Charlie's tiny head and the other over her own eyes as wave after wave of anguish and regret overwhelmed her.

It was all her fault.

CHAPTER 29

Eileen

HER FLIGHT HOME LEFT IN THREE HOURS AND HENRY WOULD BE AT the house in thirty minutes to pick her up. Her bags were packed and waiting in the foyer.

Earlier, Eileen had spoken with the lead investigator about Clare's gun and her concerns for Simon. He had assured her that, when the time came, most likely in a few months, it would be returned to her instead. Eileen wasn't sure what she would do with the 9mm. Sell it? Keep it? It had been their mother's, and so there was the sentimentality, or something like that—family tradition, nostalgia. Why else did she still have her own gun that had been, like her sister's, given to her when she had left the house for college? But when she thought about receiving Clare's weapon, currently tagged and bagged in some evidence room, the only emotions she felt were regret and revulsion. It was no longer simply a gun.

It had given her sister the means to remove her own life from this world.

It brought Eileen some relief to know that there was no way it would end up in Simon's hands. It was all too easy to imagine him one night, despondent and alone in Clare's seaside mansion. The gun stored in one of his desk drawers right next to all his dead wife's work—way too accessible. He might be in a better mental space right now, but that could change in an instant—and an instant was all he would need. She supposed that if he ever became as determined as Clare to take his own life, the absence of this one gun wouldn't stop him, but with it gone, it might slow things down. Give him time to think, to make a new choice.

She would have both her mother's old guns dismantled and destroyed.

She checked the guest bedroom one more time, under the bed, behind the curtains, behind the bathroom door to make sure she had everything before heading down the hall to Clare's study one more time. When she entered, Simon was on the floor in front of Clare's bookcase with piles of her journals all around him.

Yesterday, after the memorial service, they had come back to the house and pulled Clare's journals from two years ago. The ones from around the time she began writing her last book and Charlie's death. Simon remembered he had been out of town and Clare had been to see their mother the day Charlie died. It took them only half an hour to find the entry.

April 21

The most tragic events of my life have been my own doing. The guilt and pain and regret—it claws away at me, hollows me out, has taken away the desire to even live. I will never forgive myself. I don't deserve it. I never deserved it.

Or him. I can see now that I never could have had him. Not in any of the ways I have imagined. Eventually, I would have destroyed him because I loved him too much to ever let him go.

That's the truth I have always been too afraid to tell.

"She was driving that night," Eileen whispered when they'd both finished reading the entry. "That's what my mother was talking about, how she *took care of it*. How we needed to *protect* Clare. Because it wasn't Adam driving drunk that night; it was Clare."

"And Clare never knew that?" Simon asked.

Eileen shook her head. "I don't think so. We had just been out here for Christmas the year before. I don't think Clare could have been so—I don't know—just herself, I guess, if she'd known it was her fault." She pointed to the date of the journal entry. "I really think my mother must have said something at that visit, or at least sometime right around then. That was about the time her Alzheimer's started getting really bad. It makes sense that she could have let it slip during one of her episodes. Exactly like she did today with me."

Eileen tried to imagine what it must feel like for Simon, sitting there now, poring through Clare's thoughts about her life. She couldn't help wondering about her own husband, his private thoughts. She didn't want to know them.

"Henry will be here soon," she interrupted his reading. "I wanted to say goodbye."

Simon turned to her and then picked himself up from the floor. He seemed older, completely exhausted. "Thank you," he said, crossing the room to meet her. "For coming, for listening…for helping me try to figure all this out." He ran his hand through his already disheveled hair. "I really don't know if I could have made it through the last few days without you here."

She leaned in and gave him a hug. "Are you going to be all right here? Alone?" She looked at the journals spread all over the floor and realized that he was in real danger of losing himself in Clare's past. She pulled away from him and looked him in the eyes.

"Probably not," he said, looking around Clare's study. "It was always really just her house, and she let me live here with her, but it never felt like home for me."

"Will you go back to New York?"

He nodded. "I have a flight booked for Monday morning. I figured it was best if I didn't linger here." He stared down at Clare's journals. "I'll come back later in the year. I need some time right now, before I…deal with all this."

She reached out and touched his arm. "I'll come back then. If you want, and if you think it would help to not go through all her stuff alone."

He turned and gave her another hug. "I know I should say no, and that I'm fine, and I don't want to bother you, but I'm going to ignore all that and just say yes to your help right now." He let her go and tried his best to smile; he couldn't hold it for more than a second. "I think I'm afraid of being here alone."

"Then don't be. You don't have to be alone." She smiled at him and adjusted her purse on her shoulder. "Okay then, I'll call you tonight when I get home…make sure you're okay."

Simon nodded. "Thanks."

Eileen turned to leave.

"Oh! Wait I almost forgot." Simon called after her. He reached into his back pocket, pulled out a worn business card, and handed it to her. "When you're ready, that's the number for Clare's attorney."

Confused, Eileen glanced at the card and then back to Simon.

"Her estate," he explained. "The attorney will help explain everything."

Eileen shook her head. "Explain what?"

Simon raised his eyebrows. "Your inheritance. Clare left you quite a lot of money."

It was Eileen's turn to raise her eyebrows. "What? What do you mean?"

"She never told you?" Simon asked. "Eileen, you and I are the only beneficiaries of Clare's will."

"Me?" It hadn't occurred to her that Clare would leave her money.

Simon sighed. "I'm sorry. We should have talked about this instead of me tossing it in your lap on the way out the door. Look, call the attorney when you're ready, but you can't wait too long, okay? They want to get it settled."

Eileen nodded and she read over the card.

"Eileen?"

She lifted her head.

"It's a lot of money. It will change your whole life. You're going to need to hire your own accountant and attorney. I can give you the names of some good people."

Eileen laughed at the very idea. Her? Hiring an attorney and accountant?

"It's close to eighty-five million dollars. And that doesn't include the percentage of future royalties you'll be receiving."

She stopped laughing.

"Ms. Greyden," the flight attendant greeted her at her seat. "Can I bring you a preflight beverage?"

"A cup of tea would be nice, with milk, please."

"Of course."

Eileen sat back in her seat, closed her eyes, and hugged her complementary pillow and blanket to her stomach. It didn't seem possible, the way her entire life had changed in a week.

"A week," she whispered to herself. It had to be some mistake. To lose your sister, your husband, and be thrust into an entirely new realm of responsibility. It seemed like years' worth of upheaval.

All she wanted was to see her kids, hold them, kiss them, and tell them how much she loved them. That, and to sleep in her own bed, on her own pillow, and wake up in her busy, chaotic, messy house with her kids making noise and needing things from her.

Only, she couldn't imagine sleeping in that bed next to Eric.

"Ms. Greyden, your tea."

Eileen opened her eyes. "Thank you," she said as the flight

attendant placed the cup and saucer on the small table beside her seat and gave Eileen a smile.

"You're welcome. Please let me know if you need anything else before we take off."

Eileen picked up her cup and saucer and took a sip. The only other thing she needed right now was answers. In less than three hours, she would be standing inside her own home, face-to-face with Eric, and she had no idea what to do. She placed her cup and saucer back down and let her head fall back against the seat. Why was she the one with sweating palms, nervous and afraid to face her husband, when she wasn't the one who had been fucking Lauren Andrews?

"Mom!" Cameron yelled as she opened the front door, his feet thundering across the upstairs hallway.

She placed her purse on the table by the front door and looked up to the top of the stairs into his shiny, grinning face. He raced down, skipping steps two at a time and making her cringe, until he launched himself over the last five and landed with a thud, knees bent and hands on the wood floor inches in front of her. He sprang back up like lightning, his arms wrapped around her middle, his ear planted against her heart.

"I missed you," he said, squeezing her ribs so hard it hurt.

"I missed you too," she said into his hair as she hugged him.

Without releasing her, he turned his head and looked up into her eyes. "I'm sorry about Aunt Clare. Are you very sad?"

Eileen swallowed back a hot swell of tears and smiled down at her youngest. "Thank you. And yes, I'm very sad. I wish I'd been a better sister."

"Don't cry, Mom." He buried his face against her.

She hugged him harder and kissed his head.

"Mom?" Paige called from her room upstairs. "Are you here?"

"Yes!" Eileen called back.

"Sara, I have to go," Paige said, presumably into her phone. "Ryan!" Paige yelled, pounding with her fist on her brother's bedroom door. "Mom's here!"

Eileen closed her eyes and smiled; it was good to be home.

When Paige and Ryan came down, all three of her kids led her into the kitchen. "Dad made dinner," Ryan said. "We're supposed to let you relax." He escorted her past the kitchen and into the dining room, where the table was already set for five. With the Easter tablecloth and paper-towel napkins folded beneath the silverware.

"This is quite the reception," Eileen said as Cameron pulled out a chair for her and Paige delivered her a glass of red wine. "And the house is so clean," she noticed.

"Dad said you shouldn't have to come home to a pigsty and we had to help him clean up," Cameron confessed.

"Well, you did a great job. It's like a maid came." She smiled. "Where is your father?" she asked before taking a small sip of her wine.

"He just ran to the store," Paige said. "But he said he'd only be a minute and to go ahead and get started."

Eileen's chest hurt, but she smiled anyway. "Okay, let's eat then."

They were halfway through their plates of lasagna when Eileen heard the door to the garage close. Her heart beat hard against her chest, and her arms and legs felt weak. She didn't want to do this, face him, feel this way. She tried to swallow her bite of noodles, cheese, and marinara sauce, but it stopped halfway down her throat. Eileen grabbed her glass of wine and took a large drink to wash it down.

"You're home!" Eric said, entering the room with his arms wide and a large bouquet of flowers wrapped in cellophane from the grocery store.

"Yes," Eileen said, swallowing hard one more time and wiping her mouth on her paper towel.

He was standing right next to her seat, his arms still wide. After a few seconds, she realized he was waiting for her to stand up and hug him. Her kids stared at her, waiting for the normal response.

Eileen stood up and managed to hug Eric while evading eye contact. "I'm so sorry, honey," he whispered in her ear before kissing the side of her head and releasing her.

Eileen nodded and sat back down as Eric rounded the room to his spot at the head of the table. The kids finished off their meals, being obviously careful to behave, not fight or bicker. Each one picked up their own plate, carried it into the kitchen, rinsed it, and put it in the dishwasher without her saying a word.

"Can I take your plate?" Ryan asked her.

She smiled at him. "Thank you, yes." It wouldn't last more than a week before they'd go back to their normal, id-driven little selves, but she'd ride the sympathy wave while it lasted.

"And we'll get your bags from the car," Paige added. "Come on," she directed her brothers, who, amazingly, didn't argue with her.

It was nice to see that, when the situation was dire, every one of her kids had the capacity to behave like human beings. It made her feel like she'd done at least something right as a mother.

When all three of her kids could be heard heading upstairs, dragging her suitcase behind them, Eric refilled her wineglass and then his own. She watched the bright burgundy liquid cascade against her glass and then settle into a placid pool of alcohol that she was going to leave there. The last thing she needed tonight was another drink.

Eric picked up his glass with one hand and placed his other on top of hers on the table between them. "Are you okay?" he asked and took a drink. "How is Simon holding up?" He squeezed her hand. She could feel his eyes on the side of her face, searching her expression.

She turned to face him. "I don't really want to talk about it right now."

"Of course." He nodded. "Whenever you're ready, I'm here for you."

Eileen pushed her chair back and stood up. "I'm going to unpack and get ready for bed."

"I'm sure you're exhausted," he said, still searching her face, reading her reactions. Like on the phone two days ago, he was trying to determine what she knew. Dave must have approached him again.

"Yes. I'm pretty tired."

"I'll be up in a minute. I just want to turn on the dishwasher, put some things away."

Eileen nodded.

"Did you notice the house?" He smiled, so proud of himself for the work. "The kids even helped."

"Yes, it looks nice. Thank you." *So great to know that all this time you've been completely capable and only unwilling to help out with our lives.* She headed for the stairs, the revelations of the last week weighing on her all at once, her legs like anchors dragging.

In her room, the kids left her bags next to her dresser. She didn't feel like unpacking right now; she'd do it in the morning. She picked her tote up, carried it to the bed, and pulled her cell phone from the small pocket she was now always careful to keep it in.

She pulled up her contacts and found Simon's number.

I'm here, safe at home. Call me if you need anything, even just to talk. Anytime, seriously.

She placed her phone on the bedspread beside her and stared at the envelope in her bag. Eric was trying to read her, because he had no intention of telling her. He was trying to figure out if he was going to get away with this. Maybe he had promised Dave to do as he asked and stay away from his wife.

Never mind that they worked together and saw each other every fucking day.

Dave wanted to move on with his life and his wife. Put this affair behind them and go back to whatever their marriage had been before—or at least, whatever Dave had believed it to be before.

Eileen could understand wanting that. She had three very good reasons to consider doing exactly that herself.

Her phone buzzed, and Eileen turned it over to see the screen. It was Simon.

Same goes for you. Hope everything is okay. You'll
make the right decision either way.

She turned her phone back over and placed her palm on top of
it. The right decision. Eileen sighed; what did that mean? She tried
to imagine these choices: staying and pretending; storming out the
door; screaming at Eric in a fury of rage and horror and hurt.

How could he do this to her? To their family? And not once, not
some drunken, one-off mistake that he confessed to Eileen from his
fucking knees with promises to never, ever let it happen again. No,
he and Lauren were in a relationship. She made herself say the words
out loud, so they hurt exactly as much as they should. "Your husband
is in a *relationship* with another woman." She closed her eyes and saw
them together, naked and alone. When she had shown Simon the
pictures, his observation had gutted her.

*I don't say this to hurt you more, it's just, that look of adoration on
his face.*

Had Eric ever looked at her that way? When they first met?
When he slipped an engagement ring on her finger? No, she didn't
think so. Not the day they got married and not even after she gave
birth to their three children.

It wasn't just about her anymore. What would her kids think if
she left their father? What would they think if she didn't?

"What would you think, Eileen?" she whispered to herself.
Always knowing, never trusting, forever suspecting that every business call, late night, and out-of-town trip was only an excuse for him
to be with Lauren.

Eric was going to come upstairs any minute. She could undress, wash her face, brush her teeth, and get into bed. She could pretend she didn't know anything and that nothing had changed.

Or she could not.

The question was the outcome. Which version of herself did she imagine being tomorrow morning? Next week? Six months from now?

Ten years?

She could hear Eric's footsteps on the stairs. She stood up. In the moment and pressed for time, Eileen found that her instincts took over.

Eric walked into the bedroom with a smile. "What's all this?" he asked as he moved closer and looked at her standing next to the bed.

She said nothing. She just waited.

The smile fell off his face as his brain processed what he was seeing. He took them in all at once. Every single picture of Eric and Lauren— Eileen had laid them out in a grid across their bed, for easy viewing.

She watched her husband avoid looking at them. He stared at the floor near his feet. "You said it was insurance papers."

"I lied," Eileen said.

Eric took a breath. "I'm so sorry."

"Don't." She held up her hand. "Just get what you need and take it to the spare room. And tomorrow, you need to find yourself somewhere else to live."

"Eileen, please let me explain—"

"Honestly, I think these pictures speak for themselves. I want you to leave."

"What about the kids?"

"What about them? And don't you dare throw them in my face

after you go and do this!" She pointed to the evidence. "What about the kids here?" She held up one picture then put it down. "Or what about the kids here?" She picked up another. "Were you thinking about the kids in this one? How about here? Or here? Or any of the fucking times you decided to put your dick inside Lauren Andrews? Get out of my bedroom."

He stood there for several more seconds. Looking at the floor, then to her and the photos, he swallowed. Finally, when he realized there wasn't anything he could say that erased the pain spread across their bed, he turned and left.

CHAPTER 30

Eileen

Ten months after Clare's death

"Go, Paige!" she shouted. "Take it, there you go, there you go...all the way now! That's it! That's it!"

Eileen watched her daughter hammer the soccer ball into the corner of the net for her second goal of the day. She sat back in her chair and smiled as Paige raced back up the field, her teammates giving her high fives and side hugs as they repositioned themselves for another kickoff at center field.

"She's the terminator today," Eric said next to her.

"I know! That training clinic's made a huge difference, I think."

He nodded in agreement before turning his attention back to the game.

It had taken her four months to stop hating him. Six months to have a somewhat normal conversation with him. And nine months to forgive him.

It would take another two months before their divorce would be final. She had overheard that Dave and Lauren were also divorcing, and Eileen couldn't help herself from imagining that Lauren and Eric were still seeing each other, but she didn't really want to know. She had almost twice asked her daughter if she knew if her father was seeing anyone.

But she didn't want to ever put any of her children in that position.

It still hurt, especially thinking that Eric and Lauren might now be together. Together at last with no spouses to get in their way. Some days hurt more than others; some days she still dissolved into a torrent of tears, convinced she'd made the wrong decision that day she returned from California. But the more time that passed, the less tears there were. Maybe it hurt a little less every week.

One day, she hoped, it wouldn't hurt her at all.

The biggest problem was that she still loved Eric. That, and now knowing the facts: he had never loved her as much as she loved him.

The whistle blew, ending the game. Paige's team won by one point, and the girls were chanting and jumping up and down on the far side of the field. "So I'll swing by and get the kids at five?" Eric said, shoving his folding camp chair into its canvas carrying case.

She nodded. "See you then." She watched him sling the carrying strap over his shoulder and turn to go, but after a few steps, she forced herself to focus again on Paige. It was still painful to watch him walk away.

Her weekly talks with Simon had been more helpful than she could have ever imagined. They spoke every Tuesday at 9:00 a.m., her time. As a co-executor for Clare's estate, Eileen had been grateful to have the new job and all that she needed to learn to perform it; it helped to keep her mind occupied. Plus, it gave her and Simon a good excuse to check in and be there for each other.

"I still miss her," he admitted just last Tuesday. "Sometimes I pretend she's still out at the house working, unwilling to leave, and all I need to do is jump on a flight from JFK to San Francisco and she'll be there, sitting in her office writing."

"That's probably normal…at least I think it should be. Have you decided about going to see anyone yet? A therapist?"

"No, I don't think I'm ready. I think I'm afraid that if I do, they'll tell me I have to stop pretending she's just somewhere else. Anyway, enough about my grief. How are you holding up?"

"It's two steps forward, one step back. For some reason, this week, I really miss him. Almost like I'm telling myself that what happened was no big deal, even though logically I know it was."

"It's because the divorce is getting closer to finalized. Your comfort zone is trying to talk you away from the cliff's edge."

"That's it," she said. "That is exactly it. Part of me wants to run back into that life we had, lies and all, and just bury my head back into the sand."

"Except you can't put the toothpaste back into the tube. Do you honestly think, even if you could somehow go back, you would ever unsee those photos?"

"No," she said, sighing. "And I don't really want to go back. I just really miss that false sense of security I was drifting around in. It was comforting and familiar, and he always knew what to do when the toilet leaked or the internet went down. I hate figuring out that stuff on my own."

"Hire a good handyman," Eric said. "Speaking of the divorce, did you guys settle on a number?"

"I suggested three million, and he agreed." She had figured one million dollars for each of the three amazing, wonderful, loving children she got out of him.

"He agreed? Okay, I'm stunned, and you were right."

When Eric had first learned about the inheritance from Clare, so soon after learning that Eileen knew about Lauren, he had insisted that he wouldn't try to take any of that money in the divorce. Simon didn't think that would last. "Come on, Eileen, be serious. Do you honestly think he won't try to come for half? How good is this lawyer you've hired?"

To be honest, she didn't really know herself if Eric would change his mind once some of his guilt wore off. She felt like it was probable, given his long affair with Lauren, that she didn't know her husband as well as she thought she did.

But he never asked her for a dime. It was only last month that she had decided she actually wanted to give him something. Not half, no. But enough money to be generous and fair, and to indicate she didn't actually hate his guts. He was always going to be the father of her children.

"I'm just happy that we're getting closer to winding the whole mess up. I think it will be a relief when it's finally all said and done."

And heartbreaking. She knew signing those papers was going to open the wound back up.

Paige was heading across the field toward her, sweaty and smiling, arms linked with two other girls from her team, their huge soccer bags bouncing on their backs.

"That was a great game, huh?" someone suddenly said next to her.

"Yes," Eileen said as she turned toward the voice on her left. She sucked her breath at the sight of him. "Oh, God," she breathed. It was Samuel Cramer, witness to her husband's sex pictures and her drunken rock-bottom behavior in the San Francisco airport and receiver of a misdial outside her mother's care facility.

"Sorry, I didn't catch that." Samuel gave her a huge smile.

"Ah, nothing." She waved her hand. "I only meant to say, yes, it was a great game."

His daughter was on Paige's team, and Eileen had carefully avoided him and thus further embarrassment since the beginning of the new season. Now here he was, right in front of her. He looked relaxed in his jeans and T-shirt. His arms were a bit muscular, she noticed, and his dark hair, windblown and a little messy, fell across his forehead. He was tall, over six feet for sure, broad chest, bright brown eyes. Samuel Cramer was a very attractive man. She hadn't seen this last year. Or maybe she hadn't cared to see it.

"So." He shrugged. "Does that work for you?"

Eileen suddenly snapped out of her personal appraisal. "What? I'm sorry." God, he must think she was a complete idiot. "My mind." She laughed and pointed at her head. "So scattered right now."

He laughed, not at her, but in a sweet way. Like he found her adorably hilarious...or something. "The girls." He nodded in the direction of the three who were quickly approaching, one of which

Eileen could now see was Kimmy, his daughter. "They have cooked up ordering Chinese food and having a sleepover at our house. Is it all right with you?"

"Oh! Yes! Of course. That will be fun…except—" Eileen sighed. She suddenly remembered that it was Eric's night and he was picking the kids up later. "I'm sure it will be fine. I just need to check with her father. It's his night. But I'm sure he won't mind."

"Ah, say no more. I completely understand. We'll just keep the plans loose until we know for sure."

"Thank you."

"I'll give you my number so you can call when you know."

"Oh." She waved her hand. "I already have it," she blurted before she remembered to be embarrassed about the time he gave her the number. Eileen cringed inside at the thought of her causing the escalator crash last year.

Samuel smiled and nodded. "Right."

Thankfully, the girls arrived and filled the awkward moment with their voices and energy, and they all moved off the field in a pack toward the parking lot. She popped the trunk on her car and dumped her chair and Paige's bag into the back.

"Eileen?"

She closed the trunk and turned. It was Samuel again.

"Hey. So I was wondering, you know, if Paige does end up coming over tonight…would you maybe be interested in getting dinner with me? Or even just an appetizer, or a drink? Maybe coffee or something some other time if you're busy?"

He was asking her out. Eileen Greyden. Soon to be a divorcee.

Twenty pounds heavier than she'd like. Three kids deep. She was being asked out by this very attractive man who had been *so kind* to her on multiple occasions when he could have just as easily have walked away.

"Thank you, but no," she heard herself say.

He smiled and nodded, but she could actually see that he was disappointed.

"I'm just, right now, going through a divorce. It's been, well... really hard."

"I understand, honestly. It's been three years since mine, but I remember. It's not easy. Even though you've decided to not be together, it's still hard to not be together. Anyway, if you change your mind...standing offer," he finished with an incline of his head.

She watched him walk back to his car, actually sorry to see him go. "Samuel!" she called out before she could stop herself.

He turned around.

"Can I change my mind and take you up on that standing offer now?"

"I wish you would."

"I'll call you later."

Reading Group Guide

1. Is there a character in *Her Perfect Life* that resonates strongly with you? Which one, and why?

2. Considering what we learn about Clare, do you feel sad, triumphant, or something else altogether at her fate?

3. Have you ever wondered what life was really like for someone you admired? Discuss who this would be and if your assumptions were challenged from exploring the struggles behind Clare's outward success.

4. If you were in Clare's shoes and given the chance to reach success (but risk a close friendship), would you do so? How would you have handled the fallout with Donna Mehan?

5. Why do you think Simon stays with Clare throughout a marriage that is so obviously breaking down, and how did you feel knowing he blamed himself?

6. If you could sit down with one of your idols and ask them questions that they had to honestly answer, who would you choose and what questions would you ask?

7. Did the twist of the book surprise you, or had you guessed what was going to happen? If you had other theories, what were they?

8. Jump forward in time. Where do you see the main players, such as Eileen or Simon, a few months, a year, a decade after the events in *Her Perfect Life*?

9. Suppose Eileen hadn't ended up inheriting her sister's fortune; do you think she would have made a different choice about her marriage without the freedom this money now provides for her and her family?

10. And speaking of money, how did you feel about Eileen choosing to give Eric so much? Why do you think she did it? What would you have done, and do you think your feelings about infidelity in a relationship have changed over the course of your life?

A Conversation
with the Author

What inspired you to write *Her Perfect Life*?

I think the initial spark of an idea came to me during the 2012 Summer Olympic games. Like the rest of the world, I was getting ready to watch another of Michael Phelps's awe-inspiring performances in the pool, when the camera panned to his family cheering him on in the crowd of spectators. The announcer named the family members, and it was the first time I took note that Michael Phelps had two sisters, Hilary and Whitney.

At that time in my life, my own two children were nine and almost eight. Like many siblings, especially those as close in age as mine, the rivalry and bickering were often off the charts. Watching those two adult women cheering for their extremely talented and famous younger brother made me wonder—what was it like for them to be the siblings of The Star?

Of course *Her Perfect Life* has nothing at all to do with swimming or the Olympics, but that wonder about Hilary and Whitney Phelps was the seed that grew into the Eileen and Clare sibling dynamic. To have all those shared childhood experiences, to grow up together, to love someone that much, and then watch them go on to become a person that excels far beyond everyone else in their field. To witness them become not just great but a living legend in the minds of the rest of the world—what impact would that maybe have on a person's thinking about their own dreams, talents, and accomplishments?

Eileen is my character who wrestles with these thoughts and emotions.

Did you have to do any research to bring Clare and her "perfect" world to life?

Yes and no. On the one hand, being a writer writing about a writer was as simple as combing through my own headspace and emotions. The angst, the desire, the struggle to believe in yourself while still creating and getting your work out there—those inner aspects of Clare and her career were easy to find. More research was required with regards to her settings, homes, and the types of expensive things she would surround herself with. Although it was the best sort of research because it's like shopping for real estate, furniture, cars, and wine that are WAY outside my budget. It was fun to live vicariously through her success. As far as locations, I have traveled to Casper, Manhattan, and San Francisco but never lived in those places. So I relied heavily on internet maps, travel guides, photos, and my own imagination when creating her world in these places. My parents have lived in Wyoming for over twenty-five years—so that was very helpful when developing Clare and Eileen's birthplace.

For the parts of the book that are the "behind the curtain" world of publishing—I once was fortunate enough to work for a successful literary agent in the Denver area. Working as her assistant and helping with aspects related to foreign rights, I got a very clear and interesting vantage point of the publishing business. What I learned while working there has been instrumental to me in many ways. One, it made me realize that if I wanted to continue working in publishing, I definitely wanted to do it as a writer. Two, it made it very clear to me just how hard I was going to have to work to make a career as a writer happen. And three, it gave me the insider knowledge I would need to make Clare and Simon's fictional lives rich and authentic.

Which character did you connect with the most? Which was the most difficult for you to write?

Honestly, I really do love every one of my characters, and in case you're curious, there are elements of myself in each of them. And while Clare and I share a profession, it's actually Eileen's character that I most closely identify with.

The most difficult character for me to write was Adam because he needed to be one thing to Clare and another to my adult readers. He's the love of Clare's life, a teenage boy, and a legend in her mind. He was this, but also for my readers he was flawed, a person who made unkind choices and was also all too human. Adam's character required me to live fully in Clare's mind, a woman still mourning the greatest loss of her life, recreating different realities for that loss through her fiction, while either ignoring, denying, or completely having no memory of the very real aspects of Adam's behavior that provide the evidence to contradict Clare's extremely romanticized vision of Adam—of course, until she finally tells herself the truth in her last and final book.

Adam was a juggling act because we have to rely on Clare, a somewhat unreliable narrator when it comes to her memories and the fictions she's been telling herself for years.

Eileen is an incredibly fascinating and layered character, but any one of us could step into her shoes. What qualities did you bring to her to make her accessible, relatable, and sympathetic?

It's her life as a mother, her struggles with her marriage, her questions about her own choices, good and bad, that make her completely real to me. Eileen could be me. She could be my best friend. She could be any number of the women in my book club or living on my block. I love that she is a flawed person—but this doesn't make her a bad person, only human. My hope is that having an Eileen character gives women space to consider aspects of their own lives that are not so perfect and, if they didn't already know it, the knowledge that they are not the only ones.

Your story pulls the reader from the rocky shores of California to the small towns of America and even visits the busy streets of New York. Do you have strong connections to these places, and did you mean for them to play such important roles in the book?

I seem to always be drawn to writing stories that cover a lot of physical territory. I think this may stem from growing up in a military family and moving as much as I did as a child. Because of this,

I don't have a strong sense of "home" the way many people do and I feel connections to many places I've lived and/or visited over the years. I have loved many small towns and big cities in America and all over the world. Not unlike people, they have their own beauty, strengths, and drawbacks as well. For me, places have personalities all their own, and because of that, I feel they can't help but become one of the characters in a story.

But no, I didn't intend them to be important. I think it's more just the way I view places and settings in general—so it ends up coming across in the story.

On to questions about writing! Are you an outliner or a "pantser"?

I am both. I like to have a map, which is my general outline of the major destinations I want to hit on my way through the book. And I have to know about how long I'm going to take to get there, word-count-wise. But for the most part, when I sit down to work on a scene, I let it go where it wants as it comes to me. Some scenes I know I'll write ahead of time, some scenes I know I NEED to include, and others pop up based on events that transpired along the way, but I always know how it's going to end before starting. It might change slightly, or even completely, but I like to know where I'm going before I take off.

What does your writing space look like?

I'm very fortunate to have a designated office space in my house. It has glass French doors that open up off our main entrance, dark hardwood floors, a cream deep shag rug, a purple buttoned settee, a down-filled denim club chair, a small coffee table, and a glass desk with a white leather office chair. There are several ash-colored bookshelves filled with books, candles, lanterns, and various bric-a-brac. I recently purchased a four-by-six-foot bulletin board that I DIY'd by covering it with upholstery fabric, three-by-five note cards filled with plot points, character sketches, and scene ideas for my current book-in-progress are pinned to this.

Most days, my pug, Bella, and my Mal-Shi, Billy, are sleeping either on the chair or on the rug beneath my feet.

When you're not writing, what are you up to?

Well, the largest chunk of my nonwriting time is spent working at my job. It's not a sexy answer, but it is the truth. Outside of that, I'm also a mother, so I grocery shop all the time, pick up other people's socks, load and unload the dishwasher twelve times a day, and end up washing everyone's clothes, even though I swore many times I wasn't going to do that anymore. Maybe you can understand why I identify with Eileen so much??

But what I really love to do is read great books (of course), hang out with my kids (when they're not asking me to wash their clothes, bring them food, or drive them somewhere), watch movies, binge amazing shows, browse bookstores, sit in coffee shops, travel as much as I can, watch people in airports (it's the BEST place for people-watching), hang out with great girlfriends, and browse realtor.com for homes in coastal cities and contemplate moves I might make once my high school teens graduate.

What are some of your favorite authors and books?

Easy: *The Thirteenth Tale* by Diane Setterfield, *The Night Circus* by Erin Morgenstern, *Circe* by Madeline Miller, *The Corrections* by Jonathan Franzen, *The Wife* by Meg Wolitzer, *The Map of Time* by Félix J. Palma, *Olive Kitteridge* by Elizabeth Strout, *The Ocean at the End of the Lane* by Neil Gaiman, *Running with Scissors* by Augusten Burroughs, the entire Harry Potter series by J. K. Rowling, *The Storyteller* by Jodi Picoult, *East of Eden* by John Steinbeck, *Pride and Prejudice* by Jane Austen, *The Nightingale* by Kristin Hannah, *The Eyes of the Dragon* by Stephen King, *The Mists of Avalon* by Marion Zimmer Bradley, *What Alice Forgot* by Liane Moriarty…so, so many more. And, gosh, should I also hit on all the great books from my childhood? Because I could seriously do this all day.

If there's one thing you'd like readers to take away from *Her Perfect Life,* what would it be?

The same thing I always wish for myself as a reader: an engaging and enjoyable experience that keeps us up, turning pages, long past our bedtime.

Acknowledgments

First, thank you reader. For your time, your love of books, and allowing me to share this story with you. It really is an honor for me.

I would like to thank my agent, Kevan Lyon at the Marsal Lyon Literary Agency. For taking that pitch appointment in Orlando, signing me with only a concept and four chapters written, and the numerous reads and insightful suggestions as we got ready to submit to publishers—I am eternally grateful to have your knowledge, expertise, and advocacy in my corner.

Many thanks also go out to my publisher, Sourcebooks Landmark, and their extremely talented team of editors, designers, marketing professionals, and organizational leaders. To Grace Menary-Winefield for acquiring *Her Perfect Life* and shepherding it through those first revision rounds. To Shana Drehs for adopting *Her Perfect Life* and this grateful writer midstride and carrying us through to the publishing finish line. For their bionic eyes and exacting red pens that kept me from looking like I never passed a fourth grade grammar lesson, I am eternally in the debt of Beth Deveny, Amanda

Price, Patricia Esposito, and Jessica Thelander. Additionally, cheers to Kirsten Wenum and her marketing plans, guidance, and help getting the rest of the world to notice this book. And finally, thank you to the extremely talented Olga Grlic for the beautiful cover that far exceeded my wildest expectations.

There are writers who I very much admire that were kind enough to offer up their valuable time to read advance copies of *Her Perfect Life*: Shelley Noble, Courtney Cole, Kelly Simmons, Allison Hammer, and Anita Kushwaha. I continue to be overwhelmed with the generosity of other writers who are willing to reach out a hand and help another up. Rest assured, I will be looking to pay it forward in the future. In addition to these amazing authors, I would also like to give a shout out to all the other talented writers in my #2020debut group and the Women's Fiction Writers Association for your advocacy, connections, education, and camaraderie. I can't imagine navigating this past year without you!

Speaking of camaraderie, to my fellow authors and dear friends Aimee Henley, Shawn McGuire, and Kristi Helvig for the years of brunches, writer retreats, and support—I think you already know how much I love, respect, and value each of you, but I wanted to shout it from this rooftop as well!

To my dear girlfriends Amy Blevins, Jill Arnhold, and Lisa Sundling who are avid readers and have always kindly listened to me blather on about plots, characters, settings, and a variety of angsty writerly topics over a glass, or two, of wine—I love you ladies. And thank you Katie Broshous for all the support, belief, and cheerleading over the years. I consider myself extremely lucky to have such amazing friends.

I'm sending a special acknowledgment to Kristin Nelson and Angie Hodapp at the Nelson Literary Agency. While not my agent or agency, they are my former boss and co-worker whom I now consider friends. Thank you for the education in publishing, the always spot-on advice, knowledge, support, commiseration, signal boosting, and work experiences that have undoubtedly helped get me here. I am more grateful than you will probably ever know. Oh, and much love to our book club! Kristin Nelson, Laura Lapsys, Carrie Reedy, Angela Watts, Liz Van Liere, and Kim McCarthy: an amazingly intelligent and well-read group that make every shared dinner and book discussion both memorable and divine.

Finally, I have to thank my husband, Rod, and our two kids, Beth and Matthew. For the love, laughter, arguments, understanding, memories, adventures, and sum total of experiences that add up to lives shared together. You are my family; I love you. I am blessed with every second I get to spend with you...unless I'm writing, in which case, "Please, I'm begging you... Get out of my office so I can work!"

About the Author

© Eric Weber

Her Perfect Life is Rebecca Taylor's first novel of adult fiction. Her other works include the young adult titles *Ascendant*, winner of the Colorado Book Award, and *Affective Needs*, a finalist for the Romance Writers of America RITA Award.

In addition to writing, she works as a psychologist and serves on the board of the Women's Fiction Writers Association. Rebecca currently lives in sunny Colorado with her husband, two teens, and two tragically spoiled dogs.

Learn more about her writing at: rebeccataylorbooks.com.

Follow her on social media:

Twitter: @RebeccaTaylorEd

Facebook: @RebeccaTaylorPage

Instagram: @RebeccaTaylorAuthor